# I BURN

## And Other Stories

## Wes Laurie

# Books by Wes Laurie

Psexycho
America Goes to the Movies: the 1980s
America Goes to the Movies: the 1990s
The Monster Game
The House Under Hell
Beerasaurus Sex

# I BURN

## And Other Stories

Wes Laurie

## *ArsonCuff Press*

First Edition, 2019

For Mary

# Contents

# Country Girls Can Survive

Outlaw country isn't a music genre, it's a life genre.

Maggie Shepherd doesn't have a license, but Momma left the keys to the minivan behind when she went off to the lake for the weekend. Maggie practices getting the van to fishtail in loose gravel so she can show off for her friend Lita Boswell when she picks her up. Lita lives on a farm outside the opposite side of town and her parents are gone for the weekend too.

Maggie hits a turn in the road going way too fast and cuts the wheel. Dirt and rocks fly and it feels to her like the van is up on two wheels instead of four. Really the wheels never leave the ground and crunch to a sliding stop with a tail light bumping the trunk of a roadside tree, subtle enough that Maggie doesn't notice the impact even though the cracked plastic is something Momma will notice right away. She peels out and drives off.

The van bumps down the Boswell driveway and Lita runs outside to greet her friend. She's in boots, jean shorts, and a swimsuit top.

Maggie parks the van and bounds out of it.

"I swear I popped the van up on two wheels!"

Lita laughs and teases.

"I'm driving if we go anywhere."

She isn't old enough for a license either.

Maggie comments on Lita's outfit.

"You going swimming?"

"The rain got the creek up and I want to go jump off the bridge before it's all gone."

"We haven't done that in forever."

The stunt driving can wait, Maggie is down for splashing around in the creek. The girls used to explore the creek all the time, stepping from rock to rock trying not to fall in, always falling in, and trespassing on the private property of all the neighbors.

The bridge that Lita wishes to jump off of is a concrete affair at a crossroads where one gravel road splits into another and crosses through the creek. The slab sits in the air a few feet with walls going down to either bank of the creek forming a short tunnel underneath it with a lower slab of concrete. When the water flows through the tunnel, on the other side is a wide area that sometimes gets deep enough to swim in. It's usually only a puddle but after rainstorms like the one that passed through a couple of days ago, the water can get waist deep.

Maggie changes into some clothes that she doesn't mind getting muddy. The van stays parked on four wheels and the ladies walk away from the house and down the road.

Lita talks about an upcoming event.

"Neither of my parents will drive us to the concert. My cousin Sherri says she will, but she wants gas money. I don't even have enough for my ticket yet."

"Dang. I thought you were saving."

"Trying. How much you got?"

"None. I was hoping you'd save for me too."

"Butthole."

"My mom only gave me permission to go if I paid for it myself."

"If you see any cans on the side of the road start picking them up I guess."

They reach the bridge and survey the swimming hole from atop it. The water appears deep enough, but is dark and stagnant. Maggie's zest for swimming adventure evaporates.

"Ugh. It's stagnant."

"It always stops and moves slow here."

"It stinks. Don't you smell that? Smells like something died."

"Don't be a sissy."

"I'm not jumping in that."

Lita clucks.

"Bawk. Bawk."

Then she takes one running step and launches herself off the side of the bridge. Splash! Maggie reels back from the droplets sent her way.

Lita's feet go out from under her when she hits the water and her head bobs below the surface for a split-second. She sputters and wipes her eyes as she stands up and turns to face Maggie and the bridge. She splashes her hand down, slings water in her friend's direction.

"Come on! Get in!"

"You're going to get one of those brain eating parasites in your cooter."

Lita laughs off Maggie's concern and focuses her attention on the tunnel below the bridge. It takes her a moment to realize what she is looking at, but then she reacts quickly.

"Oh my crap!"

She tromps through the water, desperate to get out. As she exits the creek bed she continues to voice her displeasure.

"Ew. Ew. Ew. Ew!"

Maggie leaves the bridge and goes down the slope to join Lita and see what the fuss is all about.

Lodged in the space below the bridge is the rotting corpse of a drowned cow. The poor creature must have been caught in a flash flood and swept down the creek before getting wedged under the bridge. The broken, mangled corpse is definitely the source of the stench in the air.

And Lita bathed in it!

Maggie steps away from her friend, laughing hard with sympathy. She is ready to run if Lita should try to touch her with wet, dead cow cooties.

Lita has a different concern.

"There's something moving in there."

She points toward the bridge.

"I'm not falling for that."

"Serious, Maggie. There's something."

Maggie decides to fall for it. She moves to get a better view. Indeed, she witnesses movement. A piece of cow hide moves as if something might have burrowed into the carcass. The next logical step is to find a stick and get to poking; however, the scavenger crawls out and reveals itself before the stick hunt commences. The thing scuttles forward to the edge of the tunnel and stops there, takes interest in its audience.

The critter's pale body is hairless and the size of a large house cat. There is a map of veins pulsating just below the surface of the skin, but these lines also break out in many places with ends resembling frayed wires. The six legs of the creature extend from either side in rows of three like a cricket. However, at the ends of these legs are hands with digits not unlike tiny human fingers. There is a rat-like tail at the rear and the head seems a bit too plump for the size of the body with no details discernible beyond the large pincers that extend from either side of the wide mouth. Threads of cow viscera dangle from the mouth and the creature flexes a pincer to slurp in the stringy pulp. This action sets off a series of sparks at the ends of the exposed wire veins.

The creature does a little tap dance in place, then scuttles to the side edge of the tunnel closer to its human audience. It pauses there. Its companions, alien beings of similar structure, reveal themselves, out from behind and within the cow, until four of them stand in a row.

Maggie and Lita bust out of their stupor and run for their lives. The creepy freakies give chase!

The girls start up the gravel road, but then cross over, vault themselves over a fence and into a large field. This land is a neighbor's property that connects to the Boswell property at the far end. The race is on and Maggie has a slight lead.

There is a group of trees that Maggie whizzes past but Lita decides that climbing is the thing to do. She throws herself against a tree and yells to her friend as she shimmies up the trunk.

"Get in a tree!"

"No!"

Lita navigates branches and climbs higher as her friend leaves her behind. She hopes that the creatures that now gather at the base of the tree aren't inclined to ascend.

Maggie climbs over another fence and reaches the Boswell property. She dares to glance behind her as she hits the edge of the yard and doesn't see any creatures in pursuit. Eyes forward again, she isn't about to slow down again in the final stretch.

She is glad to find that the front door of the house is not locked. She slams the door behind her and peers out the glass to check once again for enemies. Nothing. A deep breath, long exhale, it is time to find a weapon.

Maggie knows where Lita's father keeps a gun. It's a Winchester 1894 .30-30 lever action rifle. It rests in a rack on the wall right next to the locked gun cabinet. She takes the rifle down and then recalls where she saw some bullets stored once upon a target shooting match.

Maggie runs into the Boswell kitchen and yanks open a drawer where random odds and ends have been collected. She pushes aside pencils, a stapler, old electric bills, lint roller, ant poison traps, and finds a bullet! One bullet, there's two, three, four, only four, no, yes, five bullets.

She loads the gun. Then she runs to the front door and after a quick scan of the visible area for combatants, rushes outside and off to give her friend an armed escort home.

Lita is as high up as she can go in the tree and realizes that it is not high enough. The aliens scale the tree, propelled not by grace or skill, but by their apparent curiosity or hunger for the human above. And their tiny fingers are of help.

One of the creatures gets the digits of one leg around the branch below the branch that Lita is perched on. She braces her back against the trunk and dangles her leg down to try and stomp the creature. She kicks out and her boot connects with the branch with enough force to break it. The branch snaps away and takes the sparking alien down with it to the ground.

Lita almost slips herself, but manages lift her body weight back on to the thick branch that she sat on. The other three aliens have not been discouraged and continue their upward progress.

The first gunshot from the Winchester booms out and the alien highest in the tree is blown away. Maggie cranks the lever of the rifle and lines up her next shot: boom! Two for two!

She strolls closer to the tree to aim at the third alien that still climbs. She fires and knows that the bullet did not score a direct hit; she "barked" the creature. It falls from the tree to the ground.

Maggie chambers the next round and can see one of the aliens on the ground. She aims, fires, and puts alien number three out of commission.

The fourth creature, the one originally booted from the tree by Lita, isn't frightened off by the gunfire. It scuttles toward Maggie through the tall grass and when she sees movement she is quick to aim toward it, too quick to fire. The bullet thumps into the ground and the alien is close enough to strike.

Maggie drops the rifle right as the alien springs itself into the air. It intends to sink its pincers into her neck.

Maggie shoots a hand out in defense and catches a hold on the creature beneath its armed jaws. The alien makes the mistake of continuing to strike upward at Maggie instead of settling for a bite of arm. She is able to bring her other hand up and two-hand the creature's neck as it struggles, kicks its legs wildly and snaps the pincers together just shy of tasting human nose.

Maggie squeezes with all of her might and to her surprise the skullcap of the alien expands and then pops with a sound not unlike a can of biscuits being opened. Brains and mush gloop out and she is quick to drop the it. The creature seems dead, but Maggie isn't taking any chances. She retrieves the rifle from the ground and uses it as a club. She smashes the stock down against the alien bug thing, squashes it up real good and gross.

Nothing else moves around the tree. The problem seems to be handled. Lita is thankful.

"Thanks."

Maggie wipes goo off her hand on to her jeans.

The next day Frank Hopper, an agent for one of those agencies that doesn't exist, walks up the driveway of the Boswell homestead. There is a gathering of folks, local yokels as far as he can tell, and he overhears a couple of lines of conversation between two good ole boys as he passes by.

"They're South American grasshoppers or whatever."

"Naw. They's fake."

Frank reaches the front of a two-car garage and workshop building that has one garage door open. In front of the door stands a teen girl wearing a Johnny Cash t-shirt. It amuses

Frank to see a "fellow man in black." Of course, Frank isn't dressed in a black suit today. Today he blends in with button up country western wear, a little too classy for the event it would seem on second, albeit too late to care, guess.

The Johnny Cash fan has a card table set up to one side of her with a small pile of generic tickets on it. Frank asks about the tickets.

"How much for a ticket?"

"Five bucks."

"What's your name?"

"That costs extra."

"Are you Lita or Maggie?"

"Lita obviously."

Frank gives her six bucks and she gives him one of the tickets.

"When you're done bring your ticket back to me. We recycle."

Frank nods in agreement with the policy and then enters the garage behind her.

The alien ship had been tracked after entering Earth's atmosphere. The running theory is that lighting from a storm system hit it, disabling the stealth and speed systems it would later engage. By the time crafts were sent to intercept the space visitors, they regained control of their systems and disappeared. However, during the brief pursuit something was seen to have been discarded from the fleeing spaceship.

Frank Hopper and company had been searching in a grid one county over with special interest in the river area that scientists guessed the discarded item had landed. They didn't know if they were looking for a broken piece of spacecraft, space aliens, or space garbage. Then came word of a hillbilly freak show some miles away.

There is a card table with a cork board on a stand beside it. Frank Hopper looks at the display and beholds the first physical, concrete evidence of extraterrestrial beings. A couple of creatures are on the table, one a little less intact than the other, and then two more have been nailed for display on to the cork board.

Frank watches as a couple of teen boys lift a piece of alien corpse from the table to better inspect and ridicule it. Maggie sneaks up on Frank and snaps him out of his amusement over the creatures and the lack of preservation in place for their scientific value.

"Would you like me to take your picture?"
She has a Polaroid camera in her hands.
"It's only a dollar more."
Heck yeah he wants a picture.

# In The Shadow of The Tunnel of Death

People fear death. In most animals this fear is an instinct, a daily exercise of reflex not a fixation. In humans it can be an all-consuming dread.

It is as natural to die as it is natural to try to avoid dying. Health and religious regimens bring comfort to some, instill a genuine wall of confidence around fear of the unknown. These folks may seem to squeeze the most enjoyment out of the many distractions the days are filled with, but the fear is still inside of the walls. Is that what life is all about then? Distracting ourselves from the inevitable conclusion of mysterious death?

Is death finality? Is there existence in death? Is there life after death? How would life before death differ if we knew the answer?

I have been without a pulse and my mind slammed a fist down to make the final puzzle piece fit. However, I warn you that the completed picture is still abstract. Read on if you think there may be comfort found in the words of someone who has taken steps beyond the mortal dividing line. Or if you have a strong constitution when it comes to facing uncertain truth. Horror, I warn you again, people lie about wanting the truth, receive it in horror as a horror.

The hypocritical may judge me with their ingrained concepts of Heaven, Hell, and Purgatory. They may assume that I am short on acreage in moral grounds. To that I state: I am not here to lecture. My presentation is open to debate, but my intention is not to join the argument. Besides, I doubt that you were appointed by God to judge me.

I am a typical person who tries to err on the side of being "good." Maybe I don't go to your church and maybe I am not always politically correct, but I am well aware of both the golden rule and the commandments, even if I do not keep up-to-date on the latest trends of what offends people. If it will help you assign me some character, understand that I died running into a burning building.

My memory doesn't serve me at all regarding the incident. Secondhand accounts from several sources suggest that I came jogging down the sidewalk and stopped before an apartment complex that was freshly engulfed in flames. The fire department had not arrived yet, though most residents of the building were in attendance on the same sidewalk as me. One woman yelled about her "baby Kevin" being trapped within the budding inferno.

They say that I went into action without introducing myself. The bystanders witnessed a jogger arrive and break into a sprint toward the building with a four word battle-cry.

"I will save Kevin!"

Firefighters found me only a few feet within the front entrance of the burning building. They surmise that I ran inside and possibly tripped or lost consciousness due to panic. And then debris collapsed on to me. I lucked out and died of smoke inhalation, burns kept to the blistering minimum.

Kevin, by the way, turned out to be a cat that had already escaped the building via an upper floor window. The fire department did have to rescue him from out of a tree. A twist of tragic comedy, right? We cry when we cry and sometimes we cry when we laugh. I doubt that I would have run into flames if I had known Kevin was a feline.

I don't remember going into the building, or jogging for that matter. I do remember WHY I went jogging. I was feeling guilty after eating a breakfast of buttermilk and vanilla waffles with a side of smoked, maple flavored bacon. I had eaten that indulgent breakfast several days in a row and felt the need to repent or else become shaped like the pig slaughtered to facilitate my gluttony. After breakfast though, my memory goes into darkness, impenetrable darkness.

You've probably already heard stories about people who have died and upon revival describe a tunnel. "Go to the light at the end of the tunnel." All that jazz, right? In darkness, that my eyes never adjusted to, I indeed found myself in a tunnel.

My body was there and I sensed that it was nude. There was a slight draft, but I never felt uncomfortable, no chill from any frozen lake, no heat from any furnace of Heaven or Hell. I could move my body and use it to feel my surroundings. However, if I touched my hand to my chest or tried to touch my body: no body. My body was not there, merely an idea of it, a phantom for me to pilot.

The tunnel was circular, something I sensed before I even explored the nature of its shape. The floor beneath my feet felt squishy, goo between my toes, though not wet, more like a fleshy rubber; something between skin and marshmallows. The floor stretched into walls on either side of me and then extended up into a low ceiling. It all felt the same.

Touch is all that I had to rely on; no sight, no sound, no smell, and no I did not think to taste my surroundings.

There isn't much more to tell. I wish I had something more poetic to recite. It remained dark. I never saw a light or any end to the tunnel. Indeed I walked, on and on. There came a moment when I thought the tunnel was constricting, but that sensation passed and I chalked it up to anxiety, a tightness formed within as my walking path seemed endless.

The tunnel seemed like an eternal line, not a loop, I only went forward, no bends. And then I awoke in a hospital bed and slowly adjusted to the pain of living. As much as I could feel my body in that tunnel, it was upon opening my eyes in that hospital that I realized the extent of numbness I had experienced. If there is to be peace found in the tunnel, I reckon that at the onset it is the lack of physical pain. However, returning to that numbness is addictive and to have "addictive" be the best descriptive I can think of is worrisome.

My first trip into the tunnel, my death, has not been my final journey. I return to it every time I close my eyes. Blinking works fine for me, but if I close my eyes even for mere seconds at a time I am returned to darkness.

Doctors explain my "falling asleep" as trauma-induced narcolepsy. It can be dangerous and it can be hard for others to awaken me. Often, I soil my pants in my sleep, an embarrassing detail, but it seems relevant. When I travel the tunnel there are not bodily functions, no need for food, no waste to excrete.

I doubt that I have brought you any comfort in relating all of this. By saying that I find peace and addiction within the darkness, I am not saying that I find any comfort myself.

Many explain my experience away as a dream within a medical condition. I ponder sleep and dreams. If I am dreaming of the tunnel, then I dream of nothing else. I recall that once upon a time I had a variety of dreams. I ponder the past and how sometimes I could wake up from sleep remembering specific dreams and then other times I'd wake up and not recall any dreams. Are dreamless nights truly dreamless? Or, perchance, might I have been traveling in the darkness of the tunnel all along?

This is all that I have for you. I continue to return to the darkness, obsession, curiosity perhaps, "sleeping" more and more each day. It's always the same. However, I don't see any other choice but to keep traveling the tunnel, to keep feeling for a way out. But, why? To keep looking for that light? Or maybe my death feels unfinished and I just want to hurry and get it over with.

# The Headless Chicken Circus

In the pecking order of the Federal Bureau of Investigation Agent Jaden Kawai knew that he wasn't above chicken feed. However, he once envisioned that his status might rise. In fact, he thought that rise began on the day he answered a phone call and gave a weirdo some advice.

"Come on down to the office and turn yourself in. Just ask for agent Kawai."

A day later and Earl Patches Bower sat in interrogation room "A" while Jaden double-checked the background check and verified that Earl Patches Bower was a real person. Jaden had initially assumed the man a crank who wished to vacation somewhere nice while cranking. However, once in the physical presence of the man he sensed a seriousness that poked into his gut instincts.

The thirty-seven-yea-old Earl Patches Bower flew to Honolulu, Hawaii from Des

Moines, Iowa. He didn't have a criminal record, owned a small house with the acreage under it, and his last verifiable employment on record was three years prior on a dairy farm. No missed taxes, no credit card debt, Iowa born, Iowa raised and, as far as anyone could tell, Iowa proud.

Earl Patches Bower wore his best pressed denim overalls over a white dress shirt. He carried himself like a proper business man, but when it came to pairing a tie with the shirt he chose a blue bandanna to match the overalls instead.

His sandy hair was neatly combed, parted on one side, though with cowlick fighting the style in the rear. He was not clean-shaven, the stubble of a future beard present and a "toothbrush" moustache above his lips.

He had waited patiently in that interrogation room with a stack of papers on the table before him. On the papers were words typed via a typewriter.

After sitting Earl Patches Bower down in the room and hearing the man confess once again, Jaden not only went about with his checks on the man, but also made sure to inform his superiors of what he was up to and informed any other agents who would listen that Earl Patches Bower was only willing to speak with him in regard to the ninety-nine murders he lay claim to. Everyone seemed casual about it, but Jaden had a hunch an event was about to transpire with him as its ringmaster.

When Jaden returned to the interrogation room he sat down in a chair across the table from Earl Patches Bower. He made a show of pulling on a pair of latex gloves and then he began to dig.

"Okay, Mr. Bower..."

"Earl Patches Bower."

"Okay, Mr. Earl Patches Bower, I'll look at your papers now."

Earl Patches Bower was a pleasant enough man, pleased to comply and share the papers.

"I have provided every name and then the location where you can find the bodies. I am cleared to do this without legal representation."

And so the ninety-nine ring circus began.

It wasn't a wild goose chase; one by one the bodies were pulled from the graves described by the papers of Earl Patches Bower. The list of the deceased sent Jaden traveling to all fifty states of the Union, while the suspect remained locked away and out of the spotlight of the media storm that shook the nation. If it bleeds it leads and Jaden, with the team assigned under him, opened wounds all over the place.

Ninety-nine human husks exhumed. They were in various states of decay and the murder methods that created them were varied when obvious.

Prior to the search, all of the names on Earl Patches Bower's list were cross-referenced and proven to be the names of people known to be missing and with open case files. However, once the corpses were cross-referenced with those names the storm blew away the ringmaster's big top and left him standing in the fierce rain. DNA tests, dental records, none of the deceased matched the names as recorded on the papers. A new list of ninety-nine names was formed.

The dead uncovered were also known missing people. This meant: ninety-nine missing people were found dead in the locations as related by Earl Patches Bower; however, none of them were the named ninety-nine people, also known missing persons, that he had confessed to killing.

Jaden returned to the interrogation room and Earl Patches Bower was returned as well. The prisoner did not arrive in cuffs or the garb of a prisoner. He wore a fresh pair of overalls and Jaden took note of that odd detail at the time, but had his concerns prioritized in a different order.

"What in the Hell is going on, Earl?"
"Earl Patches Bower."

"You gave me a list of names, missing people you said you killed, and, well, they're still missing!"

"I don't understand."

"The dead bodies you gave us aren't the people you named. Who did you kill?"

"The bodies didn't match the names?"

"No!"

"Oh."

Earl Patches Bower seemed genuinely surprised by the information. He then spoke to himself aloud, muttered a judgment loud enough that Jaden caught the words.

"A clerical error."

Jaden demanded elaboration.

"What?"

Earl Patches Bower told him what. "You'll let me go and I'll see if I can sort it out, get back to you on it."

"Yeah, no, that's not happening. I've got you confessing to ninety-nine murders and now I've got ninety-nine more that you're going to start talking about."

"The world doesn't work that way, Jaden Ray Kawai. You can hold me for the psych evaluation that has yet to have been conducted, but not much longer than that. My lawyer will explain to you that I am a nutjob confessing to crimes that cannot be proven."

"You wrote down the locations and we found the bodies."

"My lawyer will tell you that I found that paper. It blew to me in the wind."

Earl Patches Bower stood up and was very matter-of-fact, courteous, seemed like he wanted to help the F.B.I. truly sort out the matter.

"I'll try to sort things out and get back to you."

Jaden watched as Earl Patches Bower walked over to the door of the interrogation room and knocked on its surface three times. Someone opened the door from the other side and allowed the Iowan to walk free.

Jaden was told that he should be proud for having brought some closure to ninety-nine families by unearthing the bodies of their missed loved ones. He was offered a promotion complete with a raise and private office space. He couldn't fathom continuing with the job knowing that Earl Patches Bower was allowed to walk out as if he owned the place. He quit. He began his own investigation.

Jaden flew to Iowa and went to the house owned by Earl Patches Bower. No one was home. No one had been home for years according to the neighbors. The trail went cold. The storm blew over without the storyteller in charge, as Jaden perceived it, directing the narrative. Jaden wanted to blow the whistle, but he could already see what the outcome would be for a lone man crying out Earl Patches Bower.

After some time off, Jaden returned to the F.B.I. and requested to return to his job. He was granted his position, but the offer of promotion did not stand. His place in the pecking order remained acceptable to him because he saw it as the best place to be in case Earl Patches Bower decided to call.

To this day Earl Patches Bower has never been seen or heard from again.

# I Burn

When people drive by the trailer owned by Teena Farns on rural route PP they tend to assume it is a meth den hiding in plain sight. The rusty abode, tucked into the weeds barely off the road with a squat gravel driveway, has been described as an "unfortunate piece of litter" by one council member of the nearby town of Haleigh and Teena's 1982 Cutlass Supreme in the driveway is generally considered an extension of the trash, though called "a miracle" by the mechanic who did the last smog check on it.

Teena Farns is a middle-aged woman who does a strong impression of someone who "doesn't give a fuck," however, the deep stress lines on her face show that the world doesn't give a fuck if you give a fuck: "livin' ain't easy, livin' ain't free, livin' to die is the only way to be."

She sits at an unbalanced table in the kitchen area of her trailer, an area defined by where the stained carpeting of the "living room area" gives up to stained linoleum. There was once a floral pattern involving vines on the linoleum, wear and tear has made the vines look more like knots of diseased veins with clots of tumors growing from them. Teena sips from a mug of coffee, nurses a hangover, and observes how close in shade her yellowed, in need of clipping, sawing, chiseling, toenails are to the color of the floor.

It's time to light up the day. Teena reaches for a pack of cigarettes on the table, slides a cigarette out, and slides it between her lips. Then she searches the pack for her lighter. When the search doesn't yield results she gives her bathrobe a quick pat down. Nada. She barks out her irritation.

"Westley! You take my lighter again?"

The cigarette continues to hang from her lips, one of her best party tricks. When her son doesn't sound off with a response, she mumbles to Jesus.

"Jesus, light a fire in that boy."

Jesus isn't going to respond either. He probably knows that the fish decal on the back of her car was there when she bought it.

"Westley! Get your ass in here! Don't be sneaking off to school with my lighter!"

27

Westley Bush, the seventeen year old by-product of Teena coupling with a deadbeat known as "Pug" Bush, a one-night event, shuffles into the kitchen with his heavy school backpack in tow. His black t-shirt features a punk rock logo, his jeans are black faded almost to gray, shoes: work sneakers with unnecessary steel toes, and his brown hair plays as it lays, untouched by a comb in over a year.

Westley drags his backpack to the side of the table and leaves it on the floor. He sits down in an empty chair to the side of Teena. She lets him know the mood she is in in case he didn't already hear her yelling.

"I'm going to start kicking your ass more."

He looks at her, but doesn't express any interest in responding vocally.

"You think you're too big?"

He ignores her itch for confrontation and tells her of his intentions.

"I'm taking the car today."

"Like hell you are."

"I already missed the bus."

"Sounds like something to think about while you're walking. What'd you do with my lighter?"

"I haven't seen it."

"You're a selfish little thief."

Whoops. The cigarette drops from her mouth, she bobbles it, but catches it in her hand. The cigarette goes right back between her lips.

Westley gives her a dose of stank eye, but then offers to help her.

"Here, I can light it."

He reaches down into his backpack.

Teena leans toward him to put the cigarette in position to receive a light.

Westley's hand returns with a small blow torch. He clicks the flame of the torch on and though she is surprised by the sight of the torch, Teena doesn't react to save herself in the following seconds, mind not deducing a threat, expecting the first hit of nicotine.

Westley puts the torch to Teena's face. The cigarette is lit, but so is her skin as her son jumps up to keep the flame applied to it.

Teena screams and falls to floor, loses her cigarette in the process. Her son goes down after her to finish torching her face. The woman thrashes, however, loses sight of life as it is burned from her body.

Westley takes the car.

The home of the Whittaker family is a house erected in the presumed safety of suburbia within the limits of the town of Haleigh. It is modern, not an expensive sort of build, and shielded in clean, white siding. The yard is trimmed in uniform code with those of the neighbors. It's a three bedroom building with the third room providing the luxury of office space. No one is allowed to smoke in the house.

This morning Brandi Whittaker sits at the age of seventeen on the toilet. She's not making a deposit at the moment just trying to wake up some more, drifting into different thoughts and concerns.

She's a young woman blessed with a face that went from adorable cherub to attractive angel, framed by long brunette hair that holds style and shines with shampoo commercial brilliance. Every now and then someone will try to attack her looks by making fun of the small mole to one side above her top lip; however, she got over her own fixation on the mole at an early age being able to embrace it as a "beauty mark."

Brandi idly turns a ring that is on one of her fingers. The ring is a focal point for her now as she slides it off her finger. She holds the piece of jewelry up and examines, reads the inscription on the inside of the band: TRUE LOVE WAITS.

After a moment more of consideration, Brandi replaces the purity ring on her finger.

Ann Whittaker is the obvious source of Brandi's beauty queen genes. Casually dressed for the day, Ann walks into the dining room space of her home with a bowl of granola in one hand, a coffee mug in the other. She sets the bowl down before an empty chair and then sits herself down to enjoy the contents of the mug in another chair.

Brandi walks into the area. She is dressed and ready for school clutching a backpack.

Ann greets her daughter.

"I poured you some granola. Moving a little slow this morning?"

Brandi sets her backpack down and takes the seat at the granola bowl before she replies.

"Pep rally today. I'm conserving my energy."

Ann smiles. Her daughter is always a source of pride and amusement.

Dan Whittaker, the husband to Ann and father to Brandi, strolls into the room. He is dressed for business in an office outside the home. He walks over to his wife and plants a kiss on her forehead before he tells her goodbye.

"I am outie fivethoutie."

"Have a good day, dear."

Dan turns his attention to his daughter. His genetics probably had something to do with Brandi's handsomeness too. He's got a Clark Kent weighed down by the problems of Superman sort of thing going for him. If father and daughter were to sit side by side brooding with frowns one would see the resemblance in spades.

"You got gas money?"

"I'm good. Noel is picking me up today."

"Buckle up and don't be texting each other while she drives. Bye, ladies."

Dan exits the room and is off to work.

Brandi eats her granola.

Ann takes a sip of her coffee and then announces the first step in her master plan.

"I'm going to do the laundry today."

Exciting.


A candy red SUV bops down the street with overproduced pop music broadcasting out of it. As the vehicle approaches the outside of the Whittaker house the volume of the music is lowered.

Behind the wheel of the SUV is Noel Thacker. She is a peer and today's chauffeur for Brandi. Her dirty blond hair is short, but cut in mismatched lengths. She wears a Haleigh high school cheerleader uniform. The school mascot as emblazoned on the front of the uniform is a grasshopper.

Noel waves like a goofy madwoman at her friend as she sees her exit the house. However, Brandi either can't see or doesn't pay attention to the manic gesture as she walks to and gets into the vehicle.

Noel keeps the music volume down as she mashes on the gas pedal and guides her candy red rocket down the street. She comments on her friend's wardrobe.

"Shauna is going to cut your head off for not wearing your uniform."

"I guess that would save me from having to do any of her corny cheers."

Noel feigns outrage over that statement.

"Shame on you, Brandi Whittaker!"

And then Chris Owens pops up from his hiding spot in the rear seat and startles Brandi with his exclamation.

"They'll burn you at the stake!"

"Ah! Chris!"

She tries to slap him but misses.

Noel is a giggle box.

Chris is a handsome young man with his hair shaved quite short. As military as he may seem at first glance, the male cheerleader uniform he wears is not the type that gets him many respectful salutes.

As her friends keep on laughing over making their friend scream out in fright, Brandi almost smiles, but keeps things sarcastic.

"Yeah, thanks for teaming up against me guys."

Noel frowns. "I'm sorry. I'm team Chris."

"You're supposed to be team Brandi."

"Aww. I am."

Chris doesn't want Brandi to be miffed. "I'm not here to pressure you. Just needed a ride to school."

She voices more displeasure, nudges an argument forward. "Give me time and give me space, THAT was what you agreed to."

"I missed you. I'll sit back here and be quiet."

Noel fights on behalf of Chris. "Don't be mad. It's my fault. I think you guys are too cute together."

"I'm not mad."

"So, you're going to break up with Rhett today and ride off into the sunset with me and Chris happily ever after?"

"Into the sunset with both of you?"

"My love life has no wheels. I figure I'm better off being your third."

"If you want to sate Chris I won't be offended."

Chris leans forward and chimes in. "If I have an opinion on this will that put me deeper into the doghouse?"

Noel scolds him. "Shut up, idiot. I've almost got you hooked up with a threesome."

Brandi almost cracks another smile but is able to maintain her seriousness when she replies.

"Fantasize all you want, but I still want some "me" time. Me needs to not worry about boy/girl drama for a day."

Chris sits back again. "I'll give you your time and space. I'll be back here."

Brandi accidentally lets a snort slip out as she tries to hold in her chuckles this time.

Brandi makes it to her first class on time. She sits at her desk and a moment later she has company. Shauna Stevens and Kirsten Fischer arrive at the side of Brandi's desk. Both of the young women are in their grasshopper cheerleader uniforms. Brandi greets them and points out the lack of faculty at the front of the room with the final bell so near ringing.

"Shauna. Kirsten. Where's the teacher?"

Kirsten answers the question posed.

"We've got a substitute. I think it's Mr. Klepke."

Cheerleader captain Shauna demands an answer.

"Why aren't you in uniform?"

"Because I am in human mode."

"It's mandatory on game days and we've got the pep rally."

"It's silly. If it makes you feel better you can kick me off of the squad."

Kirsten continues her part in the good-cop-bad cop routine.

"We would never do that."

Shauna doesn't like Brandi's attitude.

"What is wrong with you?"

Brandi is genuine in her apology. She knows that she hasn't been "herself" as of late.

"I'm sorry."

"You mean a lot to the squad. You used to act like we meant a lot to you too."

Kirsten tries to find balance between the ladies, no pressure on Brandi, but selling what Shauna is preaching.

"It's our final year, don't you want to make some final lasting memories?"

Shauna lectures.

"It's about tradition. By not wearing the uniform you make the rest of us look silly."

Shauna grins at her own joke made at the expense of the grasshopper on her chest. Kirsten gives her a playful elbow and corrects her.

"I think she meant sexy."

Brandi does bask in the kindness in Shauna's smile. She continues to be apologetic.

"I get it. You're right. I wasn't thinking right."

Shauna and Kirsten share a look of concern with each other over their friend who apologizes with her eyes cast down.

Westley watches the trio of girls from the seat of his own desk, two back and one row over from Brandi. He doesn't care for Shauna or Kirsten, focuses on Brandi. He sees her nibble at her lip when the other two ladies walk away. He senses a sadness within her, a despair that matches the mist that envelopes his own heart. He thinks of that mist now. It is a stupid image that he conjured in some emo poetry last year: "the fog of the heart hangs over night eyes." He is over that, yet it tries to pull him back in. Romance can turn a man into a corny fool. Westley will be a jester no more!

Mr. Klepke enters the room and goes over to the blackboard to scrawl out his name for the students not already familiar with him. Brandi looks forward as if ready to tune in for a lesson. Westley stays tuned in to her, Brandi 101, and soon he plans to enroll in the advanced course.

The class passes by and Westley is caught by the bell in a daydream about dropping his pencil, getting it to roll to the back of Brandi's heel, and then licking his way up her leg as he retrieves it. He pulls himself out of the daydream, wipes at the dab of drool that formed at one corner of his mouth. However, he doesn't get out of his seat like the other students. He lingers as he sees that Brandi is slow in getting out of her seat. What could have been on her mind? If she wants escape, he's got that and more in mind for her.

All the other students exit along with the teacher.

As Brandi slowly packs books into her backpack Westley gets to his feet. He moves a hand, raises it as if he thinks to wave for

Brandi's attention. It is not a big enough gesture to be noticed and when his lips move no words come out.

Rhett Stafford strolls into the classroom. He has that big man on campus in his letterman jacket swagger. People bow down to that, but Westley glares. He hates Brandi's boyfriend. The stank eye that he shoots at Rhett goes as unnoticed as his complete presence.

Rhett calls to Brandi as he approaches her. "Brandiiiiiiiii!"

He holds out his arms as if she should rush to him in celebration. Her response is less than ecstatic.

"Hey, Rhett."

"Did you have your phone off all weekend or what?"

Rhett suddenly notices the fly on the wall, catches Westley staring at them.

"Queerbait, quit standing there looking like you want to shoot up the school. Get out."

Brandi flicks a quick glance toward Rhett's target and then says the name of the high school basketball superstar in a scolding tone.

"Rhett."

Westley decides to comply with Rhett's order. He grabs his things and walks toward the front of the classroom. As he passes by Rhett feigns a punch at him. Westley flinches, bumps into a desk, trips, and falls on to the floor.

Rhett laughs, but Brandi doesn't approve. "Don't be a jerk!"

She shoves Rhett with both hands, but not with enough power to topple only irritate him.

"What the hell?"

She turns her attention to Westley on the floor.

"Are you okay, Wes?"

She sort of knows his name. He hates his name. She called him "Wes" instead of "West," an improvement, could she be more perfect?

She holds out a hand, an offer to help him off the floor. It is her left hand. He appreciates that. He appreciates her fingers, lovely fingers, and one of them wears a purity ring. He has seen it many times before, but never so close. He wants to smell her fingers and then shove them into his mouth.

He does not take her hand. He gets himself up to his feet without a word, like a cool man, and then after a brief scowl at Rhett, walks toward and then out of the room.

Rhett is amused. Brandi isn't finished punishing him for that.

"You're a bully."

"Pssh. He's one of those kids my dad caught doing satanic rituals down at Hobbs creek."

His excuse doesn't soften Brandi on the interaction.

The school bell rings and they are both going to be late for class.

Rhett issues an apology.

"I'm sorry, I'll apologize if that helps. I've got too much testosterone running through my system right now."

She is ready to move on.

"I'm late for my next class."

"What are you thinking about?"

"What do you mean?"

"I can tell you've got something on your mind. Something smart, college and all that. Maybe you're thinking about whether or not I'm a jock cliché peaking in high school and destined to work the cash register at the hardware store. Or worse, work for my dad."

"I know better than that."

"I'm small town raised, but I see the big picture. I love you, Brandi."

Mr. Klepke interrupts.

"What are you two doing in here? There's no second period in here."

Brandi takes that as a cue to skip out on the conversation. She clutches her backpack and hurries to the exit. Rhett chases after her.

In the hallway Rhett watches Brandi hurry away. It is obvious that she wants to put distance between them. He lets her have it. His class is in the same direction, but he'll slow roll and maybe wet his whistle at a water fountain. It'll give him time to come up with a joke to crack when he enters class late.

Before the pep rally Brandi puts on her cheerleader uniform. She takes a moment after lacing up her shoe to sit and experience the emptiness of the women's locker room.

Noel enters the room and launches right into conversation with Brandi.

"Shauna is complaining that you're not out there. She told 'em to tell you that this is another reason we wear the uniform to school."

Brandi hops up off of the bench, claps her hands together, and responds with a classic cheerleading opener.

"O! K!"

Both girl's laugh. Then Brandi shares a thought about cheerleading.

"I like cheerleading, but it's for school.

She tugs on the fabric of the uniform.

"I don't want to put this on at home. At home, it's not me."

Noel has a juicer topic on her mind.

"Did you talk to Rhett this morning?"

"Briefly."

"Annnd? Are you now single?"

"Honestly, he said he loved me, and it still felt good."

"Chris is so great though!"

"It's complicated. I kind of want to run away before it blows up and I become a town scandal and a disappointment to my parents."

"I don't think that anyone is going to freak out about a girl with two suitors on the hook. Do you think Rhett knows about Chris?"

"No."

"Nothing to worry about then."

"I wish."

Kirsten walks in as Shauna's messenger.

"Pep rally! We need your spirit on the floor!"

The gymnasium rocks with energy during the pep rally. Brandi and company put on the rap infused cheer performance that was written by Shauna. Due to all of the noise it seems to go well. Specifically the part about how "grasshoppers will never be squashed." Most of the students are stomping their feet and clapping due to their love of not having to be in a class.

Underneath the bleachers Westley watches Brandi and her dance moves. The way her hips sway in her skirt is mesmerizing. He is impressed by the way that she is able to fake "joy." It is infectious. He almost wants to yell out "go grasshoppers!"

After the pep rally Brandi and Noel return to the locker room together. Brandi's backpack is on the ground next to the bench where she left it. There is a hairbrush on the bench over it. Brandi walks over to her backpack and right away registers that something is "off."

"Do you smell that?"

Noel sniffs the air as Brandi moves her investigation along. The charred remains of a book are on the end of the bench down from the brush.

"It looks like someone was burning a book or something."

"Huh. Weird."

Noel walks over for a closer look.

"Any of your stuff been ganked?"

Brandi picks up her backpack and quickly sorts through the contents.

"I don't know. I didn't have my brush out I don't think."

She picks up the hair brush and Noel advises against tampering with the potential crime scene.

"I wouldn't touch it."

"Why?"

"What if some weirdo like Mrs. Perkins was down here shoving it into her cooter?"

Brandi drops the brush. Noel pushes her theory and teasing.

"I mean, I didn't see Mrs. Perkins out there at the rally."

"I have her for next period."

"Woof. Awkward for you then."

Brandi does her best to make her face express: "I am grossed out."

Westley returns home from school, fishtails his mother's car down the driveway, high on dust cloud nine.

Inside the trailer he sits down in a kitchen chair and holds up the hair he plucked from Brandi's brush. He smells the hair and even gives it a little nibble. Then he tells the corpse of his mother, still in the floor, about his day.

"She called me Wes. Not stupid West."

He sniffs the hairball again.

"I will be able to smell her through the brimstone of Hell. She's the one. She is pure. All of my waiting, all of my preparations, it's finally coming true."

He is too excited to stay in his seat. He paces and exclaims to his dead mother what will be.

"I will be reborn by my true father! Brandi Whittaker will be the queen at my side! We will set this world on fire!"

Westley gathers what he needs from the trailer and then pours the gasoline. He stands in the driveway and watches the flames as they absorb the trailer into their heat. He screams obscenities into the fire, at the corpse that burns inside of it. Then he gets into the car and drives away from the only home that he has ever known and always knew was never home.

At the Whittaker house Brandi is still in her cheer uniform, but is comfortable enough lounged on a couch in the living room. The television is on, but her cellphone screen has her attention.

Ann Whittaker walks into the room with a glass of treat in each hand—pink smoothies.

Brandi sets her phone down on the arm of the couch as her mother approaches and hands her a smoothie.

"Virgin strawberry daiquiris. The taste of the thrill with none of the ill."

"Thanks, Mom."

Ann sits down on the couch to converse with her daughter between sips of smoothie.

"Do you have a game tonight?"

"Yeah. Apparently I have to wear the uniform all the way until it's over or else we lose."

"Do you want me to go? We might be a few minutes late, but your father and I could make it."

"No. That's okay."

Brandi picks up her phone to check the latest text to arrive.

Ann glances at the television, but the program doesn't interest her either, maybe

Brandi will share some of her world from the phone. "Is that Noel?"

Brandi nods, keeps her eyes on the phone, fingers working the buttons.

"You should invite her to church on Sunday. I haven't seen her there in a while."

"I'll ask her."

Brandi sets the phone down again. She gives her attention to her mom, sees that her mother's interest is in her and it's a perfect time for some serious mother-daughter chatting.

"Mom."

"Daughter?"

"Dad commutes like an hour to work, why don't we just live in the city?"

"Because it doesn't feel like home."

Brandi nods to this as if she understands, but the nodding is in silence, a moment of silence in which she musters up the nerve to approach what she really wants to ask.

"What would you think if I stayed home and took a year off before going to college?"

"What would you do?"

"Work at the ice cream shop? Figure out what I want to do?"

Ann hears Brandi's doubt, but does not have any doubt of her own.

"You want to go to college. You'll have your pick of the litter too. I know, I made sure all of your applications were perfect and mailed off. It's natural to have cold feet, but you'll see what it's like when you get there."

"You're right."

"We're invested in you becoming a big shot lawyer so that when your father and I are old you can afford to put us in a luxury home."

"And if I don't become a big shot lawyer?"

"We'll still love you even if you only become a non-profit lawyer."

"Well, that's good to know."

Mother smiles at daughter, proud of the blossoming adult who sips from the smoothie that she made for her. Brandi smiles to hide her dread, but it turns into a grimace due to the onset of a smoothie-induced brain freeze.

The fire set by Westley destroyed the trailer, but did not manage to spread too far beyond a weeded ditch line behind the structure. Firemen reached the scene in a timely fashion after a passing motorist called in the blaze. Flames still flicker, but it's akin to a dying campfire.

Now Sheriff Merle Stafford, father of Rhett, stands in the driveway and surveys the damage with Levi Coontz, a good-ole-boy volunteer fireman who smokes a cigarette.

"It was a hot one, Sheriff. It tried to spread to the woods, but we got it snuffed."

"I was told that I'd want to come out here personally."

Earl gestures toward the ash heap where the trailer once stood.

"Think we found human remains in there."

"That's not good."

"Teena Farns and her boy lived here."

"They both in it you reckon?"

"Can't say for sure. We saw the body and figured we should run it by you before we piddle around digging too deep."

"Better safe than sorry. I'll call in the crime scene fellers."

He looks around and a question pops into his head.

"Was there any type of vehicle that burned up?"

"Don't seem to be."

"Do you know what Teena drove?"

"Not off the top of my head. A car maybe?"

"Maybe. Okay. Well, this might be a long night."

He pulls out his own pack of cigarettes.

Teena's car is parked in the driveway of a rural lake house. Westley doesn't know the name of the lake, has always known it as "the lake," and the name must not be that well known despite its size because a lot of the rental houses remain empty of tourists all year. The lake is a long bike ride from the town of Haleigh, but the distance teenage legs will pedal for adventure is a much farther distance.

Westley has snooped around the lake properties for years.

Tonight he entered a house that he saw listed as having a vacancy for renters on the Internet. He unlocked the cabin by smashing a rock through a window pane in one of the doors. Even with everything on his mind, as he put his hand through the broken window to unlock the door, he gives a second of judgment to the stupid people who still design doors with such windows on them.

The decor of the house is rustic disarray and taxidermy. The owner of the place made sure that the online listing showed off the owl that got stuffed and turned into an unfortunate centerpiece on a decorative table. However, left out of the photos are the other small animals chucked into piles for lazy storage: squirrels, lizards, a cat. The decapitated head of a grand buck leans against one wall waiting to be hung.

The materials of Westley have been spread out in the living room area of the house. He has journals, books, drawings, all reference materials that point toward an interest in dark arts and the catacombs of Hell. Aside from these items there are also some boxes of mechanical odds and ends, tools, a propane tank, and plenty of containers for gasoline.

In the rear yard of the property, which travels all the way down to a private dock on the lake, Westley has arranged himself a ceremonial pentagram. The symbol is painted in thick white on the grass and encircled by black candles that have all been lit. He doesn't have Druid robes to fit himself perfectly to the scene that he has laid out, but Westley does wear a black hoodie with the hood up for imitation.

The teen gazes beyond his pentagram and toward the lake. He marvels at the colors reflected off the lake's surface as daylight and twilight conduct the slow changing of the guard.

His eyes then direct his attention to a floating wooden platform out in the lake. It is the type of structure that people dive from or rest on for sunbathing. Westley has never seen anyone ever actually use it for those purposes, but he's seen summer camp movies. He pulls out the clump of Brandi's hair from his pocket and smells it as he thinks about his plans for that floating platform. First he has some business with the pentagram. Time to get busy being born.

He holds Brandi's hair up, extends it skyward to be blessed by the dying light as he speaks aloud to the pentagram.

"Tasa reme laris Satan."

He pauses for a moment and then repeats the words.

"Tasa reme laris Satan."

He steps over the candles and closer to the center of the pentagram. He continues to hold up the hair, but alters his chant.

"Ganic Tasa fubin, Flereous."

He listens. The words are out of his mouth and he is on the edge of great things, perhaps existence as he knows it has already been altered, he listens for a clue, hears his manic heartbeat. He barks out those words again.

"Ganic Tasa, fubin, Flereous!"

He stoops down and places the hair into the center of the pentagram.

"I honor you."

Once he stands straight again, again he continues.

"Ganic Tasa, fubin, Flereous."

Next he steps outside of the circle of candles and retrieves a canister of gasoline. He unscrews the cap and tosses it aside. The fluid inside the can sloshes as he walks it back to the circle and stands on the pentagram.

"Ganic Tasa fubin, Flereous. Come over me, Flereous. Empower me!"

He jerks his head into a nod that shakes the hood off of his head.

"Ganic Tasa fubin, Flereous. Come over me, Flereous. Empower me."

He lifts the gas can up over his head, a wobbly procedure for he hasn't been lifting many weights in recent years. Some of the gas splashes out too early, but he manages to heft the rest high enough to then pour over his own head. As he showers in the gasoline he continues to yell.

"Ganic Tasa fubin, Flereous!"

His muscles weaken and he lowers the can, makes sure to drain the rest of the contents on to his body, legs, shoes. When the can is empty he throws it aside. He spits, gags on fumes, but still proceeds with his ceremony by pulling out a lighter.

"Ganic Tasa fubin, Flereous. I am fire. Empower me!"

He soaks in a moment of silence, takes in the burn that is in his eyes, his nose, takes in the sunset, the lake, the flames of the candles, and then he flicks the lighter's flame into being.

He touches the flame to himself and ignites.

"Ahh!"

The scream comes before the pain, the pain comes in a flash thereafter. He doesn't bother with a secondary scream as he becomes a human fireball.

He runs off of the pentagram, hurdles the candles without disturbing them, and streaks across the yard toward the lake.

The young man in flames sprints across the dock and leaps off of the end of it into the lake.

After the splash an orgy of bubbles rise furiously to the surface of the water. However, they dissipate in short order and the lake is once again calm.

Darkness strangles the last of the sunlight.

The cheerleader squad of Brandi, Noel, Shauna, Kirsten, and Chris hang out in the bed of Chris' junker pickup truck. They debate their school mascot with Shauna being a leader happy with their program as it is.

"Our mascot is as strong as we make it. We could be 'the cupcakes' and still be fearsome."

Kirsten is cool with that viewpoint.

"I like grasshoppers just fine."

Noel suggests an imaginative new element to be added.

"Can we at least be magic grasshoppers?"

Brandi votes for Noel's idea.

"I'm in for that. We need to draw little wizard hats on them."

Chris disagrees.

"No. We need to change it. I vote for making it a dinosaur."

Shauna poops on that suggestion.

"Being 'the dinosaurs' would sound dumb."

"It would be a specific type of dinosaur."

"Give us one dinosaur name that would be short enough or that people at our school could even pronounce."

"Ballasaurus." He is able to maintain a straight face as Kirsten dares him to elaborate.

"What would Ballasaurus look like?"

"A t-rex with gold chains around its neck."

The girls laugh at him and Brandi voices her disapproval.

"I'm not voting for that."

Kirsten offers up another outside of the box concept.

"I think Creepy Pete down at the gas station should become our mascot."

A group chuckle ensues and Noel changes her vote.

"Eww, totally. Creepy Pete all the way."

Shauna cuts their chill time short.

"We better go sit in the crowd and support J.V."

She hops up to get out of the truck and the others all move to follow her. Chris, however, is going to let the girls go ahead of him toward the school.

"I'll be right in. I've got to get my water bottle."

He goes over the side of the truck bed and then walks toward the cab.

Brandi at first follows the other young women, but then turns around. She walks back to have an alone moment with Chris by his truck. He has his water bottle and greets her.

"Hey."

She is apprehensive about delivering her message.

"After the game, there's something I'd like to talk to you about."

"I'm not sure if that sounds great or ominous."

Brandi shrugs. She's not ready to get into it yet. Chris has assumptions to fill in the blanks with.

"This town can be a dream killer. You've just got to survive a few more months and then you can move on to amazing things. I want you to know that, as your friend, I won't let that fall apart for you. Rhett is already your boyfriend and that makes sense. He's the safe choice. If you're going to break it off with me, I understand."

Brandi admires his eyes for a moment. She searches for her response, finds it.

"That makes you the safe choice, Chris. After the game, okay?"

Chris pumps a fist and gives her a wink.

"Go grasshoppers."

Gloria Ipple, an older woman who gave up eating meat, but not collecting roadkill and collecting it as art, has seen some weird things in her time, but the pentagram surrounded by still lit candles at her feet ranks high in weirdness to her. She stares down at the arrangement and speaks into the cellphone that she holds to the side of her head.

"It looks like they're gone. The punks have vandalized the place. Thanks for the neighborly heads up, Donna. I'll call you back later."

Gloria hangs up her phone and clips it to the holder on her belt. She grumble-mumbles on her way over to where the water hose is stored against the house. She goes through the pain in the butt process that is unfurling the hose and getting it connected to the water spigot. Then she drags the hose over to where the candles burn, the trigger of the hose nozzle gets pulled, and water sprays at the tiny flames.

The water pressure suddenly cuts off. Gloria yanks on the hose to free it of any kinks, but is surprised to find zero tension. The severed end of the hose flops over to her and splashes her pant leg and shoes with water.

"What in the hell?"

Gloria drops the hose and turns to investigate. When she sees what stands behind her Gloria experiences true terror for the first time in her life. Her hands fumble for the phone clipped to her side, the programming of instinct trying to save her while her brain shuts down as if it is already dead. The phone gets freed.

A sword blade whooshes through the air and strikes with impressive precision, separates head from neck with impressive might, the blade must be goddamned impressive sharp indeed. As Gloria's head topples off, her hands bring the cellphone up so that the blood spurting stump at her neck can try to call for help. The hands forgot to dial any numbers and the headless body gives up and collapses to the ground.

What the crowd inside of the high school gymnasium lacks in size it makes up for in enthusiasm. The proud parents of ball players and cheerleaders mingle with sports fans and perverts to take pictures and yell out encouraging support to the youngster there to provide entertainment.

One section of the bottom row of bleachers is reserved for the cheer squad and also serves as the player's bench. Brandi and company currently sit and watch the varsity basketball players finish their warmup drills.

Rhett and his teammates are doing layups when the referee calls on the attention of coaches and athletes to let them know it is time to huddle up off the court and get ready to rumble.

As the players walk over to their bench the cheerleaders stand up to show their unity with the team and offer encouragement. Rhett detours over to Brandi with a request.

"Can I get a good luck kiss?"

He puckers his lips and smooches some air.

Brandi hesitates in fulfilling his request, but then leans in and delivers a peck to his cheek.

Chris watches this exchange of affection and Rhett catches the male cheerleader's stare.

"No thanks, Chris. I only kiss the ones with pom-poms."

He grasps both of his own breasts in case the innuendo wasn't clear enough.

Chris lifts up one of his hands to show that at that exact moment he actually does hold a pom-pom. He gives it a little shake for Rhett and the basketball player laughs.

"Ha."

Rhett offers his fist for a fist bump and Chris is polite enough to bump it. The Rhett gives Chris a playful warning.

"Don't let me catch you looking up my girlfriend's skirt."

After the basketball player hustles away Brandi turns to Chris and they share a brief look of complicated feelings.

Spotlights have been erected to shine down on the ruins of the trailer turned crematorium for Teena Frans. However, there isn't much activity going on beneath these lights yet in way of investigation.

Volunteer fireman Levi Coontz stands around in the driveway with his fellow firefighting buddy Garth Butler. Garth has an idea on how the night could be hurried along.

"I've seen enough forensics shows, if the Sheriff wants to deputize us, we could get this show on the road."

Levi teases his buddy.

"You got one of them DNA kits? Going to sniff out semen amongst the ashes?"

"Semen? You think this was a sex thing?"

"Maybe. Right now I reckon it was a fire."

Garth nods to that truth.

"Yep. He should deputize us."

Sheriff Stafford exits his patrol vehicle and rushes over to his two new unofficial deputies.

"Levi, you got your radio on? There's another fire call. Somebody is burning the hay bales on Donna Jones's property near the lake."

Levi and Garth both flick their cigarettes off into the crime scene as Levi shouts out the call to duty for the others who meander about.

"Boy, mount up!"

The Sheriff leads with more orders for Levi to consider.

"Ya'll follow me out. The firebug might still be there."

The property of Donna Jones butts up against the property of Gloria Ipple. While the Ipple plot is just a lakeside feature, the Jones land extends farther into a vast sum of acreage with a massive hay field being a current feature. The hay field is ablaze, and on the route that the Sheriff and his firefighter backup team drive they can see the individual bales as fireballs, but the flames are going to be dancing around with any flammable partner and spread across the land in a sheet if a valiant fight is not organized before winds start flirting with any intentions.

The red and blue lights on the top of the Sheriff's vehicle lead the parade toward the best field entrance where Donna Jones has already had her son-in-law open the gate.

At the high school the basketball game is underway.

Brandi and the cheerleaders do their best to keep the crowd energized. They stomp their feet and wave their hands in the air. It's Brandi's turn to hop like a grasshopper and she squats down and pops up like a pro with joy too incredible to be true plastered on her face.

Sheriff Merle Stafford goes into the fire field with his gun out, ready to duel with any torch-bearing demons. He wants to make sure that the firemen are safe from any threats, but it seems to him that the fire is just as big a threat as the being that set it and they should act quicker than a clearing of the area will take to extinguish that threat. It's not like the swirling smoke and flickering flames make searching the field for arsonists an easy task.

Levi walks up to the Sheriff for direction. "See anything?"

"You boys go ahead and get to watering them flames."

While his father is stepping into a deadly game in the field, Rhett Stafford plays some defense on the basketball court. An opponent dribbles the basketball and tries to work by Rhett. Rhett gets a hand in and strips the ball free. It's his now!

Rhett dribbles the stolen ball across the court and on the other side he lives out every aspiring athlete's wet dream: he shoots! He scores!

A line of fire shoots up behind the gathered firemen and the armed lawman within the field of Donna Jones. Even as visibility becomes hazier with fires already set, it is obvious that someone just lit an accelerant between the men and where they parked their vehicles.

Garth Butler thinks he saw something. "I think I saw something!"

The Sheriff keeps his gun out and he squints around, seeks movement outside of the gathered group of men. He worries that they are being surrounded in their position.

He breaks off from the fireman as he observes a bulk of shadow moving along the perimeter as he understands it with the nearest burning bale.

A Molotov cocktail sails through the air and lands at the Sheriff's feet. The bomb explodes and flames shoot up the lawman's pant legs.

The cheerleaders do some pom-pom pumps and sway their hips on the sidelines. Chris is at the end of the line, the sole male cheerleader, and he seems checked out of cheering. He watches the action on the court and it is less about being a sports fan and more about letting himself indulge in a moment of jealousy as his romantic rival Rhett gets to showcase himself in a way that people find easier to admire. No one is there to see Chris; woe is he.

A tossed pom-pom hits Chris in the face and snaps him out of his dramatic indulgence. He turns and sees Brandi smiling at him. He tosses her pom-pom back to her with a smile and joins her in once again proclaiming to the world within the gymnasium that grasshoppers are invincible.

A barrage of Molotov cocktails disunite the firemen and send them off on "every man for himself" trajectories around the burning field. Some of the homemade bombs break on impact as intended, but one bottle conks Levi in the head without bursting out with explosion.

A hand to his aching head, Levi loses his sense of direction as a wall of smoke wafts into his route. He stumbles and loses the cigarette that he held between his lips.

A figure moves toward him out of the haze and darkness. Levi hunkers down to get himself below the smoke, a maneuver taught to firemen in pre-school. A cowering that makes him an easier target for the approaching entity.

The humanoid figure that steps closer to Levi smells of barbequed flesh and Levi can indeed see that the epidermis on it is charred. However, what Levi is awe-struck by is the battle sword held in the hands of the being. The blade has been doused in accelerant and flames swirl around the blade. It is awesome for a moment and then the moment is over, the last moment of Levi's life. He is struck dead by the flaming sword.

Rhett breaks a sweat as he dribbles the ball on offense. He jukes his way past an opponent and a second defender steps in. This leaves

Rhett's teammate Allen Pippen open and Rhett ends his drive toward the basket with a skillful pass. Allen shoots, Allen scores.

As Rhett hustles back on defense he looks to his girlfriend on the sideline and forms a heart symbol with his fingers.

Brandi celebrates and there is no doubt that in that moment she is his cheerleader.

Sheriff Stafford has lost some skin, his shoes, and his pants, but underwear, uniform top, gun, and his life are intact. He relies on his internal compass to help lead him through the inferno that the bale field has become.

Fireman Garth Butler suddenly lunges into view. His back is on fire and his torso has been cleaved open. The man seems to scream, but gargling blood is the only sound effect he can make. The Sheriff shows restraint in his trigger finger as the wounded man spills out his guts and falls down at his feet. The Sheriff considers flipping his restraint into brutal mercy, but the fireman lies still, perhaps already gone from pain, and executing the wounded isn't a world that the Sheriff wants to live in just yet.

The death yelps of another fireman can be heard nearby. The Sheriff chooses to run in what he thinks is the opposite direction.

The star basketball player that is the Sheriff's son has the ball again and edges his defender ever closer toward the goal. He senses that he is within range for a nice Michael Jordan moment, and pulls up the ball as he stops. He pivots and spins toward the goal and does a pump fake to try and entice his opponent off his feet too early. However, the defender doesn't bite and when Rhett follows up the fake with an actual jump shot an open hand slaps the ball easily. The shot is blocked and the ball spikes back into Rhett, hits off of him and rolls toward a sideline.

Rhett isn't hurt and adrenaline taps him to chase after the ball. He makes a dive that results in some floor burns to his body, but the ball goes out of bounds as a turnover.

Sheriff Stafford closes his eyes to run through a section of flames. His calculations were correct and he finds himself tripping and falling to the ground into clearer air near the fence line. The fence is wooden, probably best to get over it before it too is engulfed.

The Sheriff gets to his feet, uses a fence board as a rung, and steps up, however, he's not as graceful as he was in his youth and tumbles over the top of the fence. When he lands on the other side he loses the grip on his gun.

As the Sheriff sits up he finds himself facing the burning field and at the edge of the fire that he just ran through stands an ominous figure with a sword. The sword is no longer on fire as others got to see it, but the vision is just as intimidating to the mind. The Sheriff quickly searches the ground for his gun, not as easy as it would be if the grass weren't so overgrown.

Westley charges toward the fence, a dark mess of seared flesh and melted clothing, pasted together with boiled blood and cooked fats. He is both wet and crispy. His eyes are sheer redness, but it seems to be red vision not blindness.

The Sheriff finds his gun and as he rises up, Westley reaches the fence and jabs the blade of the sword between the wooden slats. The sword pierces through the Sheriff's chest and impales his heart. Merle Stafford manages to fire a bullet up toward the Heavens, a violent prayer that does nothing to stop the Hell on Earth before him.

Westley withdraws the blade and the Sheriff flops over dead.

The basketball game is over and the gymnasium has been cleared, as well as most of the parking lot of cars. Chris, still in his uniform of cheer, walks alone to his truck. When he reaches the vehicle he leans against the driver's side door and watches as Brandi, Noel, Shauna, Kirsten, and Rhett exit the school building as a group. None of them have used the school showers or changed their

clothing, the girls in their cheer clothes, Rhett
in his player jersey and shorts, though he has
donned a jacket. They walk into the lot, but
don't get far from the building before they
linger in place.

Noel pouts. "I can't believe that we lost the
game."

Her sympathy seems spoken directly to
Rhett and he responds.

"We? Maybe you should have scored more
points for us."

Shauna defends the work of the
cheerleaders.

"Our energy is out there on the court
helping the players."

Rhett pulls a fifth of whiskey out of his
jacket pocket and shows it off to the group.

"How about I share? This is meant for
celebration, but losing doesn't have to cancel
the party."

The "party" is news to Brandi.

"What party?"

"They're leaving the doors unlocked for
me. I thought that we might have a date. I
guess it can be you, me, and the skirted three
though."

"I do want to talk to you alone."

Rhett likes the sound of that.

"Let's get our alone time then."

Noel steps up and yanks the bottle of
booze out of his hands.

"I'll take care of this."

Kirsten is in but has a question. "Do we get shot glasses?"

Noel doesn't see the need for such things. "I'm chugging this bastard like a real lady."

Kirsten gives Shauna a flutter of her eyelashes, a cross between asking for permission and a flirtatious invite to the party. Shauna is in. The trio of Noel, Shauna, and Kirsten link arms and head back toward the unlocked school building.

After the trio reaches the doors, Rhett takes Brandi by the hand.

"Come on, we can talk inside."

She doesn't let him guide her. "Alone, Rhett. It's important."

She nods in the direction of Chris at the truck. Rhett is confused.

"Alone with Chris?"

"Yes."

"Why would we need Chris?"

Brandi can't get herself to answer that yet. Rhett's confusion ramps up in anger.

"Has he been making moves on you? I had a feeling, but I wasn't sure."

"There's just, like, really something I would like to discuss with both of you."

"Is it good or bad?"

"I don't know."

"You like him? Is this why we've been having problems? This why you ditched me this weekend?"

"It's not like that."

He gets louder.

"Not like what? Tell me what it's like!"

His yelling only inspires her to stay quiet on details. Rhett moves into action.

"I'll beat it out of him."

He walks toward Chris and Brandi runs to get in front of him. She pushes her hands to his chest and he slaps them off, a little too hard for even his own liking and that gets him to stop walking.

Chris calls over to them. "Is everything okay?"

Rhett yells a threat.

"I'm going to break your teeth out of your face!"

Brandi tries to sedate the aggressiveness.

"I need the three of us to talk like adults."

"You want to break up with me for a cheerleader boy? Is this because he goes to your church? He's a part of your Jesus purity ring circle of jerkoffs."

"Stop it!"

"Yeah. No. You know what? I'm going inside before they drink all of my buzz. I had a shitty weekend and was looking forward to tonight. You and pom-pom boy can talk if you want. You already know how I feel and if that's not gay enough for you, then I guess there's nothing else to say."

Rhett turns and takes long angry strides toward the school.

Brandi does not follow after him. Chris walks over to Brandi's side.

"You okay?"

"Please take me home."

The drive to Brandi's house doesn't feature any dialogue between the two, both let their minds float along with the country music that emits from the radio. It must be depressing ballad hour because the country station gives the duo many of the soft strings of lost love and violins of lost dogs that the genre has to offer.

As Chris's truck swings up in front of their destination, Brandi is drawn out of her mind by flames reflecting on the side door glass before her face. She stares toward her home.

"My yard is on fire!"

The truck brakes into park hard and Brandi doesn't waste any time throwing the door open and rushing out.

The fire on the front lawn burns in symbol of unknown meaning to the cheerleader. The flames stay in their neat design, do not seem to be an immediate threat to spread.

Brandi moves around the burning symbol and sees that her front door is ajar. She goes to the door and calls out to her parents as she pushes it the rest of the way open.

"Mom! Dad!"

Once she enters the living room Brandi hears 80s synth pop playing from deeper within the house. She stands in the room for a moment and surveys it for danger. A lamp is on, but it seems that most of the lights in the house have been left off.

"Mom! Dad?"

Brandi moves on to continue exploration.

The source of the music is her parent's bedroom. The door to the room is shut but Brandi turns the knob and finds that it is unlocked. She pushes into the room with caution.

Daddy Dan Whittaker has mommy Ann Whittaker bent over the bed and pounds her from behind to the beat of the music.

Brandi covers her eyes.

"Mom!"

Her mom and dad scramble out of their erotic coupling, scurry on to the bed, and do their best to wrap a blanket over their nudity as Ann yells back to their daughter.

"Brandi! Privacy!"

"Our front yard is on fire!"

Dan Whittaker, in his "lucky" robe, steps out of his front door to see about a fire. Brandi exits the house after him. They discover that the fire is out and Chris stands there with a fire extinguisher in his hand and an explanation.

"I keep this in the truck."

Dan likes the guy.

"Good boy. Do you kids have any clue who would do this?"

Chris shakes his head and Brandi vocalizes her lack of suspects.

"No."

Dan will work with a basic theory.

"Brazen vandals. Your mom is calling the Sheriff."

Dan goes back inside and Brand speaks with Chris.

"This is freaky. I thought my parents were murdered. Oh God, I walked in on them having sex."

"I don't know what to say to that. But, I'm here, if you want to talk about it?"

Dusty Tate, a chubby fellow with his affection for death metal emblazoned across his t-shirt, calls out to Chris and Brandi as he crosses the street to meet them.

"I know who did it!"

Chris makes sure that he positions himself between Dusty and Brandi. Dusty is a "weird" kid from their class, one of the "quiet ones."

"What are you doing here, Dusty?"

Brandi is kinder than Chris in tone and explains for Dusty.

"He lives across the street."

She doesn't need Chris to shield her, steps around him to question Dusty herself.

"You saw who did this?"

"It was Westley Bush. I didn't see him light it, but I did see his mom's car circling the block. He and I used to be friends."

It makes sense to Brandi; she seems to accept it like she deserves it.

"I saw Westley at school today. Rhett was mean to him. Maybe he's getting his revenge against me."

Dusty doesn't agree with the tone of her read of the scenario.

"Doubt that. You're like his fantasy woman. He has a huge crush on you."

"Really?"

Dusty points to the burnt lawn.

"That's the sign of Flereous, lieutenant of Hell, fire God to some. Westley is into demonology, satanic black magic stuff. That symbol means that he's marked you to be his fire queen."

"Fire queen?"

Chris is still suspicious of Dusty.

"Where did he go, Dusty? Is he at your house?"

"We're not friends anymore. He probably went to find Brandi, probably forgot that there was a basketball game tonight. I think he's finally flipped out."

It all sounds kooky, but Brandi is worried.

"What will he do if he finds me?"
"Burn you."


The Whittaker family gathers in their living room, Ann and Dan now fully dressed, and Chris has accepted an invite to stand in on the meeting.

Brandi lowers her cellphone from her head and updates the group on her failed call.

"Noel isn't answering her phone."

Her mother speaks in a tone meant to ease any worry.

"The sheriff's department are sending someone. We'll tell them everything."

Brandi doesn't want to sit around and wait for someone else to take action.

"Can we go to the school and see if Noel is still there? Rhett was there too. Westley might hurt them."

Ann doesn't have the utmost confidence in the reliability of the neighbor boy.

"Dusty Tate is a troubled boy."

Chris offers to help.

"I can go check on them."

Brandi wants permission to go with him.

"Dad?"

Her father isn't onboard.

"Brandi, you're staying in."

His wife backs him up, tries to soothe Brandi again.

"I'm sure everything is fine."

Mr. Whittaker has some thoughts on law and order.

"Dusty and his friend are going to be sorry that they played with matches."

Chris offers his services again.

"I'll see if they're still at the school. Is it okay if I come back by here after?"

Dan answers. "Thanks for the offer, Chris, but we'll manage as a family. You should head home afterward."

"Yes, Sir."

Brandi lets Chris know that she expects to hear from him.

"Call me."


Rhett Stafford lies on his back in the center of the school basketball court and meditates on his misery. Noel, Shauna, and Kirsten play around shooting a basketball at a goal at one end of the court. The bottle of whiskey stands at the three point line nearest the young women.

Noel breaks away from the other cheerleaders and scoops up the whiskey. She takes it with her to go and talk with Rhett.

"Get up, Grasshopper. Maybe it's not all bad."

Rhett looks up at her.

"What would you know about it?"

"I know what's worth holding on to."

Rhett sits up with interest.

"What has Brandi said to you?"

Noel extends a hand down to him as an offer to help him to his feet.

"Get up."

He takes her hand and uses her to find his balancing in standing. Once he is on his feet Noel continues to speak.

"Let me show you something. You'll forget about being Mr. Sad Pants, Grasshopper."

She tugs on his hand and he allows her to lead him away from the court.

Shauna and Kirsten take notice of the duo leaving with the booze and share a look that translates their understanding of high school hormones and scandal.

Noel leads Rhett into the women's locker room and has him sit down on a bench. She sets the bottle of whiskey down and then sits herself down as well. She straddles the bench across from Rhett which gets him to turn to her as he voices his impatience.

"What do you have to show me?"

"Close your eyes."

He complies with the request.

Noel examines Rhett's face for a second, but then she leans in and presses her lips to his to deliver a kiss.

His eyes open and he pulls his face back ever so slightly from hers.

"What was that?"

She answers by leaning in with her lips available to him. This time he returns the kiss. However, he ends the kiss, pulls away, and stands up.

"This is wrong."

Noel defends it.

"It's right. It's how you should be treated. Appreciated."

"You're drunk."

"I've wanted this sober, Rhett. We can have it."

"You're Brandi's best friend."

"We should all be happy."

Noel stands up to get closer to Rhett again. He wards her off.

"I'm in love with Brandi."

"But, what if I'm in love with you?"

"I like you as a friend, Noel."

"That sounds like a good place to start."

She reaches out, wants to caress his face, but he doesn't allow it. She is disappointed.

"You're right. I'm drunk."

She hangs her head and leans toward Rhett. He lets her rest her head against his chest. She puts her arms around him and at first he doesn't know how to accept it, but then puts his own arms around her, holds her in a gentle hug. Noel confesses a somber fear.

"She might leave both of us."

Brandi treads back and forth in her bedroom with her cellphone in hand. No texts, no calls, no status updates, the world seems broken, silent, a moment of peace within knotted nerves.

Brandi sits on the edge of her bed and checks the screen of the phone once again. To send out a transmission of her own is a dead end that she contemplates going down again. Instead she puts the phone down on the bed.

She kicks off one shoe, then the other, a simple relief, it feels good. Then she peels off her socks and lets them drop to the floor by the shoes. She breathes, lets her feet breathe, there is time to relax within this time of stress, the texts will come, the calls will come. It's time to take off the cheerleader costume.

Brandi gets up from the bed and walks over to her closet. When she opens the door she discovers that Westley stands inside as an option to wear.

She screams and stumbles away.

Westley steps out of the closet, charred bits of skin flake away. He is a mess of sticky and dry, burnt and oozing, blood and dirt, some of his flesh cooked away to reveal knobs of bone.

Brandi runs from him, her footing wild, but she manages to stay on her feet and get out of the bedroom.

In the living room she collides with her parents who are en route to investigate her scream.

"There's something in the house!"

Dan whips out his car keys and holds them out to his daughter.

"Take my car. Go."

Brandi takes the keys and runs to the front door. Ann stays at her husband's side, but he doesn't want her there.

"Ann, go with her. I'll handle this."

"Dan."

"Go!"

Ann obeys his wish.

The determined father balls up his fists and proceeds toward Brandi's bedroom to throw some blows if need be.

In the driveway Brandi gets into the driver's seat of her father's car. She turns the key in the ignition and the engine comes to life. Then she leans across the car to pop the handle of the passenger side door, opens it to let her mother in. Ann gets into the passenger seat and shuts the door behind her.

"Wait for your father."

"I am."

Ann lowers her window and sets her eyes on the house: she left the front door open.

A throat cracking scream that no man should ever have to make in his life emanates from the house. Dan's scream is long and shrill and Ann is hypnotized by the terror within it all the way until the scream ends. Then she bolts out of the car and runs back into the house. She has left the car door open.

Brandi stays in place. Her hands shake and she grips the steering wheel, an anchor to try and settle them.

Ann's scream is no less gut-wrenching than her husband's, it is merely cut off shorter.

Brandi whimpers and her brain delivers a dose of survival instinct through her body. She stretches, shaky, across the front of the car to get her hand on the passenger side door handle. Fingers on it, hurry, hurry, hurry, pulls, hurry, pulls the door shut.

Nerves splintered, brain cells scattered after the initial shock of action, Brandi gets herself back behind the wheel and manages to pop the gear shift intro reverse. No mom or dad onboard, she reverses the car out of the driveway and then slams on the brakes, cranks the gear into drive. She almost runs Dusty over as he runs up to the front of the car and puts his hands on the hood.

"Oh God."

Dusty runs to the passenger side of the car and knocks on the window.

"Take me with you!"

She pushes the button to unlock the door and Dusty gets inside, slams the door.

Brandi's bare foot mashes down on the gas pedal.

Shauna and Kirsten walk away from the school building hand in hand. Chris approaches them from the opposite direction and stops them with an inquiry.

"Anything weird been happening here?"

Shauna blabs the truth right away.

"Noel and Rhett went down into the locker room together."

Kirsten scolds her.

"Tattle-tale!"

Chris continues to probe.

"No one else in there?"

Shauna answers again, flashes him a goofy smile that is rare for her face.

"Nope. Why do you wanna know?"

Chris can smell the whiskey.

"You're funny when you're drunk."

Kirsten lets out a drunken giggle.

"She didn't even drink any."

Chris fills them in on the latest activity from the side of town he has traveled from.

"Somebody set Brandi's yard on fire."

Shauna isn't going down for the crime.

"It wasn't any of us."

"Have you seen Westley Bush around?"

"Eww. No. We haven't seen anyone."

"That weirdo is out and about."

Shauna assures him that she and Kirsten plan to be safe.

"We're heading home."

"Cool. I guess I better go tell Rhett and Noel."

Kirsten gives him a warning that he already assumed was the case.

"Careful. Rhett seemed upset with you and Brandi."

Shauna isn't worried for Chris, has fun with being the gossip girl and catty.

"I'm sure Noel has gotten him over it."

Kirsten is very amused.

"Who are you and what have you done with Shauna?"

"Thanks for the heads up, ladies."

Chris heads toward the school while Shauna and Kirsten continue on to Shauna's car in the parking lot.

Noel and Rhett walk into the gymnasium by way of the locker room area. They travel with space between them.

Chris waits for them on the basketball court and Rhett wants an explanation.

"What are you doing here?"

"It's about Brandi."

Rhett doesn't want to hear it. He charges at Chris with his violent intentions clear.

Chris choose to run and try to talk sense into his pursuer.

"Listen to me!"

Noel is not impressed as she watches the boys go into their laps.

In the parking lot Shauna and Kirsten are in the front seats of the car turned toward one another. They pass a joint back and forth and gaze into each other's eyes. The weed makes Shauna contemplative.

"Have I been on a power trip with the squad?"

"What?"

"I write all of the cheers like I'm the leader of the band or something. You can write cheers."

"I don't want to write cheers."

"Maybe the others do."

"I don't think they care like you do."

Shauna absorbs that as a sweet compliment.

"Thanks for noticing."

Their fingers mingle, hands come together in the center area between the seats.

Chris feels silly and lets Rhett catch him. Rhett shoves him right to the floor and then pounces down to straddle him. He slaps at Chris's head, but most of the blows hit arm.

Noel yells at them.

"Cut it out!"

Rhett releases Chris and steps away.

"He's a coward. Sneaking around behind my back and then running from me."

Chris doesn't argue.

"You're right. I deserve to be punched in the face."

"You admit it? You're trying to steal my girl?"

"She's awesome, Rhett. I don't know what else to say."

Rhett tries to kick him, but Chris rolls out of the way and gets up to his feet. He isn't about to fight Rhett; however, he is still going the route of reason.

"You need to talk to Brandi. She's your girlfriend not mine and I'm stepping back from that. Okay? Sorry if you think I'm trying to hurt you."

"You can't hurt me."

"I came to tell you that Brandi might have a stalker."

"You."

"Somebody set her front yard on fire. I was told it was that Westley Bush guy."

This information clicks with Rhett.

"That demon worshipping punk was eye-balling her this morning."

"Maybe you should call your dad. Is he in town?"

"He's in town. Someone's trailer burnt down and he said they'd be cleaning that up until late."

Noel connects the dots for them.

"A trailer burnt down? Fire in Brandi's yard? Hello! Where does Westley Bush live?"

Rhett might know.

"Shit. I think he lives in a rat-ass trailer. My phone is in the bleachers."

Rhett goes to find his phone.

Shauna and Kirsten have moved on from gazing to kissing. There is a lot of passion from mouth to mouth, touch to touch. They are oblivious to the vehicle that Brandi pilots into the lot. Dan Whittaker's car goes past Shauna's car and closer to the school building. Shauna gets her hand around third base.

Rhett is on his phone and this gives Noel and Chris a moment alone. Chris asks about a rumor he has heard.

"You and Rhett do anything interesting in the locker room?"

"You should hope we did."

"I'm putting myself above the drama."

"If you want the girl you have to fight for her."

"It's not a competition. She knows me. If it's meant to be, it's meant to be."

Noel scoffs at that.

"Who knows anybody?"

The doors to the gym bang open and Brandi rushes in with an announcement.

85

"There's a monster!"

Dusty enters the gym behind her.

Noel, Chris, and Rhett rush over to meet Brandi. Chris and Rhett both move to get their hands on the girl, but Noel gets her arms around her and catches the sobs.

"My parents."

The boys turn their attention to Dusty. Rhett grabs Dusty by an arm and Chris questions him.

"What happened?"

"I couldn't see, but I heard screaming."

Brandi cries out one of the details responsible for her trauma.

"His skin was peeling off."

Rhett turns to look at his girlfriend and when he does Dusty is able to pull his arm free from his grasp. Rhett wants to better understand.

"What do you mean, Brandi?"

Noel tells him what to do. "Call your dad."

"He's not answering. Dispatch told me they've had several calls from town and they're on it."

Brandi pulls away from Noel, snorts up some snot, tries to compose herself better as she relates a gory detail again.

"His skin was peeling off."

Dusty tosses in two cents. "Westley has been playing with fire."

Noel seeks a plan. "Should we leave? Will he find us here?"

Chris is the realist. "If he wants to find us it's not like there's that many places in town to look."

Rhett steps up to Brandi and pulls her to him, his turn to console. "You'll be safe here."

Shauna and Kirsten kiss their way into the rear seat of the car.

Shauna takes charge as a giver and gets Kirsten to relax as she ducks her head down below the young woman's skirt.

Outside of the car a murky liquid cascades down the glass of the windows as someone pours it.

Kirsten moans.

The liquid on the car ignites. Shauna's car, over the top from front to back, is ablaze.

Caught up in each other, Shauna and Kirsten do not at first notice that they are now inside a burning car. However, Shauna comes out from between Kirsten's legs for air and discovers the peril.

"We're on fire!"

Kirsten opens her eyes and both women take in the experience.

Shauna snaps them out of their stupor. "Get out!"

They each reach for separate doors and bail out of the vehicle, feeling the heat, but no burns.

Kirsten sprints toward the school. However, she pulls up and turns around to seek her lover.

Shauna stands a few feet away from the car with Westley behind her. His flaming sword is through her. In shock she looks down at the blade, watches as fire licks from it to the fabric of her uniform.

Westley withdraws the blade and blood slops from out of Shauna's gut.

She doesn't fall. She looks ahead and sees the horror on Kirsten's face. Shauna wants to give Kirsten a chance to escape. She whirls around and attacks what she sees as a deformed goblin creature of some sort.

Westley cuts her down with the sword.

Noel sits on a bottom bleacher seat with her arm around Brandi. She comments on her friend's bare feet.

"We should see if anyone left shoes in the locker room."

Dusty and Chris stand together and watch as Rhett yells into his phone.

"That doesn't make sense!"

Rhett ends the call and chucks his phone away into the bleachers. He informs the others of the advice given to him over the phone.

"They said sit tight."

Noel has an idea.

"We should lock the doors."

Rhett is familiar with the doors.

"They lock from the outside with a key."

The doors in question bursts open and Kirsten enters with a declaration.

"It's the goddamned devil!"

Noel and Brandi jump up from their seat as Kirsten hurries to them with more bad news.

"It killed Shauna."

Kirsten is antsy, ready to bolt away at any moment.

Rhett postures up.

"I'll beat his ass."

Kirsten has seen the devil's tool.

"He's got a fire sword."

Dusty knows about the weapon.

"It's a badass sword."

Kirsten doesn't wait for a group vote.

"We've got to run."

She runs across the gym, opposite from where she entered, and goes out of the doors there.

In the hallway Kirsten doesn't hesitate to pick a path, she turns right and goes and goes.

Brandi and Noel exit the gym into the hallway and do not see Kirsten. However, Westley growls to them from up the hall.

"My love!"

The girls see Westley in all the gory glory of his reborn sled; a half-processed slaughterhouse refugee. The flames have gone out on his sword. He strolls forward and drags the large blade against the wall, clanks it against a bank of lockers as he reaches it.

Dusty, Chris, and Rhett join the girls. They all see the slow and steady pace of Westley. All of the tough talk is forgotten and the four of them dash off in the opposite direction.

The killer stalks, determined for the world to be laid at his feet, not exerting any more effort than he wants to in the circular contest of life, a plane of existence already faded in importance to him.

The group that is prey turn a corner and following Noel's lead duck into a classroom. Chris slams the door behind him and then presses his back against it to make sure it stays shut. Rhett has a better idea and shoves the teacher's desk toward the door. Chris moves to help him and they get the barricade into position.

Once the desk is in place Rhett sits down in front of it and presses his back to it, takes over the hero position from Chris.

"He's not getting in here."

Chris goes over to check out the windows with Brandi and Noel. He thinks they offer the solution to their problem.

"We go out the window, circle around, and get in my truck."

Rhett disagrees.

"We sit tight. We'll see him coming."

Dusty points out an issue with that.

"He'll burn us out."

Chris turns on Dusty.

"What all in Hell were you two into?"

"I was on drugs, I don't remember. His master plan was some ritual out at the lake. I think he just wants Brandi not the rest of us."

"All we'll give him is you."

Brandi eyes the blocked door, not at ease with being stationary.

"Where did he go? He was right behind us."

No one answers. They will sit tight for now.

Brandi thinks aloud about her friend Kirsten.

"I hope Kirsten got out."


Kirsten is out. She ran right out of a side door of the building and then down the road. Her shoes clap on asphalt and the bright lights of the gas station ahead of her is a beacon in the eerie silence of the town.

Kirsten gets past the automated doors and goes straight to the front counter of the business. The clerk is currently more invested in sorting through a box of cigarettes than paying attention to the latest customer. Kirsten slaps the counter to get his attention.

"There's a killer loose!"

Creepy Pete turns away from his sorting task and lumbers over to address Kirsten's concern. Her joke nominee for school mascot, Creepy Pete, grew up being told that he looks like Sloth from *The Goonies* who had a baby with a mutant from *The Hills Have Eyes*. Yet, here he is a local fixture whom a cheerleader comes to for comfort in her time of need.

"Can you give me a ride home?"

He doesn't appreciate the severity of the plot that she has become embroiled in.

"I can't leave the store."

Kirsten's tears catch up to her and drip. "Okay."

"I can call your parents to come and get you."

"Okay."

He lifts up the phone and she wanders away with the mantra of "okay" in her mind. If she is going to be okay, she needs to get out of sight of all the front windows of the store. She goes over to the beverage cooler section and slumps down to the floor to hide and cry.

A moment later and Creepy Pete looms over her. He hands down a brilliant blue slushie which she accepts.

"Your father is on his way, Kirsten."

"Thank you."

She sips from the treat and is grateful for Creepy Pete.

Chris paces while Noel and Dusty keep watch at the windows. Rhett is on guard on the floor before the teacher's desk and Brandi sits in a front row student desk. Rhett watches the way his girlfriend taps a foot with anxiety. He wishes that he could relieve her of all fear and hurt. Ideally doing that would wipe him clean as well.

"Brandi, I'm sorry for always being stupid. Can I hold you? I want everything to be okay."

Gasoline flows under the door of the room and around the teacher's desk. Rhett smells the fume and gets up to his feet at the same time that Brandi launches up and alerts him.

"Rhett, get up!"

The students gather together near the windows and watch the puddle grow. Dusty cannot help himself.

"I told you."

Whoosh! The liquid turns into flames as it is lit from the other side of the door.

Noel is one step ahead of the others, pushes a window open and hikes her leg up to work her body through the acute angle.

The drop out of the window isn't a graceful descent for any of them but they don't break any bones and flee together around the building to the parking lot. They skid to a stop as Mr. Klepke steps into their path with a hunting rifle. He aims the gun at the students.

"Hold it!"

Brandi pleads with him.

"Mr. Klepke, help us!"

The teacher is high strung and not a natural action star.

"I saw fire. Shauna Stevens is dead. What have you kids done?"

"It wasn't us."

Rhett tries to project that he holds some of the same authority as his known father.

"Quit pointing that gun at us."

Mr. Klepke is not convinced that the people before him aren't arsonists and murderers.

"All of you line up over there."

He directs with the gun, points them to an area beneath a lot light. The students obey, but Brandi continues to plead their case.

"Mr. Klepke, there's someone after us."

"It'll get it sorted out."

A plastic bottle that erupts into flame arcs through the night air and strikes Mr. Klepke. When the fire strikes him, the teacher fires off a shot from his rifle toward the students.

Westley gets a passing grade in Molotov cocktail concocting, combining a flammable with a vessel for perfect distribution in the moment, heck, the timing of his throw this time should make one wonder why he never tried out for the football team. He launches a second bomb as the teacher spins to see who has just lit his pants on fire. The second Molotov is a bottle that shatters against the ground and sends Mr. Klepke reeling backward, unable to maintain his balance. The teacher falls down hard on his butt.

Brandi and her friends run for their lives.

Mr. Klepke doesn't think to use his rifle anymore. He slaps at the flames that eat at him. A third explosive device rolls up to him and when it explodes it shreds away all of the man's consciousness with nails.

Dusty stumbles in the pursuit of escape, but Brandi is quick to help him back to his feet. This puts them at the rear of the pack.

Chris reaches his truck and gets in on the driver's side. Noel enters the passenger side and Rhett jumps into the bed of the vehicle. Rhett holds his hand out as a target for Brandi to run to. He can see that Westley stalks onward with his hand wrapped around another bottle that features a rag fuse at the ready in it. The killer's sword is nowhere to be seen.

Brandi reaches the tail of the truck and accepts Rhett's hand to help lift her inside. Dusty runs to the cab of the vehicle and Noel lets him in on the passenger side.

Westley lights the fuse of his last bomb and continues to walk.

Rhett pounds his hands on the roof of the cab, keeps his eyes on the advancing maniac, and yells for Chris to get them moving.

"Start the truck!"

He's trying. He's trying.

Chris turns the key in the ignition, but the truck doesn't seem to want to cooperate. Classic.

Noel echoes Rhett's demand.

"Holy crap, start the truck!"

He's trying. He's trying.

Westley lobs his last bomb in the direction of the truck; however, it is obvious that he does it for show not to actually strike the people in the bed of the vehicle. Brandi and Rhett watch as the Molotov strikes the parking lot just behind the truck and explodes into a tiny burst of flame.

The truck engine roars to life. Chris has always been adept at driving in reverse. He slams on the gas pedal, cuts the wheel, and aims the rear of the truck toward the exit of the parking lot. As he sees the distance grow between them and Westley through the front windshield he considers whether or not he should try to run Westley over. Too risky.

Truck tires hit main road and Chris cuts the wheel again. Brandi and Rhett are almost tossed out of the bed. The truck is put into drive and hastens away in a forward direction.

Rhett yells at Chris through the open driver's side window as they go.

"My house! I have guns!"

Chris nods his head in agreement with the destination.

Brandi and Rhett sit down in the bed of the truck. She leans against him and he gets a chance to hold her.

The Stafford house is located outside of town. The truck starts to weave miles before its destination. Noel realizes that their driver appears to be nodding off.

"Chris, what's wrong?"

He turns to her, but instead of saying anything he faints. Noel grabs the wheel as the truck drifts toward the ditch. She shoves her leg past Chris's and gets his foot off of the gas and her foot on to the brake.

When the truck comes to a sudden halt, Rhett stands up in the bed and comments on where they have arrived.

"We're stopping by the cemetery."

The truck engine shuts off.

Noel goes from turning the key back in the ignition to checking Chris for vitals. He is alive with some consciousness, but she can now see that he bleeds from his side.

Rhett is out of the bed of the truck and opens the driver's side door. He can see the blood; it drips off of the door. Rhett leans in to scope out the damage to Chris and forms a quick conclusion.

"Dude, you were shot."

Chris finds the strength to reply to that.

"It hurts now."

In a night of panic, Noel fights against the next surge, but the edge is obvious in her voice.

"What do we do?"

Rhett takes charge.

"Scoot over. Dusty, get out, switch places with Brandi."

As Dusty climbs out Rhett pushes Chris over enough that he can squeeze in behind the wheel of the truck. Noel holds her hands to Chris' wound as Rhett tries to start the truck. He turns the key, but no dice.

Brandi appears at the open passenger side door and Noel fills her in.

"Mr. Klepke shot Chris."

"Oh God."

Rhett keeps trying to bring life to the engine.

"Chris, how do you get this beast started?"

Chris responds in a whisper.

"I don't know anymore."

Rhett gives up on the truck.

"We can't sit here on the road. My house is two miles. Chris, do you think you can walk?"

Chris doesn't answer. Noel, cradles his head, tries to coax him into having more energy.

"Chris, sweetie, stay with us."

Chris manages to lift a hand and give the group a thumbs up. Rhett doesn't have confidence in that gesture.

"He's bled too much; we can't move him. We leave him. If we cut through the cemetery and woods we can get to my house faster."

Brandi doesn't like that.

"I'm not leaving anyone else behind tonight."

"I'm not letting you stay here."

"Then we all go."

Rhett doesn't bother to argue, tries to start the truck one last time.

The backwoods Haleigh cemetery is considered romantic by some, a lover's lane for the young and young at heart. Tonight the gothic charm is not illuminated, the glow of the moon across the mossy stones forms a sinister aura.

Chris has one arm around Rhett, Rhett carries most of the weight, and Brandi is on his other side, tries to keep pressure on his wound with her hand, as they walk down the gravel road that goes into the cemetery. As they reach the first row of headstones Chris attempts to battle his pain with a sense of humor.

"Guys, I would prefer the hospital."

His chuckle transitions into a groan of pain. Rhett notices that he has gone slacker.

"We've got to keep moving."

Chris feels that he has reached his exit.

"I can't. Down."

His insistence scares Brandi.

"Chris, no."

Rhett helps Chris ease down to the ground. Chris doesn't just sit; he lies down on to his back and gazes up at the night sky.

Brandi goes to her knees at his side and holds on to one of his hands.

Chris shifts his eyes from the stars to the eyes of the woman he loves. She squeezes his hand and he shudders with a sudden warmth that he very much appreciates.

"Thank you."

Brandi doesn't understand.

"For what?"

Chris isn't there anymore. In a blink he is gone into the warmth and Brandi holds the hand of a cold shell.

"Chris? Chris?"

Noel absorbs the sorrow from where she stands.

"No. No. No. No. No."

Rhett suggests that there still might be hope.

"We'll get him help."

Rhett aches for Brandi but as she leans down and whispers something into the ear of Chris's corpse he cannot stave off the flare of jealousy that signals his temper. Then he watches his girlfriend kiss the dead young man on the lips and it hurts, a selfish hurt, a dark and miserable hurt of love.

The headlights of a vehicle appear at the entrance road of the cemetery and the group all turn their concern to this new development. Rhett goes macho.

"All of you hide. I'll take care of this."

Brandi worries.

"What if it's him?"

"I'll kill him for you."

She has seen him in this mode before.

"Don't, Rhett. I love you too."

Noel grabs Brandi by the hand and pulls, coaxes her away from Rhett's side. Rhett and Brandi share a look. His eyes are hardened by the determination to end the horror of the night. Brandi goes with Noel, Dusty absconds with them instead of confronting the incoming vehicle with Rhett.

The young women go deep into the rows of the cemetery and split apart in order to take advantage of two decent-sized headstones. Brandi ducks down and peers around her chosen stone and she can see Noel across the aisle from her. Dusty flops down a few stones away on the same side as Brandi. His hiding approach seems to be: lie his bulk down as flat as possible and hope for the best.

The car has parked and Rhett's night-vision has adjusted well enough that he can tell it is Westley who climbs out of the driver's seat.

"Come get some, freak!"

Rhett keeps his distance and continues to taunt as Westley walks around to the rear of the car.

"Try to firebomb me! Pull out your pansy sword!"

The trunk of the car is open and Westley rummages through the contents of it. Rhett realizes that he has not put enough thought into his valiant stand; Westley might be getting a gun for all he knows. Rhett readies his fists, no backing down now.

"It's just you and me, freak! She'll never be yours!"

Westley walks into full sight once again and now has a cylinder tank strapped on and aligned to his spine, a thin hose line stretches from that and connects to a tube shape held in his hands. At first glance Rhett thinks: *The Ghostbusters*. Then Westley squeezes the trigger of his flamethrower and shows off by spewing a line of flame into the air.

Time to run. Rhett runs toward Westley not away.

Brandi dares to watch the event unfold from her hiding spot.

Rhett thinks that he can zig and zag his way close enough to knock Westley out. Rhett zigs and Westley triggers out a stream of fire and has no problem catching the athlete mid-zag to bathe him in flames.

Brandi bites one of her knuckles hard enough to draw blood as she suppresses a scream.

Rhett drops to the ground and flops around, life out of his head, last will to live creating spasms of action in an attempt to get out of the fire. Westley steps over the burning body and keeps spraying hot death.

The killer decides that his victim is well done and doesn't empty his tank. He steps away from the burning corpse and decides to investigate the cemetery.

Brandi is about to jump up and yell for Noel to run away with her but Dusty gets to his feet first and draws Westley's attention.

"She's over here!"

Westley turns to the sound.

Dusty continues to point at Brandi.

"I've got her!"

Brandi gets to her feet and Dusty throws himself against her, grabs, gets a hold on one of her arms. Brandi twists to free herself and Dusty struggles, but maintains a grip. Then Noel swoops in to the rescue. She smashes a vase of plastic flowers into Dusty's skull. The blow dims the lights in his head and Dusty releases Brandi, drops to his knees and both of his hands go to clutch his headache.

Noel and Brandi flee toward and then disappear into the woods that border the farthest reaches of the cemetery.

Westley reaches the chubby traitor and Dusty quits touching the tenderness of his head wound to try to tap into the friendship he once shared with the killer before him.

"Remember when we drew the flamethrower blueprints together? I see it turned out awesome."

No words come out of Westley's lipless mouth; a disturbing hiss is all that Dusty gets in reply. He tries another negotiation tactic and pledge of allegiance.

"Hail Beelzebub."

Westley points the flamethrower at Dusty's face and pulls the trigger.

Whoosh! Dusty's scream peels away and disintegrates with his flesh.

Nature's carpet isn't kind to the bare soles of Brandi's feet. She crunches over a branch and then pulls up to a stop next to a tree. She indulges the pain in her feet, uses it to tether her to the world, catch her breath, reality, clear her mind. Noel stops with her friend and asks for directions.

"Which way do we go?"

"It's no use anymore."

"We're going to make it."

"It's me he wants. I'm going back."

"No."

"I'm not running anymore."

"You selfish bitch. Rhett just sacrificed himself for you!"

"I didn't want that!"

"You don't ever know what you want!"

Noel slaps her.

The blow elicits a whimper, but Brandi has made up her mind.

"No one else is dying over me."

"Fuck you. Seriously."

Noel shakes her head in disappointment, but holds out hope that her friend will follow her. She points off into the darkness.

"I'm going that way."

Brandi nods, an indication that it is the right direction to go. Noel hurries away in that direction, doesn't slow down to see if her friend will follow. Her friend does not follow.

Westley shucks the flamethrower off as he sees Brandi exit the woodlands and return to the cemetery. She slowly walks toward him and he knows that she sees a monster, but soon she will see herself as he sees her and the magnificent power that they will be together.

The cheerleader trembles before him. He offers a hand, grotesque in appearance, yet gentle in motion. She hesitates, repulsed but she understands that he is the way of the future and she must go his way. She takes his hand and together they walk amongst the gravestones and return to his vehicle.

Noel sees the initial interaction between Westley and Brandi but she doesn't wait for them to start their journey because she has circled back around on a stealth mission. She runs ahead of them toward the entrance of the cemetery. She is hidden by the darkness of the trees that line the highway side of the cemetery. However, if one were to stop and listen to the night, surely some sound would give away her movement.

Noel considers fleeing down the highway, but if she wants to escape she already had her opportunity. Instead she makes her way close to the gravel drive of the cemetery and hides behind the thickest tree she can find with a vantage point of the drive and Westley's car in it. Now would be a good time to form a plan if she plans on rescuing her friend. Nothing comes to mind.

As the odd couple of a cheerleader and burnt man of horror reach where Rhett's body is a dwindling campfire, Brandi falls to her knees and sobs. Wesley does not release her hand but gives her a solid set of seconds to mourn. Then he yanks hard on her arm and forces her to her feet.

At the car Westley opens the rear door on the driver's side for Brandi. He lets her step up to the opening where she can see within the interior of the car's assorted garbage. The sword is positioned as the passenger in the front seat and there is what appears to be a box of fireworks.

Brandi assumes she is meant to get into the car. She stands there, unable to force herself to enter. Westley has no problem with forcing her. In fact, he has procured a chemical from the deep web to help with the task.

He grabs her from behind and smothers a chloroform soaked rag over her mouth and nose. He pushes her toward the car door and as she loses consciousness she becomes more pliable and he is able to tuck her into the vehicle and shut the door.

He doesn't figure that it will ever be needed again once he assumes is other-worldly powers in full, but Westley isn't going to leave his flamethrower behind. Call him sentimental, the device served him well as a hobby building it and as a vanquisher of foes and he'll hold on to it as a trinket of history. He walks away from the car, heads out into the cemetery to retrieve the flamethrower.

Noel sees her chance and runs toward the car. Westley is distracted enough by his excitement over his conquest that he doesn't hear her shoes against the gravel and does not catch any hint of the movement happening behind him.

When Noel reaches the car she looks inside. She had seen Westley overtake her friend and assumes her to be drugged. She gives herself a split-second to decide whether it is worth the risk to try and wake Brandi. No. And the keys do not appear to dangle from the ignition.

She runs around to the rear of the car and searches for a weapon in the clutter of the trunk. Spastic, not seeing anything to give her armed confidence, Noel does the next best thing, the dumbest thing that she can think of and crawls into the trunk. She scrunches in as far as she can go to the side of a box and covers herself in the musty blanket that is there.

Westley lugs his flamethrower back and crams it into the trunk without checking for stowaways. His mind is on to greater things, the trivial detail of how his trunk is organized doesn't even register to his eyes. He slams the trunk shut and goes to the driver's side of the car where he left the keys on the seat in plain sight.

The chaos and confusion surrounding and in the town of Haleigh aren't too far away yet Westley finds the return to Gloria Ipple's lake house to be the serene eye of the storm. In all of his life he cannot recall ever having felt on the verge of such happiness as what now tickles him. The destruction of his flesh has helped numb him to the nerves of the old world and awakened him to the pleasures to come.

Westley motors a small boat across the lake and toward the floating dock that he has converted into a ceremonial pyre. He is in the process of delivering a final bundle of kindling which he will soak in the sacred kerosene blessed by his desires. Then he shall chauffeur his lady out to present her to the entrance of their kingdom.

Brandi awakens inside the lake house. She is in the main living room area and she is hogtied with her dirty feet up in the air behind her. A rag has been shoved into her mouth and taped over to keep her quiet in discomfort. She wiggles and yells, but is indeed a captive.

Meanwhile, tired of waiting for the right moment, Noel makes her moment for escaping the trunk of the car parked in the lake house driveway. She kicks down the rear seats of the vehicle and worms her way out; sweaty, thirsty, kind of has to pee. She scopes out her surroundings outside the car windows and judges the coast to be clear enough.

Noel wills herself into stealth ninja mode and exits the vehicle. She travels to the lake house and eases open the front door, creeps inside.

All caution is thrown to the wind when she sees her friend tied up in the floor. Noel runs over and the first thing she does is rip the tape off and pull the gag from Brandi's mouth. Brandi exclaims the name of her hero.

"Noel!"

"Merry Christmas."

"You shouldn't be here."

"That makes two of us."

The rope bindings are tight and Noel seeks out something to cut them with. She spies Westley's sword where it rests across the couch, however, she also notices a hacksaw also rests on the cushions and goes to pick that up as a more reasonable tool.

As she cuts the ropes, Noel seeks a little more information about their current predicament.

"Where is Westley?"

"I don't know."

Brandi turns and does her best to help Noel work through the bindings. When they break and she is freed she has to stretch her limbs, work out the kinks.

Noel tosses the saw aside and apologizes to her friend.

"I'm sorry that I called you a bitch. I know you loved Rhett. I loved him too. And Shauna. And Chris. And I know you've lost a lot tonight, but you can't give up. Because I love you too, Brandi."

Brandi is thankful and ready to escape. They punctuate the motivational apology with a hug. They have dallied too long. Westley charges into the room to make it a group hug.

As the women let go of each other Westley throws his arms around Brandi and swings her off to one side, shoves her hard to the floor in the direction of the couch. His focus is on the interloper.

Noel backpedals away and her legs bump up against antlers of the buck piece that is in the floor. She decides that the gruesome home decor might as well be used as a weapon. Noel flexes her biceps and lifts the animal head.

Westley chooses to go for a weapon as well. He goes for his sword that is on the couch. Brandi tries to intercept him, wobbles on her knees to get the sword for herself. Westley detours from the blade and goes at Brandi, strikes out with his leg and smashes his kneecap into the side of her head. Brandi bounces against an arm of the couch and crumples to the floor.

Noel rams Westley from behind with the antlers of the buck. The horns do not spear him as Noel imagined that they might and Westley even manages to stay on his feet as he pushes them away.

Westley bumps against the decorative table with the owl on it and lifts the bird by its head to use it like a club; the wooden base that the creature is affixed to is solid with deadly corners.

Noel has some issue with trying to control her awkward weapon but she is able to use the severed head to deflect the first blows as Westley attacks with the owl. His advances have her on the retreat and he takes advantage of this by grabbing on to the antlers of her piece and wresting the severed head from her grasp.

Noel slips and cracks down on to her tailbone. Westley still has the owl and she throws her hands up in desperate defense anticipating the blows he is about to punish her with.

As Westley looms over Noel the blade of his sword rips through his torso, splits his charred flesh open like it is a burnt on the outside, pink in the middle roast. He is stunned. Brandi stands behind him with the hilt of the sword held tight in her hands. She withdraws the sword and Westley drops to his knees.

The cheerleader has the upper hand, yet hesitates in killer instinct. But, the execution must go on. She lifts the sword and prepares to chop the death blow.

Westley seems resigned to his fate but it ain't over until the devil sings. He turns around and punches Brandi in the gut as her momentum moves forward. The wind is knocked out of her and the sword slips out of her hands.

Owl still in hand, Westley rises and clocks Brandi in the head with it. Winded and rattled, she sprawls out on the floor incapacitated with nausea and pain.

Westley pivots his attention to Noel before he can be blindsided again. She is up to her feet. She runs and he chases with the owl raised above his head.

Noel gets the front door open and is quick enough to get one step beyond the portal. The owl arcs down and catches her with a blow at the top of the spine. She drops forward on to the porch.

As Noel tries to crawl away Westley slams the base of the owl against her cranium. Her face smacks against the porch hard enough to split her lips and put splinters into her mouth. The thunk sound satisfies Westley and he discards the owl. He grabs Noel by the legs and drags her body inside the house. The fight and flight are out of her.

Once Noel is rolled over on display in the main area of the house, Westley squats over her. He smooshes her cheeks together with one hand to toy with her suffering. The blood that oozes from her mouth becomes a paint that he smears as a mask over the rest of her face. He senses that Brandi is on her feet behind him and his hand next goes to Noel's throat.

Brandi can see that her friend is still breathing. She has the sword once again but does not lift it. She lets it drop to the floor as Westley turns to look at her, his hand around Noel's throat, a threat that doesn't need words, but as all of humanity before her, caught in the turmoil of existence have asked, she poses a "why."

"Why are you doing this?"

His gravelly voice is not domineering in response; he sounds like a young man in pain.

"I'm saving us from the world."

He releases Noel and stands up. He faces Brandi and examines the wound she created in him. He picks at, peels off a charred chunk of himself. The portion of blackness falls to the floor and the wet pink inside of him is better revealed.

Brandi gags on the urge to be sick.

"Let me and my friend go."

"You're mine."

Brandi keeps her emotions and bile in check, steel gaze on the burnt one before her, wanting to get him away from her best friend.

"Okay. I'm ready. Woo me."

He wishes that she would say his name again in her special way: Wes. However, it doesn't count if you have to ask for it, it loses its magic. Something more to look forward to, it's the little details that make a relationship wonderful, prizes to be won daily, and they will have eternity together. He steps to her and holds out his hand just as he did for her in the cemetery.

She takes his hand. Then she uses his extended appendage as leverage to yank herself toward him. She strikes at his open wound, shoves her hand into the gory hole. Blood slops over her wrist as she tears band digs into the meat.

Westley roars with the shock of pain and then rages into it with a burst of strength. He forces his hands around Brandi's throat and shoves his weight against her. The couple stagger to the couch where he falls on top of and strangles her.

Brandi loses the fight and her consciousness.

Another bump to her noggin brings Brandi around. She opens her eyes and finds that Westley is dragging her across the lawn. When they reach the private dock area he checks on her, and once he sees that she is awake gestures for her to rise. He holds his hand out. She sits up and decides to get to her feet rather than have herself drug over the wooden planks ahead. She ignores his hand.

She can see that he carries a new blade, a thick, ornate dagger with skulls laid into the handle; very Hot Topic.

Brandi is directed to the boat and after she crawls into it Westley binds her hands behind her with rope. Then he works the boat motor and out on to the lake they motor.

Branches, brambles, brush has been collected and arranged over the surface of the floating platform in the lake. An opening has been left for one to climb aboard the platform and there is a path to the center where a makeshift bed of blankets and pillows awaits. Around the bed, the inner circle within the circle of kindling are gas canisters, propane tanks, and, essential for romantic occult ambiance, lit candles.

Brandi is helped out of the boat and steps on to the platform, observes the arrangement. Westley nudges her forward with a command.

"Lie."

Independent spirit, fiery to match his own, he appreciates that in doses and doesn't correct the woman when she sits on the bedding, but does not lie down. He wants a woman not a dog.

Westley stands before her and lifts up a candle, holds the candle in one hand, his ceremonial dagger in the other. Time, it is. He kisses the blade of the dagger, exposed gums to metal, and then hovers the point of the blade over the flame of the candle.

"Tasa reme lairs Satan."

Blade away from flame, voice shouted to Hell.

"Ganic Tasa fubin, Flereous!"

He tosses the candle into the brush at one side of the platform. The accelerant ignites and the woody pile crackles with the fire.

Westley lifts another candle and repeats the process to turn the platform into a bonfire.

Noel, alive and unsteady, staggers away from the lake house and looks toward the lake. She sees the flames out on the platform. She walks toward the water.

Brandi fears that she might not find an escape from the ring of fire. She considers springing up, charging forward, and ramming headfirst into her captor, perhaps he would shield her hair from catching too much fire. However, she fears that he would drag her to the bottom of the lake with her bound hands after slicing her open with the dagger. She eyes the gas cans and propane tanks around her, to do nothing is to explode. The heat intensifies.

Westley bellows out to his Lord, eyes skyward, hell above, heaven below.

"Flereous! I bring my virgin queen to you! Ganic Tasa fubin, Flereous! Accept my virgin queen!"

Brandi interjects.

"I'm not a virgin!"

Westley looks down to her, assures her of her value.

"You are pure."

He bends down and displays the lethal edge of the dagger. Brandi lets herself die, thinks her throat is about to be slit, however, he does not kill her, he reaches behind her and cuts the rope away from her hands. He grabs her hand and holds it up to show her the ring that she wears on her finger. He yells into her face, covers up her protest to keep the ceremony on track.

"My virgin queen's purity ring! Flereous, bind us in fire!"

Brandi yells right back into his disfigured face.

"I'm pregnant!"

Westley drops her hand.

"No. You are pure. Perfect."

He points the dagger, close to the tip of her nose. She doesn't cross her eyes to look at it and yells even louder.

"I slept with Rhett and Chris!"

She can tell that she has struck him a devastating blow of truth. She releases more.

"I'm pregnant and don't even know who the father is!"

He moves back from her and lets the dagger fall loose from his hand. Dejected, heartbroken, his belief in her as what he wanted is a disappointment that he will not overcome.

"It won't work."

He reaches a hand to the nearest propane tank and prepares to twist the valve wheel.

His cheerleader, no cheer for him, is beautiful against the fire canvas. He turns his head and looks away.

Shoes left on the shore, Noel moves in the shallows of the lake, woozy, hesitant to let the cold water go over her knees. She doesn't know what the fire means; it does not call to her, it frightens her toward it.

Boom! An explosion sends the flames on the platform higher and Noel throws herself forward into the water.

Brandi swims as fast as she can toward the distant shoreline. Another explosion erupts from the platform, hard enough to rain flaming debris around her.

Pace too frantic, swimming form not recently practiced, Brandi's muscles cramp and she has to tread in place for a moment. Noel swims up to her and splashes to a stop. She too is ready for a breather and gives an arm of support to her friend so that they may remain afloat together until they are energized enough to finish the swim ahead. Nothing else swims toward them, the threat of Westley assumed to be incinerated. Snakes, normally the girls wouldn't go into the lake due to a fear of snakes, but snakes don't come to mind.

Brandi and Noel crawl out of the lake, drag themselves through the mud. The cheerleaders stop and sit up together side by side. They look back toward the lake and the fireball that was the floating platform.

"He let me go. I'm not pure enough for Satan."

Brandi slides off her purity ring and tosses it into the lake.

Noel turns and hugs her friend. They hold each other up, each one wanting to cry, yet sensing it is not yet the time. After a moment Noel suggests a course of action.

"Let's go home."

There is a lot more horror to face in that direction.

"I'm afraid."

They sit in a spell of silence, watch the flames go lower.

Then Brandi decides that it is time to stand up again.

# A Hot Meal

His breath smells like truck exhaust and that worries him. One problem at a time though, right now he's fixated on getting some vittles in his belly. Last night he dumpster dined, but he doesn't want a second-hand meal tonight. The charity has been slow, his savings are zilch, and as the hour grows late the prospect of a hot meal being placed at his feet dwindles.

Walter Dewitt, a son of Arkansas, sometimes claims that the city of Dewitt, Arkansas is named after a relative. Not a stretch, may be true, he's never visited the place himself, is now a resident of the streets of Los Angeles. He relocated to the City of Angels to break into show business. He never thought he would land right into the movies but figured that the movie roles would be offered to him after he gained his fame as a movie critic. Walter grew up obsessed with Siskel and

Ebert and once upon a time thought himself the successor to their thrones.

He wrote and wrote, criticized and criticized, watched some movies, networked, pitched, and no one cared. The format of his movie review show didn't matter to him for his wit was the secret sauce that would have people falling in love with him via their television screens and smearing his review quotes all over the Internet. America, nay, the World would seek out his opinions on movies. An extra dose of sex appeal never hurts either and his favorite pitch, the golden ticket he thought, involved him paired up with a swimsuit model in each episode: *Dewitt and the Babe.*

He lost interest in himself along with most everything else. He came to realize that his reviews were all about himself and not faithful to the reality of the projects that he criticized. Assumptions ruled over facts and blah, blah, blah. Depression sucker punched him and he turned to drugs to pick himself back up. They sunk him.

Walter is seven years sober now and treading the streets of Los Angeles. Maybe one day he will get a bus ticket back to Arkansas, but his pride has inflated the price of bus tickets beyond his means.

"Homeless Vet," "Will Work 4 Food," "God Bless / Anything Helps," nothing seemed to help on this day and he eventually went the comedy route of "Will Twerk 4 Cash" to no avail. He wouldn't give his effort a thumbs up though. He had propped his signs up and napped, no enthusiasm to his panhandling performance.

Hangry, Walter decides to mosey along to a new spot. He'll find his pal Tony and see if Tony is up for some clubbing. They've had some success lingering within sight of a disco and then presenting themselves to drunks who parked far away in order to avoid paying the valet. This approach doesn't usually invoke compassion from the donors, but fear-induced charity spends the same. Private taxi cellphone aps may be all the rage, but it's a big city and there's always some moths fluttering around the edges of the lights with their wallets.

They don't rob drunk people in order to get their cash, they intimidate drunk people into thinking they are being robbed. It's a morally sound operation if you look at it through hangry eyes.

Walter's pal Tony was a real estate agent until he raped a woman who showed up to an "open house" that he hosted. Tony doesn't seem to have learned remorse while serving his prison sentence because he enjoys telling the rape story to anyone who will listen and he always makes sure to inform them that the woman wasn't a real home buyer, just a looky-loo wasting his time.

Tony has the most bulbous eyelids that Walter has ever seen. On some days they are quite purple-ish in color. A short man with a craggy face, not a ladies' man, but a man that loves the ladies, a rapist imp really is how Walter thinks of him, but a good pal. Tony helped Walter adjust to survival on the streets and gifted him a nice pair of gloves once.

Tony doesn't like to shit where he eats, but doesn't like to shit too far away either. Walter knows his shitting grounds and it doesn't take long to find him. It doesn't surprise him that Tony is in the act of chatting up a lady.

Walter sidles closer, doesn't know what might be in the works, doesn't want to spook anyone. It appears that Tony, Walter interprets the hand gestures, wishes to coax the woman into the narrow alley behind him. She seems content to stay right where she stands. Walter can see that she is in a long, weird dress and doesn't get the impression, as he squints, that she is a "lady of the night."

Tony catches a glimpse of Walter and waves him on over to join them.

Upon closer visual Walter can tell that this woman is not going to be prey for Tony. Even if they teamed up against her Walter doesn't think pulling the woman into the alley would be an easy task. Tony knows that Walter doesn't rape, therefore, a different angle must be getting worked.

The woman is strong in the arms, muscles evident, a weight lifter, but not too masculine or bulging with veins, tight, lethal biceps. Her arms are the only part of her below the jaw that is exposed. Her sleeveless gown, baring large polka dots of florescent yellow against dingy white fabric, covers her from neck to toes and bells out in such a way that Walter cannot fathom the outline of her figure. It is almost like a stiff moo-moo, though it looks soft enough, hiding all curves, unique in Walter's fashion observing experience. He guesses in his mind that her body is a fit to her arms and would wager that Tony thinks that as well. He'd wager Tony's curiosity is hard in his pants.

The woman is taller than Tony, five feet six to seven inches perhaps. Her skin is olive and Walter sees a single splotch of discoloration on her right cheek, a pinkish blemish. Her hair, black, is too short for Walter's general taste when it comes to attraction and what the opposite sex should wear on their scalp. However, even with that hairstyle and the blemish, this woman's face speaks of goddess heritage. The alignment of her facial features are a phenomenon no less easy to gaze at than the stars seen when the smog parts. Her eyes are sharp, one amber and one blue, gorgeous, aglow with life.

Tony makes introductions.

"Walter, buddy ole pal, this here is Coco. Coco is new to the neighborhood."

Coco speaks to Walter. When she does she brings a hand up and holds it over her mouth to shield any view of her teeth. Walter takes note of her long fingernails, pointed on the ends, painted black, no doubt that they could scratch an itch to the bone.

"Your friend Tony is quite lecherous."

Her words are clear enough, voice garnished with some rasp, yet there is some constraint, not only is she using her hand as a guard, but she probably isn't parting her lips very wide. Walter assumes that the blemish on her cheek is not the flaw that makes her the most self-conscious. Rotten teeth and rotten breath most likely. She'll find that they have that in common.

Walter apologizes for the rapist without needing to know what lewd propositions were made.

"I'm sorry."

Tony defends himself.

"She wants it."

Coco surprises Walter with confirmation.

"I'm offering handjobs if you'll help me move some furniture. I've also got hot food at my camp."

She lowers her hand away from her mouth and Walter considers them once again. Strong hands, petite, the fingernails are worrisome, yet the finger meat, palm space, those arm muscles, she can probably pump him empty in short order without scratching too deep with the nails. Hot food sounds great.

Tony commits them to the deal.

"Lead the way, hotness. We're your movers."

Walter smiles, allows Tony's answer to stand for him.

Coco leads the way. Walter watches the hem of her gown and realizes that it never touches the sidewalk, yet never reveals any peek of her shoes.

Tony appears to watch where, in best estimation, the woman's ass might be. There is a gentle sway to the fabric, but still no hint of body shape swaying beneath it.

Walter also notices that there are more discolored patches of skin on Coco's elbows that match the one on her face. The name of the condition eludes him at first, he knows it, he ponders over it for much of their journey.

Vitiligo! Yeah, that's it.

Coco may have been new to the neighborhood where they met her, but she has led them out of that region and through a few more neighborhoods. She isn't lost.

Walter surmises that they are headed toward the L.A. River. Walter's inner compass is correct.

The L.A. River mostly flows over a concrete channel. It is mostly unfamiliar ground to Walter. He prefers to stay dry and is not a connoisseur of graffiti.

Coco shows the men how to best navigate down into the river area. Some moonlight reveals that the water travels a narrow path here, not much over a trickle of sound made by its flow, and as she descends the concrete embankment Walter is again fixated on the magic of her gown. He notes how the garment creates the illusion that the woman almost floats within it, fabric not rumpling at all, her head held at an angle indicating perfect posture is maintained. Of course, the darkness of the night does help gowns play tricks on people's eyes sometimes.

She is nimble. Walter is shaky, but lucky. Tony falls, scrapes his knee, and farts.

Coco leads the men to the entrance of a drainage tunnel. The walls are wide enough for a maintenance vehicle to pass through the concert maw. Beyond the entrance is inky blackness. Walter has come this far in an easygoing enough state of mind, but now as he stares into the tunnel, all things considered by his sober mind: bizarre fashion, shadows, the L.A. River, an elegant woman offering handjobs, Tony's fat eyelids, Walter starts to get the willies. If her legs match her arms, she probably doesn't need much help lifting things. He has a question.

"Where and what is the furniture?"

She doesn't hesitate to respond, hand flashing up to her mouth, tone honest.

"A mattress and a chest of drawers. They're in the tunnel and I need help lifting them up some stairs into my camp."

Maybe she really does need some assistance. Maybe she just likes feeding people and giving them handjobs.

She takes a step into the darkness of the tunnel and stoops down to lift something. A battery powered lantern returns in her hands and lights up with the twist of a knob. Tony takes the initiative and reaches out, withdraws the lantern from her hands.

"I'll lead the way."

Walter likes that idea. They can't be led into an ambush if they take the point position and control the light.

Tony enters the tunnel and Walter follows close behind. A blink of imagination has Walter casting himself into the shoes of an archeological explorer entering some ancient Egyptian tomb. The adventure begins! Treasure awaits!

Walter is struck in the back of the head, a powerful punch by one of Coco's fists. He staggers, doesn't want to hit his head on the concrete below, however, knows that he is going down, the air is out of his balloon. He loses consciousness. Curses!

Awareness of self and surroundings eventually flickers back to Walter, in part ignited by the sound of Tony's screams.

Walter opens his eyes. Tony sounds as if he is close behind him and in severe pain, ongoing pain, something hurts him currently.

Walter takes inventory of himself. He discovers that he is tied, wrist to wrist, ankle to ankle with rope, and then wrists to ankles via more rope, while enough duct tape to repair many ducts wraps his chest to the chair on which he is propped up. The chair is rickety and there's no way she needed anyone's help moving it.

The tunnel alcove in which he sits is lit by the battery powered lantern. The area of light forms a weak circle, which Walter resides in, with darkness hiding all that is beyond the circle. There are critters out there, Walter can tell, ginormous rats or sewer raccoons perhaps, they move in the darkness ahead, flitter shadows into the light, in a slight frenzy of excitement, encircling, yet not daring to investigate closer and be illuminated.

Tony's screams taper off into whimpers and then cease with a wet gargle and a crunch. Walter turns his head, stretches his neck to see what horror show may be in production behind him.

Tony's eyes are sealed away behind his fat eyelids. His mouth is twisted open in an unnatural display of the mighty pain he suffered. While Walter can make out these details of Tony's head, Tony's body is a blur of a shape disconnected into the darkness. Bloody strips of gore stretch from the stump of Tony's neck, the head is severed unclean.

Coco steps out of the darkness behind Walter and circles around him, stays within the light so that his eyes may track her. He turns away from Tony's detached head and focuses on the strange beauty in her, now blood spattered, strange dress. The blood is not only on cloth, it is splattered across her face.

She stands in the light before him and opens her mouth, this time not bothering to conceal the contents with her hands. Coated in Tony's blood are rows of fangs, so many, so sharp, so more befitting a mutant wolf than a woman of grace.

Coco has more to reveal. She grips her gown at either side and hitches the fabric up into bundles at her waist. The pulling, the strength it seems that she must muster for the job, explains the muscles of her arms, a toughness needed to remove and probably fashioned by the garment.

Her legs are thinner than Walter expected. They are furry, knobby knees. Her feet are paws, not unlike those of a large dog, but there are deformities that grow from the tops of them. As Coco struggles to lift her dress up farther Walter gets time to deduce that the growths are not gnarled tumors but rather human toes, complete with nails as dark as those of her fingers, poking out of the beastly paws, useless mutations or perhaps evidence of a transformation never realized.

She has her gown up, rips it over her head, shakes free, and then tosses it aside. Coco continues to bare her fangs, drool Tony's blood, and poses for Walter to behold the rest of her in shock and awe.

The discolored splotches are plentiful across the length of her body, as are patches of coarse fur that match the somewhat denser coat on her legs. Her torso is well endowed. Dual rows of breasts hang heavy from her, three plump on each side. The teats leak blood.

Walter averts his eyes downward, not to stare at her abnormal feet, but to will power into the heels of his own shoes which he does his best to click together in their bound state. There's no place like Arkansas, there's no place like Arkansas. He is fooling himself, shit like this would totally happen in Arkansas too.

Skittering feet, whispers, giggles sound out of the darkness.

New movement draws Walter's attention forward. Coco lowers herself to the ground, acrobatic yoga on to her knees, folds herself back, aims her crotch toward Walter. Her pubes are a tumbleweed of brambles.

Coco strokes her hands down her engorged breasts. The blood trickles from them, squirts in excited streams, as she continues to stroke, rub, caresses.

Out of the darkness Coco's children emerge. Her brood gathers to her, eight toddlers, warped creatures caught between human and canine with lipless cleft holes in their faces for mouths.

Six teats and eight children leads to a shoving match, primal squeals as greedy mouths seek nipples. Coco moans as the children suckle, feed on the blood that secretes from her Mommaries.

Walter's tummy growls. The runt of the litter hears this and walks over to Walter to investigate.

# Bioluminescent

Dear Leonard,

We were once inseparable chums and I hope that you can visit the memories without tasting the poisons that divided us. I am a changed man.

You know me better than anyone else could ever dare. You know that my mind is reliably sound and educated. My head has always been hardened against mysticism, claims of the occult, fanciful spiritualism, and paranormal phenomenon that go against what my eyes have seen. Reality has been for me a scientific plane and constant reflection of healthy self-awareness. I have never been susceptible to nervousness or quick to excitement or seduced into the type of emotional instability that leads to the imagination forming experiences of the supernatural. A professional skeptic is something I could have called myself.

Yet, here I have a tale for you that I of all men could never have anticipated writing. Please consider this an apology and embrace this correspondence as not only sincere, but to be considered as such with urgency.

You are familiar with my home. It is a house that has been in my family for generations. While it is not a mansion, it does have grandeur unlike any other within the city. They built the suburbs up to and around the property. It is unique in that I am tucked in with neighbors, but in a world all my own.

You are also familiar with my reluctance to travel, even though traveling is a necessity in our line of work. However, I actually went on a vacation. Take a moment, Leonard, and gently lift your jaw back off of the floor. My reasons for leaving my home were always more about getting back to it. This time I tried to focus on staying away without becoming stressed. Remember how we swore that we would never venture to Florida? Well, I decided to see it once before it is lost to the ocean.

You would appreciate all of the sweat to be found in the parking lots of the topless taco hut establishments in Tampa Bay. It was at such an establishment that I met a young man calling himself Richard. He invited me to a house party at which his band would be playing. A simple stop for tacos and the fate of my skepticism was sealed.

I won't bore you with the trivial masturbation that was the rest of that day spent sightseeing. Eventually I made my way to the address that young Richard had dictated to me. It was a few blinks past the witching hour when I arrived in a middle-class neighborhood teetering on the sinkhole of poverty. There were lights on in some of the windows, however, the street lights were all blown out. If this were the starting point of a novel it would read: "it was a dark and desolate street."

The address given to me for the house party turned out to be a false one. The sour woman in a wheelchair who answered the door knew nothing about a party or my specific Richard. She bid me a "buzz off" and slammed the door in my face.

I had not parked close to the woman's house; thus, a bit of a dark walk lay ahead of me. I had enjoyed it well enough on arrival and there was no reason to doubt that the return journey would be any less trivial. I am somewhat nocturnal by nature. You've heard me brag about my night vision. It is legitimate.

Yes, Leonard, my old friend, you of all people know of my pride, of my habits, oh, my ways, of my ways. I am going to surprise you. I know your ways as well. It is because of this intimate knowledge that we share of each other that I know you will believe me. I do not distrust my own sanity; I wish I could.

I walked. Suddenly I was touched across the face and I knew that touch: spider webs. I waved a hand to brush them away, however, they were not there. I did not find any strands on my fingers. It did not strike me as peculiar at first. The next steps changed that attitude. I found the next touch to my face to be quite peculiar. More spider webs arrived with each step that I took, yet, as I felt them on my face, I never found them on my hands. I did not see any webs floating before me, no hovering arachnid artists spinning in my path. Every step closer to my car produced thicker invisible webs.

I turned toward the street itself and found that the air stepping in that direction was clear of obstruction. By turning my head I found my eyes aligned with a house on the opposite side of the street from where I stood. Richard stood outside the house.

Previously I had seen enough in the young man's eyes to make me want to go to his party, still, in that moment I thought about how minor the doe-eyed boy had been to me as a person of interest. He had been a vacation trinket. His eyes had changed. They were glowing, pulsating with florescent swirls of green not unlike the bioluminescence of a firefly.

I stood there and deduced that only I and Richard partook of this moment in the night. Had I been the only one to receive the party invitation? It is a mystery that steps on my fingers as I try to hold on to the edge of the cliff that was once my reality. I do not back down from a challenge and I've found out that I do not back down from ghouls.

Richard with the glow eyes turned and walked toward the house behind him. I followed without hesitation. The house seemed to be in decent shape, the lawn kept trimmed, however, I did notice upon closer inspection that the front door and all of the windows had been boarded over.

We crept around the side of the house to the rear. My guide bypassed the boarded over back entrance and stopped to stand before a low basement window. His firefly eyes lit on to me again and the message was clear. The key to entry was that low portal. I found one of the boards to be quite loose and after some prying popped it free. Then I wedged that board behind the others and used it to pry them loose and then free as well. The glass of the window could not take the pressure that I applied against it with my board and it broke. The sound froze me in place, but the night remained still, no neighborhood watch rushed to investigate.

Richard, if that was his name—I have not since made inquiries—had vanished at that point. Alone and without a flashlight, I still felt compelled to stoop down to the broken window and reach inside to unlock it. The rusty metal frame that still held some shards of glass pushed inward and an opening was provided that I could squeeze through. Perhaps I am not as slim as I used to be. Perhaps I have packed on no less than seven pounds since you last saw me. However, I passed through the window without suffering a single nick or cut to my sucked in gut.

It seems that I should have considered what fall awaited me in the darkness beyond the window. I blindly dropped inside and as luck would have it thumped easy-peasy on to a washer and dryer set. Of course, luck may not have been involved, my guide would have warned me I think if there had been peril waiting to impale me. Of course, of course, the immediate trust I had in Richard seems odd, don't you think?

Fear entered my gut. The type of fear I haven't known since childhood. The certainty that nothing would ever be the same was what I sensed. We fall into our patterns certainly, but there is no certainty. This is the change in me that can't be denied. It doesn't matter what you choose to believe in, existence is not a solid state. Rules and structure do not form impenetrable defenses.

Richard returned by way of illuminated eyes. The darkness peeled away and there stood a count of fifteen young men crammed into the basement with fifteen sealed oil drums before them. Some of them were younger than Richard, but all of them shared the firefly eyes that illuminated the basement.

Richard and his band began their performance for their audience of one. They pounded their hands in rhythm against the lids of the barrels. The created a thunderous melody that will hum in my mind every day for the rest of my days and whatever may be thereafter.

The end of the performance is not something that I can recall. There weren't any goodbyes, no chance for me to offer critique. The men, the barrels, those eyes, they were all before me and then they were not. I found myself walking in the street toward my vehicle. I must have left the house party in a trance.

Now this is where one could theorize that I was drugged or under some form of hypnosis. Even if either of those elements were in play, the theory does not matter because of what followed after the event. The event was a puzzle, though simple enough to solve in terms of message. The message had been given to me and I felt compelled to deliver it.

An anonymous phone call was made to the police. A hot tip about where they could find at least one dead body. Yes, I directed them to that basement and I'm not sure how it went down procedurally, but I am sure it was my persuasive tone that got them to investigate with haste. You are the only one, Leonard, I admit it to you now, that has ever been able to get past my skills of persuasion. You have lasted until the final rounds of arguments and perhaps you have never taken me to the mat, but you knew how to walk away without giving me satisfaction.

They found fifteen bodies in that basement. Each oil drum contained the corpse of a young man. The property owner confessed to the murders all too willingly; one of those types I guess.

And there you have the story. The truth. I implore you to act upon this information. If queer happenings such as this are possible, then you and I seem ripe for selection when it comes to future hauntings.

I will act. I will not be a victim in some perverse line waiting for the cosmic powers or wheel of chance to choose to ruin me for me. Thus, I am removing all of the bodies from the basement of my home and giving them a proper disposal. I suggest that you do the same.

    Your pal,
    Bartholomew

# Cheater's Box

Tim cheated on Penelope. He revealed the affair to her in order to take their relationship to the next level. The marriage proposal really put her on the spot. She loved him before she knew that he cheated on her, one time only, he swore, and she couldn't figure out how to not love him afterward. Therefore, she accepted that he loved her too and that his mistake would never be repeated.

Trust is an important part of a marriage and she made him promise a new level of openness in their new level of commitment to each another. She made sure he knew he could trust her to kill him if he ever betrayed her again. She showed him the gun she would use, a nine millimeter gifted to her by her mother the day her father went to prison.

Tim gave her all of his passwords, access to all of his devices, all of his accounts, all of his heart. Yes, they married.

One year and two months into the marriage and Penelope has grown suspicious. Suspicion has gnawed at her for the entire year and two months, tortured her with her inability to forgive and forget, forget she forgave.

Tim has his man cave in their house. It is a private space, but he keeps the door open, never locked. The problem is a secret in a shoebox.

Penelope has noticed the shoebox for quite some time now, never paid it any mind, but then out of the blue it dawns on her that the shoebox is never around without Tim. He never leaves the box out in the open when he is absent. She concludes that he either takes the box with him or hides it.

She shouldn't have to search for the box to discover what is inside. They trust each other. She will ask him. She goes to the man cave where Tim is lounged in a recliner before his television, sports tuned in, at only a glance by her it appears to be some sort of swimming pool football match. The shoebox is within Tim's reach on a side table.

Penelope tries to sound casual, but gets right to the point.

"What's in the shoebox?"

Tim divides his attention between television and wife, but doesn't give Penelope the greater percentage when he replies.

"Nothing."

He's lying.

"Tim, show me the nothing."

"It's work junk, honey."

"Let me see it."

He looks at her now. He's sweating.

"No. It's personal client information and not something I can share."

"We share everything."

"I don't ask you to write down credit card numbers from customers at your work do I?"

She steps forward and reaches for the box. He is quick to snatch it up and hold it close to him.

She demands it.

"Give it to me. Open it."

He doesn't argue back, doesn't comply, sweats, awkward. She accuses.

"Tim, you're cheating on me again."

"Don't be stupid."

"Don't call me stupid."

"You're never going to let me live it down. I married you. I love you."

"I warned you about keeping secrets. What's in the box?"

"You have to trust me."

"Is it a secret cellphone? Phone numbers? Love letters? Pictures of your whores?"

He tries to put his foot down and exert some "man of the house" power.

"This conversation is over, Penelope. You go calm down and we can talk about your paranoia later. There's nothing in the box."

Rage. It's been inside of her for a long time. It gets into the pilot seat and steers Penelope out of the room: "ladies and gentlemen this is your Captain speaking, down your shots, we're going full throttle." She goes straight to the bedroom and spins the combination on her own special box: the gun safe. She pulls out her nine, loaded. Penelope, the gun, and the rage fly back to Tim's man cave.

Tim is still in the recliner. He looks up to Penelope and sees the gun barrel pointed at his face. The shoe box is held in his arms.

No words are spoken. She can tell by his eyes that the contents of the box are more important to him than she ever will be. It's over.

She pulls the trigger. Blam!

Tim's unfaithful brains splatter out of the back of his skull. He slumps over dead in the chair, grip on the box loosened.

Penelope is numb. She drops her gun to the floor and picks up the shoe box.

She removes the lid of the box and peers inside. At first she is confused, but her brain forms an explanation for the contents: Tim was a nose picker too lazy to get up and get tissues.

Or, maybe he enjoyed the picks, no one will ever know the full truth of it. Inside of the box, however, is a collection of boogers, many boogers, dried globs of booger, blood flecked booger, boogers with nose hairs attached, and boogers with some shine still on their slime.

Penelope is stunned by the discovery, but still does not get overly emotional. She had assumed wrong, sure, but a box of boogers is disgusting and Tim still deserved what he got.

# Mo

## 1

Forty-five acres of wooded land represents the world of Gilbert Ryan. Years of monthly payments to the bank led to the realization of the dream: ownership. It's his land. Paying property taxes never disillusioned him in regard to the value of holding the deed; taxes on his land are a patriotic privilege.

One of the first projects that Gilbert undertook after moving on to the land, at the age of thirty-seven, was to build a fence. He had never erected a fence before, but he had enthusiasm for the job. He bought a rickety old tractor to haul around his posts, pre-shaped posts purchased in affordable batches when he could afford them, and toiled under the sun many, many days working with a post hole digger. In some places trees became makeshift posts for holding the fencing.

Barbed wire is what stretched from post to post to tree to tree to post to tree to post. There wasn't a specific purpose for choosing barbed wire in regard to any neighboring livestock— Gilbert merely wanted to mark the borders of his territory with authority. The fence started at the edges of the highway, but did not seal off the yard from the road and did not run parallel to the road in front of the home area. Instead the fence went away from the road perpendicular and then to either side of the house and yard area, sectioning those areas away from the woodlands. The fencing also branched out from the starting posts, indeed running parallel to the road for a spell, before turning along the property line into the woods to encircle around at the backside as a signal of where Gilbert's land ends and his neighbor's begins.

The property bordering Gilbert's land belongs to the widow Meta Bradbury. Her property encircles his on most sides and his plot cuts a rhombus swath into hers starting at the highway. The real estate agent had informed Gilbert that the Bradburys had once owned the land themselves having relinquished it to one of their children to live on before that child then sold it to another family from whom Gilbert bought it.

The realtor had also informed Gilbert that - Meta Bradbury was a witch. He never followed up on that bit of information, did not travel in the gossip circles within the nearest town to see what cultivated such a label. As neighbors far removed from too many other neighbors, - Meta's property butted up against state forest land, though only fifteen minutes away from the nearest city, only ten away from the nearest State Penitentiary, the Ryans and Bradburys did not associate with one another too often. They waved in passing whenever passing occurred.

The journey to becoming a property owner had involved Gilbert working many jobs and moving from many homes before landing a solid position at a car manufacturing plant. The commute had been worth the pay and while his alternating schedule left the brunt of child rearing to his wife Kristy, she and their two kids, Molly and Daniel, never wanted for life's necessities and were even afforded items of hobby and entertainment.

When Gilbert wasn't working he liked to sleep and he liked to "putter around" on his forty-five acres. The land had come with a patched together house that required a constant flow of repairs. Kristy found as much meaning and seemed to derive as much enjoyment from the responsibility as he did. The kids, each born before the move to the land, but getting to spend the bulk of their growing years living there, developed a strong sense of duty around the chores allotted to them.

Gilbert did his best to involve himself in his children's lives as they grew, finding windows of time between work shifts to dole out fatherly lessons. He knows he instilled a strong work ethic in them, something that gives honor to the family name.

Their home was heated by a wood-burning stove; therefore, both children learned the art of stacking wood at a young age. Eventually they were shown how to harvest it from the trees on the property. Daniel embraced the chainsaw, Molly shied away from it.

Gilbert cut down only dying trees from his own land and often purchased loads of wood or made deals to cut down trees on other people's property so as not to strip his own bare. Meta Bradbury had denied him access to her property for lumber, but she had been reasonable about it and Gilbert respected her preference for privacy.

The wooded area of Gilbert's land, aside from the fencing, the thin trails he crafted, and some hunting blinds he set up, remained undeveloped. He has always kept salt blocks and piles of corn as "feed stations" within the woods to attract deer. He is not a true hunter even when he dresses the part and heads off into the woods with a shotgun. Gilbert sits in his blinds and watches for deer, never aims the gun, never pulls the trigger, a ritual that has always warmed him with a sense of balance: master over his land, yet a gentle observer of nature and its will upon said land.

The children did not play in the woods generally or share in their father's interest in them. They saw that portion of the property as a place for poison ivy, ticks, and work. Of course, Daniel did utilize both the woods and one of his father's blinds to lose his virginity during his late teens. As for Kristy, she mainly took pride in the house and yard, leaving Gilbert alone in his pride for the woods.

Once Molly and Daniel reached adulthood most financial obligation to them faded. Neither child went the college route and both held steady jobs and formed steady family units of their own. It did not bother Gilbert that his children moved far away and rarely came to visit. His relationship with them had been loving, but always slightly distant.

He was too distant for Kristy's taste. The divorce came as a shock, but throughout the process Gilbert had something to focus on: keeping his land. The court proceedings were not without some drama and hurtful statements; there were attempts to draw out emotional weakness and admittance of shortcomings as a parent and spouse, but Gilbert weathered it all and Kristy did not contend his desire to hold on to his property; at the cost of a generous financial split that he could make payments along with the alimony.

Routine had dictated Gilbert's activities before his family went away and he found it an even more reliable engine in their absence. He did not search for a new lover, did not seek any enlightenment within his free time, directed his focus on the "puttering around." His thoughts were fairly mundane, though an interest in animals did lead to him purchasing some books about birds, squirrels and such. He was under the impression that hermits should also hoard treasure and so whenever he could justify the investment, he would seek out small gold coins to purchase with no specific collecting angle, just the gold content was of interest. The life of a hermit suited him for a spell.

After Gilbert retired the shell of numbness began to flake. "Boredom" isn't the right word, words are not adequate in conveying the swirl of thoughts and emotion that began to fill the seconds of his days; however, "without purpose" is a pair closer to definition than "bored." "Withering away" also fits the aches he felt in mind and bones.

To his surprise the child to return to him was Molly. Daniel seemed content in his grudges, but Molly moved back into the region and initiated contact. She introduced Gilbert to his granddaughter Nianna and rejuvenation began.

Molly, without her husband Greg, whatever his attitude problem was, would stop in from time to time to chat, Nianna tagging along. Eventually she began dropping Nianna off for overnights—free babysitter—and this led to week long summer visits for grandfather and granddaughter to bond.

Talking with Nianna made Gilbert realize just how long he had spent talking to himself. She brought outside perspective into his world and he shared his simple world with her, the generational gap generating new philosophical and observational abilities within the duo in regard to existence and day to day matters on the blue marble Earth. Gilbert put more thoughts into his thoughts, more considerations. Nianna even got him to vote for the first time in all of his years, skewing his political preferences toward issues that mattered most to her and her future.

Nianna enjoyed exploring the woods with her grandpa and as she got older enjoyed venturing into them alone as well.

He taught her how to stack firewood and she convinced him to install a central heating system instead.

When she was fifteen going on twenty-four Nianna forced Gilbert into dating again. She created a dating profile on the Internet without his permission. She never told him, but the fact was that she became worried about his lack of companionship after she discovered his stash of clothing catalogs in which he had placed bookmarks to keep track of his favorite pages on which ladies were modeling undergarments.

Gilbert himself had never ventured onto the Internet, did not have it installed at his house, but once the potential matches began calling the man found himself intrigued.

A woman named Lucille Harris swept into Gilbert's life, the rock and roll to his country, a woman who dyed her gray hair vivid red and loved to keep everyone up to date on the latest Hollywood stories that she read in the grocery store tabloids. Their romance burned for the better part of a year before ending in Lucille's death. She perished in an automobile accident, not her fault, a pileup that shocked the county and headlined the local news several days in a row. Lucille's dog Mr. Stinkles had been in the car with her when she perished. The dog had escaped the accident unharmed—a miracle? Gilbert thought it a wonder, but he also wondered about how many dogs die in car accidents each year, their names omitted from the official press releases.

Lucille had never moved in with Gilbert, but after her death he did inherit the Labrador Mr. Stinkles. Gilbert called the dog Buddy. He also got to calling Nianna "buddy" which amused the girl, often getting her to respond with "what's up, Pal-pa?" A sense of humor had grown on the man and sometimes he would inquire whether or not Nianna was hungry for some dog food.

Gilbert mourned Lucille, but his world did not crumble; her passing had enriched it. He did not see himself as someone participating in the "outside world," however, the amount of "outside world" he was letting into his own, as mainly inspired by his granddaughter and Lucille, gave him fresh energy. No one would be calling him the "happy hermit" anytime soon, but there was for sure more zippity to his daily doo-da when he stepped out of bed each morning.

At seventy-six years of age Gilbert stands on the backside of his wooded property with his seventeen-year-old-granddaughter Nianna, buddies bonded by blood, dressed in their camouflage, he armed with a 12 gauge shotgun and she a .410, weapons they had planned to use on some targets, but now feeling like wise protection in their hands as they survey the damage that has been rendered near and to the fence. Amateur tracking enthusiasts, the trail had led the duo to the breach, to the scene of the crime.

Moments earlier Gilbert, Nianna, and Buddy had traveled together to one of the deer feeding areas, not expecting to see any wildlife, due to Buddy's constant need to vocalize his enthusiasm about woodland hikes, merely to check out the feed level, enjoy a stroll, and then to set up some paper targets for blasting away with the shotguns.

At the feed spot Buddy went bonkers. The dog barked and yelped at something on the ground and then he took off into the woods after a scent. Gilbert and Nianna hurried over to the place Buddy had initially clued in on, not bothering to chase after him. On the ground they discovered a bloody patch of furry scalp with broken off antlers shattered around it. A nine point buck, by Gilbert's estimation, had somehow lost the top of its head and its rack, with the rack not only being detached, but smashed into bits.

Buddy's barks grew distant as grandfather and granddaughter rooted next to the disturbing find to theorize. Could it have been a poacher with poor aim? Or was it a rabid animal that had inflicted damage unto itself? The nearby trees did not have any marks to indicate self-mutilating headbutts. Could there have been a vicious fight between two bucks? Gilbert has seen photos of bucks that have decapitated other bucks. The ground is not torn up with an abundance of tracks really. Wait. Where did Buddy go? Quiet. Too quiet.

They went after the dog and that tracking is how they came to be at the rear fence.

Never in all of his years has Gilbert replaced or repaired the fence around his property. The barbed wire rusted and it sagged, but now before him it has been torn free from posts and trees altogether, removing all sign of boundary and providing a large gap of passage from his property on to the property of Meta Bradbury. Lying in that gap, surely having chased off the fence mangling intruder, is the former Mr. Stinkles, Buddy the Labrador, in a fatal state of mangle himself. The dog is in chunks, the body seemingly exploded and spread about, the decapitated head in pristine enough state for easy identification. Eyes shut, tongue lolled out of his mouth, Buddy's expression is still cute even in the aftermath of violent death.

Nianna is horrified, yet stands her ground and allows anger to hold back the tears. Someone is responsible for the death of her friend—what has happened to the dog is not natural—she will avenge him. Gilbert has another idea.

"You better get back to the house, Nianna."

No. Nothing will stop her. She WILL avenge him.

Nianna does not reply to Gilbert's suggestion. The elderly man seems somewhat stupefied as he surveys the damage to fence and dog. She follows him as he inches closer and closer to trespassing.

Gilbert is indeed mystified by the scene, but the emotional swell within him is analogous to the determined feelings of his granddaughter. His world has been violated, a declaration of war. He senses danger; however, he does not again suggest that Nianna should leave his side. He knows that she is a capable young woman and if there is danger to face two shotguns are better than one. Also, something he has never mentioned to Nianna is that he doesn't actually go into the woods alone anymore, not since the day he fell down and lay on the ground for over an hour wondering if the strength would come back into his legs to carry him. It had, but slowly.

His mind wraps around the situation as best as it's going to wrap and Gilbert puts forth a hypothesis.

"Maybe it's a bear. We do have black bears in Missouri."

The conclusion that he has come to is shaky, but he is sure of what he must do. Gilbert continues to walk forward. He walks off of his property to hunt down whatever murdered his dog.

Nianna's eyes scan the shotgun in her hands, a weapon used to stop squirrels on a rampage not bears. Her thirst for vengeance suddenly dries and is replaced by fear. The shock of discovering the carnage has caught up to her in full. Buddy is dead and she wants to cry.

Nianna hurries to catch up to her grandpa. She doesn't voice any concerns about their quest.

The trail grows confusing in a short amount of time, the quarry did not leave ample blood evidence or tracks as one might assume, and while every broken twig should be considered a directional clue the fact is there are lots of broken twigs in the woods, none sticking out as obvious evidence of passage. Gilbert isn't lost in the unfamiliar territory of the Bradbury land, just "lost." A sense of adventure lures him along for half an hour—the enticement of adventure fades as the pain in his knees amplifies—they may fail him at any moment. He has pushed himself past his daily threshold for exercise. He decides to halt their trek, but then he sees something of interest on the ground. He hobbles closer and draws Nianna's attention to the find.

"Look."

In a patch of exposed dirt there is a print. The back heel of a large foot is apparent, yet going forward whatever made the print seems to have drug its foot hiding further markings of identifiable species distinction. Nianna questions the find.

"Is that a bear track?"

"Maybe. We should head back and report all this."

"Bears poop in the woods."

Gilbert doesn't know what he is supposed to say back to that nugget of knowledge and instead gazes ahead into the woods, travels a little farther with his eyes to spare his knees. Yards away he spies what may be the edge of a creek bed. Gilbert wants to check it out; a quick peek and then they will retreat home. He gives his granddaughter a gentle command as he walks toward the creek.

"Wait here."

Nianna abides.

When Gilbert reaches the edge of what is indeed a creek, he is surprised to see how deep the indentation is and that there is water. The flow of the water is lazy enough that depth along the winding creek bed is probably inconsistent. The man forgets his knees for a moment as he feels the temptation to hop down into the creek and follow it to confirm where the water pools or vanishes along the way. He doesn't do any hopping, but Gilbert does walk over to investigate the nearest bend in the creek. He thinks he might have a peek and then ploop a pebble down into the water before calling off the expedition.

Around the bend the creek widens and the buck that lost its antlers is revealed. The creature is down in the bed, partially submerged in water and partially alive, with a bloody cap of exposed skull where its antlers and scalp used to be. Gilbert's own jaw hangs somewhat open as he watches the lower jaw of the animal slowly move up and down as if the buck wishes to speak on what its glazed over eyes have seen. Gilbert doesn't want to linger on the pathetic sight, wants not to decide that he must shoot the deer to put away its misery.

When he looks away from the buck Gilbert puts his focus on the damp earth around the edges of the creek. He wants to see evidence of the animal having fallen in after a flight of panic, surely induced by its grotesque wound. Nary a hoof print is to be seen. However, he does see a clear impact in the mud of a shape and size that astounds him.

Nianna screams.

Gilbert spins around as something rushes toward him. It does not occur to him to fire his gun. His only thought is: "That's a strange bear."

Nianna sees the beast wipe grandpa off his feet. She fires her shotgun in the general direction of the attack without true aim. Then she drops the weapon and runs for her life.

## 2

Eric Bradbury is who he is and tries not to catch his reflection in mirrors because of it. His dull, brown hair is thinning and the meat on his five foot nine frame is pudgy. He's not fat—overweight, sure, but he can still see the outline of the thinner man he is. He has been meaning to get into better shape, but it's hard to find the time when you're the manager at a fast food restaurant. And the food at Nachogee's, home of the "world's best nacho hot dog burger," is too convenient too many days of the week.

When he was a kid he thought he could grow up to be "anything." Therefore, he chose to be a superhero with the secret identity of the President of the United States of America. Eventually he changed course and hoped to become a celebrated comic book writer and artist, at the latest by the age of twenty-two. Now at twenty-five he is still at Nachogee's; first job, been there since the age of sixteen. Eric Bradbury isn't who he isn't and tries not to catch his reflection in mirrors because of it.

He catches sight of himself in the mirror and a staring contest ensues. He didn't go into his bedroom to contemplate the meaning of life within the eyes of his reflection. But, there attached to his dresser is a mirror and there he is in it. It's an antique that was given to him as a child, kept and hauled around as if it had earned value beyond the bargain price his mother paid for it at a yard sale. Of course, the meaning of life is a mystery and that question to a mirror just makes him reflect on the past. Damn it, he only meant to grab his deodorant not crash backward into the vise of history.

Raised in a popcorn kernel of a town in Missouri, at sixteen Eric got his license and permission to drive twenty minutes down the road to where industry went franchise; a primer town before one goes the full hour away into a metropolis. He landed the job at Nachogee's. He wished to escape the rural lands and while twenty minutes down the road wasn't far enough he still believed in dreams to come and the paycheck helped keep him supplied in his first drugs of choice: comics and movies.

By seventeen he was proud to be the youngest shift leader at Nachogee's. In the quick service world his star shined bright enough to attract Jessica Sapp, a co-worker, into becoming his first real girlfriend. The way it felt to push against another body with passion, well, that was a new drug of choice and he rerouted most of his money to keep his dealer showered with gifts.

Fast forward out of high school and on the cusp of attending the only college to offer him any sort of scholarship, a small college, but in the big city of St. Louis, and Eric found himself intimidated by the classes scheduled for him, math outside of his interests in art and literature. Change, the truth in change, one of life's ultimate challenges, finally taking real steps toward being who he fantasized about being, that scared him. Also, he feared losing Jessica. Their relationship was already one of slight distance, but escaping to the city would make it long distance.

Jessica helped Eric out by telling him that she was pregnant. The out, an escape from his escape, he could see himself being happy with her. His job was stable, he could provide for a child, and the challenge of the "hard road," refusing the networking privileges of college and working on his graphic novel alone, there was something romantic in the thought of that journey. He would make it a journey not stasis. He bailed on college and rented an apartment to be closer to his love. Side note: his younger brother Luke Bradbury, designated black sheep of the family, reveled in Eric's troubles and the grief they caused their parents.

Jessica failed to mention that the baby might not be his. She had been sleeping with no fewer than three other guys. After a few more months Jessica gave up her ruse and let Eric know that one of the other fellas had actually paid for an abortion not long after she had first discovered her state of being with potential child.

Eric loved her and asked her to move in with him anyway. She left him. She moved to Florida with a carnie named Texas.

He knew that he had made a mistake and he knew that his scholarship was still available, but Eric did not have the will to conduct another severe pivot.    Deep down he worried that anxiety blended with laziness of spirit were preventing him from reversing back to the exit ramp of higher education that he understood was "the right thing;" however, he also didn't want to discount his ambition and the strength of getting by on his talent without some official degree in this or that. Heartbreak can cloud a person's judgment as much as it can twist a person's belief in their judgment, and Eric stayed the course that felt safe, the comfort of smelling like XXX french fries and ketchup.

By the age of nineteen Eric's pride in being the youngest shift leader was gone and by twenty-one when he got promoted to Assistant Manager, there was more money, even less pride. Old enough to drink alcohol, no friends to go drinking with, he can remember working the night of his birthday. He had not dated anyone since Jessica. His world was the space between the walls of Nachogee's.

Lonely, disappearing, his existence no longer relevant to him, ego slain, clean the shit of strangers off the bathroom walls because the cleanliness of the restroom is one of the first things by which a potential customer will judge a business, a cycle of cheese and shit splatters.

He tied to turn the pain into art, forged a comic book concept around a depressed fast food worker with super powers and sent it out to be judged by publishers. He grew numb to the rejection until one reader decided it was their duty to send him a two page letter criticizing his nerve to even dare try his hand at the art form. He threw away the rejection, kept his comic, got rid of the character's super powers and made him a shotgun toting agent of rampage, three issues worth, then he stuck it in a drawer and applied for a transfer and a promotion at work.

Eric's boss asked him to hold off on the transfer, convinced him for the better part of a year not to depart. Heck, maybe it had been longer than a year, he didn't take those college math classes and he had to have been twenty-three when he transferred to the assistant manager position at a St. Louis store.

During the wait for transfer he self-published a black and white one-shot about a carnie named Texas. No one cared.

The move to St. Louis brought some swagger to Eric's step. He had nothing to lose in reinventing himself as the new same old Eric. He even found the time to go on a few dates outside of work, though none of them panned out. It ended up being another co-worker who stole his heart. Life plan B was back on, the center of the world was a woman, Nachogee's was the necessary evil that paid the bills, and he was sure that his real career would blossom on the side at any moment because talent finds a way.

Then at twenty-five years old the promotion came through bumping Eric up to General Manager status. He'll run his own store and prove he has what it takes for the next promotion of District Manager. He was lucky enough to be granted a week of vacation before the full transfer of power. The man that he sees in the mirror has things going for him. And he's got a stick of deodorant in his hand.

Eric breaks eye contact with himself and walks out of the bedroom before he gets too depressed. He hasn't written or truly made art in the past year.

Eric arrives at and lingers in the entrance to his living room and admires Lilly Knowles. She is gorgeous, out of his league and he hopes she never realizes it. She does. She has to. She's just that sweet not to care, just that soulmate, he just has to keep telling himself that, keep the faith, keep the confidence.

Strands of golden blonde hair twisted around her finger, bare feet propped up on the ottoman, Lilly lounges on the sofa and watches television. She doesn't acknowledge Eric as he lingers.

They didn't acknowledge each other the very first time that they met. Lilly was introduced to Eric on the day she was hired at Nachogee's, he waved, but kept his focus on the rush of business to be dealt with; hamburgers and French fries complicated by all those different types of spiced cheese substance. They were not scheduled to work together her first week on the job.

Lilly didn't care for her job and it showed to those around her. She was contemplating quitting, but then when she saw that her second week had only a single work day scheduled it seemed manageable. The single day of work came about because the other managers, the shift leaders, had requested that Eric, in charge of scheduling, cut her hours. He scheduled her to work his weekend shift knowing that he had more patience than the average crew trainer. They had told him she was slow and as dumb as a rock. He likes an underdog. Their fates were sealed.

At first sight her eyes seemed too big and she kind of smelled like she needed to take a bath. The stench he would learn came as a result of her coming to work straight after color guard practice for her high school. As he became familiar with the expressions of her face, listened to her voice, admired her smile, and stood in close proximity to her showing her how to best fill food orders, Eric accidentally fell in love with her. Her eyes weren't too big, they were the most beautiful he had ever seen, weird that he did not see that right away. Her smell triggered something within him, suddenly a perfume better than oxygen. She wasn't dumb at all and while she lacked enthusiasm for the work at first, she sped up, and they had fun.

Eric had made the job fun for Lilly. Sparks did not fly for her, but the smiles sure did. To her the assistant manager was a cool guy and the way he powered through the job with skill and sarcasm amused her greatly. Her life outside of work was hectic with a busy senior year schedule. Also, she lived with a step-mother who loved butting heads with her over everything and a father who tended to cow to the step-mother.

When the summer came Lilly realized how much she looked forward to going to work and hanging out with Eric. She took on more shifts, a star employee, most of them during Eric's work hours. She sensed that it wasn't a coincidence that he scheduled her to work the hours that he did. She entered the summer as a single lady, screw Todd Lattner and his pushy dick, and a guy who had his shit together could be cool. She invited Eric to a party on a night that she knew they would both be free. He wasn't the party type, but he wanted to be her type and went. They had fun. They kissed during a slow dance to a fast song. They dated thereafter.

Eric made her feel appreciated. He listened like a co-conspirator against the world. Relationships between managers and employees were forbidden and breaking the rules added to the early excitement of the bonding; the snuck looks, touches, and sex in the storage room, the office, the cooler, the freezer, the storage shed, the dumpster area, and on the roof. She kept him a secret from her parents. Sneaking him into her house was another level of thrill.

When it came time for her to go to college she stayed local and kept some hours at Nachogee's. They saw each other less. She quit after a month of trying to juggle higher education and work. They did their best not to see each other less.

They have been together for shy of two years. She's on break from school and he's on break from work.

Her eyes drift away from the nonsense on television to look at her own toes, nails void of paint, maybe she will paint them, purposefully ignoring Eric as he continues to stare at her from across the room. Is it a game? Is she playing or not?

From where he stands Eric looks at the soles of those same feet, considers her perfect from head to toe, never been a "foot guy," but maybe he will worship them before they leave, find her smell underneath the new perfume she has been wearing.

The television remote is on the ottoman next to Lilly's feet. Eric breaks away from his position and walks over to scoop up the remote. He powers off the television.

Lilly gives an indifferent protest.

"I was watching that."

Eric sets the remote back down as he questions his girlfriend's sluggish posture.

"Do you have all your stuff packed?"

An awkward flash of realization punctuates the question within Eric's mind: "I sound like her dad or something." She probably agrees, but doesn't complain her way into that argument, merely throws his question back at him.

"Do YOU have all your stuff packed?"

"Ha. Don't act like you're waiting on me. You don't even have your shoes on."

Lilly yanks her reclined body up and pulls her feet off the ottoman in a twitch of deft athleticism. She drops her feet down to her flip-flops on the floor, scoots her tootsies into said foot attachments, then props her now adorned feet right back up on the ottoman. She crosses her arms, a pose that goes well with her smirk.

Eric takes another moment to simply stand there and adore her.

She goes ahead and taunts his preparedness.

"If you'd hurry up and call our ride, we could be over the river and through the woods to grandma's house already."

"I did. We took a vote and decided that after granny's we'd rather go to Branson instead of Las Vegas."

"Hick, no. I'll be finding a new ride to Vegas then."

Eric reaches down and tugs off one of her flip-flops. She doesn't appreciate that.

"Ow!"

"You don't want to go to Vegas, you don't even have your shoes on yet."

"It's your grandma's house I'm not ready for. Meeting family makes me nervous."

"If she bites, she doesn't have teeth."

"I don't know proper etiquette. Do I let her gum me or punch her?"

"She's old, let her have her thrills."

Eric sits down on the couch next to Lilly. She swings her legs around to where her feet are in Eric's lap.

"Gimmie my shoe."

He removes her other flip-flop and tosses both to the floor.

"Eric, come on now."

He lifts up one of her feet, pushes to get a bend in her knee, and turns his head to deliver a passionate kiss to the sole of the foot.

Lilly yanks her foot out of his grasp, scoots, retracts both legs from his lap.

"Ack! Freako!"

Eric crawls over to her, slides himself against her in an attempt to bring some kisses to her face. She pushes back against him, denies him lip access with an excuse.

"We're going to fall behind schedule."

He's ready for romantic theatrics.

"Damn the consequences."

He goes in for another kiss as she struggles to keep him at bay. After a moment Eric decides to retreat, but not without punishing her. He reaches in and tickles her sides. Lilly squirms, laughs, and roars out a command.

"Stop!"

She kicks at him as he moves to give her space. Eric ends up back in his sitting position with her legs across his lap. She's not smiling and he's had a question on his mind for some time that slips out.

"Are we having intimacy issues?"

"Don't ask stupid questions."

"It's been almost a week."

"You just had your mouth on my foot."

"I'll put it wherever you want."

He gently bends her leg and presses a kiss on her knee. Then he looks at her with all of the seduction he can muster, seeks the "green light" to continue.

"Hmm?"

Lilly pulls her legs away once again, sits up with her feet on the floor. She tries to get the conversation back on the topic of their trip.

"Did you call your brother?"

"Yeah."

"He could be here any minute."

"We could make it an amazing minute."

Lilly stands up.

"I've gotta pee. If our ride isn't here after that, I guess you can suck my toes if that's what you want."

The offer lacks enthusiasm and just leaves Eric feeling disheartened and weird. He watches her walk out of the room and tries to do as she did, change the topic in his mind back to the trip ahead.

The itinerary: get picked up by his brother Luke, drive from St. Louis to Owensville to pick up their cousin Clint and his wife Indigo, then farther into the wilds of central Missouri to visit their grandmother Meta Bradbury, and after that quick visit they drive straight on to Nevada to experience the razzle dazzle of Las Vegas for the first time. It is the first real trip and vacation Eric has ever planned out in his adult life; extra special.

Her foot that he kissed had smelled like dog shit.

3

175

Luke Bradbury grew up in the same household as Eric Bradbury; however, he got the left-handed experience to Eric's right. His being left-handed was "a curse that came out of left field" according to his mother. No one on either side of their family had ever been left-handed as far as she knew. She blamed the curse for his behavioral issues and poor grades; always the public attention seeker and class clown.

At first his parents tried strict discipline and privilege depravation. Dad spanked him with a yard stick once, seemed to regret it, never apologized, but never did it again either. Once he hit his teens Luke's possessions were sparse and his state of being "grounded" was permanent. However, he still made noise for himself.

One time, the precise time a few seconds past three in the morning, the police brought fourteen-year-old Luke home after he got his arm stuck in a vending machine trying to steal candy bars. An extra quirk added to his criminal mischief was the fact that he was in drag: makeup, tight dress, and a bow in his hair. There was no setting the boy straight.

A full confession over what he had been up to never materialized; however, Luke did come out as gay. His mom and dad accepted his sexuality on the surface, but the boy sensed he had wronged some belief inside of them and their smiles were as warm as those of cheap puppets. Also, it wasn't too long after his reveal that he got shipped away to a boot camp program, followed by an "academy," that he is pretty sure was some sort of mental health facility, but cannot recall the details of because of the drug cocktails they tested on him during that time.

The vending machine incident had been a Robin Hood mission for the homeless camped outside the warehouse where the rave that Luke went to that night was being held, by the way. And dressing in drag isn't something Luke did because of being homosexual, it was the theme of the rave: Gender Bender. He's put on a dress only one other time in his life and that was a Halloween gag.

After being rehabilitated a few times Luke did some time in juvenile hall thanks to drugs not prescribed to him and vandalism.

His parents signed off on his emancipation at seventeen after he became a pizza delivery boy and started living with a masseur named Terry. Everyone thought Terry was gay. Terry was never gay. In fact, Luke ended up having to get his own place as soon as he was eighteen because Terry wanted to move his girlfriend and her kid into his house.

Luke became a long-haul truck driver on a whim and that whim has provided him with a steady paycheck for years along with giving him the chance to see most of the Eastern United States. And lots of weird stuff at trucks stops. Truck stops are like different worlds within the world and Luke doesn't exactly feel like he belongs in either one, but finds it damn interesting traveling between them.

Luke and Eric ran in different circles and from time to time shared brotherly moments of chit-chat, nothing too intimate or profound. They didn't argue too often, but they never bonded over philosophical discussions or sought each other out for specific advice. Luke has always looked up to his older brother, maybe because in the golden years before the teenage spiral, the time in youth when they spent hours mashing their action figures together, Eric proved to be an admirable leader in fantasy fiction. They fought enough imaginary wars together to cement an unspoken trust.

Eric never involves himself in Luke's affairs, which means he never judges him or treats him as a "lesser than." Maybe he scolded him a time or two and Luke knew how to annoy Eric in return, but never with such force as to create an obvious rift. Eric accepted his brother as his brother without fanfare or judgment. Luke in return was appreciative without ever having to explain such a feeling or thank his brother for being a brother.

Of course, on the flip side of the positive is that Luke and Eric's close relationship is at times imaginary. Luke will sometimes reflect on things and realize that with most things unspoken between them they don't have much of a relationship in regard to keeping up with each other's lives. There is a distance kept between them that has only grown wider with age.

After the rumors printed as fact in the newspapers and the police investigation, Luke found that his brother was still his brother, got a surprise call from him and Eric didn't even mention hearing the information that had been spun out into the wind. Luke was delighted to get invited on a trip with the only caveat being that they got to take his van: Dessi.

Dessi is a 1994 Chevy Astro, the last model of the first generation of that model. Eric knows this because Luke is a proud van owner. However, Dessi's paint job is new to him as he spies the vehicle entering the parking lot of his apartment complex.

As a celebration of the miracle that Dessi still runs lane to lane with any other beast on the road, Luke got a custom paint job. On a palette of glossy purples are angels, warrior angel women, who pose with swords while wearing string bikinis on their curvy bodies.

At first sight Eric is amused, takes in the art with boy wonderment: "awesome." He is ready to roll with it, going to Vegas, letting in some crazy isn't like letting in some vampires.

Then Lilly sidles up behind Eric and looks out the window, sees the van as it gets parked. Eric turns to her and her frown quickly changes his own presented attitude toward the vehicle: Dessi is an embarrassing monster. He unifies with her in frown. He remains secretly amused.

Outside, Luke stands next to Dessi, a showman presenting the main attraction with two thumbs up and a smile as full throttle as he can muster. Lilly ignores him and rolls her luggage to store it in the vehicle while Eric pauses to greet his brother and acknowledge the achievement in art.

"It looks like it was painted by Michelangelo himself."

Luke is instantly inspired by the comment.

"Ninja turtles! You're right, I should have gotten her painted up like the Ninja Turtle van."

The name Michelangelo as a famous painter did not go over Luke's head, it's just a twist of fate and comment that the brothers were big Teenage Mutant Ninja Turtle fans growing up and the name Dessi also happens to comes from what Luke named his pet box turtle when he was in Kindergarten. Why he named his turtle Dessi is a mystery to him. Dessi was a three-legged wonder, a speedy lettuce muncher that always impressed the other kids at Show-and-Tell no matter how many times, every time Luke brought her to school for the event.

Heavy metal chaos screeches out of Dessi's speaker system. The only distinguishable word amongst the vocal ramblings is doubled up, smooshed together each time it is belted out, "mother-mother" repeated as the hook. Both Lilly and Eric cringe against the decibel level, she in the rear of the vehicle, he riding shotgun, while Luke jerks the steering wheel from side to side violently and sings out.

"Mother-mother! Mother-mother!"

Luke takes both hands off the wheel and turns to Eric. He signs devil horns with each hand and then shows off his headbanging skills. Lilly can't believe they have volunteered to be the hostages of a lunatic. She thinks about bailing out of the vehicle.

They have not pulled out of the driveway of the apartment yet.

Eric turns down the volume knob on the stereo. Luke keeps the volume of his voice loud, but rubs his neck from the headbanging stunt.

"Are we ready to launch?"

"Yeah. You okay to drive?"

"Whiplash builds character. I accidentally got the edited version of this cd. They're not really singing mother-mother. When you get censored music you've got to play it full volume to rebel."

He turns his attention to Lilly in the back.

"State of the art sound system made the hair on your back stand up didn't it? Like the tunes?"

"I prefer my hearing."

"You'll get over that."

He turns his attention back to the front of the van and grips the steering wheel once again.

"Ladies and gentlemen, this is your Captain speaking, Dessi will now be leaving, buckle up, and wave your hands in the air like you just don't care. Let's go get Clint and Indigo!"

He cranks the radio volume back up, introduces Eric and Lilly to a new song, gibberish to them, a galactic opera about the wild horses that fly out of black holes to him, cranks Dessi into reverse, and mashes on the gas pedal. Luke roars the van backward for show, but then quickly becomes the more conservative driver that he actually is.

Eric turns down the volume of the stereo once again.

They are out of the driveway, trip underway.

The trio don't fall into conversation. Eric and Lilly both pull out their cellphones and put their attention on the small screens. Eric does so with an excuse for his brother's benefit.

"I've got to catch up on a last few work things."

Lilly's attention drifts from her screen toward the front of the vehicle. She eyes a sprig of Eric's wayward hair going rogue off the side of his head. She thinks he should wear hats more.

Earlier he had brought into question the state of intimacy in their relationship. She doesn't want to think about that. Why is she thinking about that? What else does she have to think about? School.

She's not making the grades that she had hoped for. The social scene, even though she hasn't left her home city, has been eye opening. She's been doing her best to have fun with all her new friends, and juggle classes, and juggle a relationship with Eric, and she's not adept at juggling. Crap, school and Eric are connected thoughts; what else does she have to think about? The future.

She is curious as to what the world has to offer. She's trying to get a business degree while dabbling in computer information science, but along the way she has forgotten to be motivated. She would like to craft some lifestyle brands and understand how to bring customers into the fold but has begun to doubt that success in such ventures can be possible without living life to the fullest to begin with. There are adventures calling to her, so many, and she can't tell which direction they are calling from exactly.

Her brother is in the army and she knew she had a problem the day she found herself seriously considering going down to the enlistment office herself. She'd prefer world travel without the experience of war, but her father, having been a navy man himself, always spoke of how well the military helps a young soul find direction. She didn't realize that she had been paying attention to his subtle nudges of career advice.

Maybe she could survive boot camp and see herself holding a weapon. She had been in color guard rather than cheerleading at school. She did not spin flags as a part of her troop, rather a plastic rifle facsimile. If terrorists had ever attacked her school she could have dazzled them with her spinning skills for sure. It was fun. No, joining the military wouldn't be fun. The thought of committing to something and then realizing too late that it was just another wrong turn scares her, especially when you tie on the perils of war.

She got a job offer modeling for a boutique clothing line. The owner's ambition impressed her. There could be travel involved representing the brand and spreading its profile from city to city. Someone liked her enough to want her to be the face of that. Another avenue to consider.

She hasn't shared any of her thoughts with Eric. He's never really asked her about her schooling. Sure, he makes polite inquiries, but she can tell he's not really listening if she does describe events from her classes. And she knows he doesn't trust her, he's bad at pretending, and she doesn't know if he should trust her either. He's going to try and pull her in yet another direction, a path of his own forging. And she really wants to lean forward and pat that waving piece of hair down on the side of his head right now, but she refrains.

She doesn't want to think anymore. She seeks out music on her phone to try and combat the insult of what Luke considers music. She realizes that she doesn't know where her headphones are.

Eric turns around in his seat like the perfectly telepathic gentleman and hands her some headphones for her phone. His smile is warm, makes her feel loved, and that makes her feel sad.

# 4

Clint Morgan is the son of Patty Morgan who originally hails from the Bradbury clan, Aunt to Eric and Luke Bradbury, which makes Clint a cousin to Eric and Luke. Oddly, the family never got together and the cousins never really saw each other aside from if they were at their grandmother's at the same time. Clint is the same age as Eric and would mostly hang around him when hanging around with cousins was being done. Eric picked up some premature baldness genes, Clint ended up with gray at the temples of his otherwise black hair before he was twenty.

He doesn't always act as mature as his hair may indicate, but Clint did take on many adult responsibilities at a young age. His father died and Clint inherited several rental properties to manage. When he met and married his wife they were both only eighteen.

Indigo Morgan married Clint without hesitation. Their romance was as fairy tale to her as reality ever gets, true love at first sight. They met not in school, but rather in a grocery store parking lot when her cart rolled away from her and somehow stayed on the perfect trajectory to travel four cars lengths away and plow into him from behind. She says that love at first sight came by instinct, he says the freckles on her face made him swoon.

After some dating they moved in together; when it's right it's right. She hails from a large family and while they are taking their time getting around to it, she figures she and Clint are going to have a whole litter of puppies at some point. Literally puppies, she doesn't want children, just wants to open a large scale animal rescue. She works with Clint expanding the Morgan real estate empire of blue-collar condos.

Owensville is a small Missouri town, home of the Flying Dutchmen, where Clint and Indigo manage some properties, and chose to buy up rural plots of land in the surrounding region for potential development; an acre here and there for maybe a mobile home to be placed or a dog shelter. Their own home is on one such piece of property, a double-wide that is under what they can actually afford, but they are saving up for the future and it has vaulted ceilings so that's fancy enough for now. One day they will have a nice house and, if Clint has his way, an elaborate system of bunkers underneath it, not because he wants to prep for the end of the world, but just because it would be cool to have.

It is at the city park in Owensville that Clint and Indigo await pickup. They are getting picked up there out of consideration for travel time and path trajectory; Vegas awaits, no one wants to get lost in the wilds of

Owensville. They caught a ride from a friend and wait in a picnic bench area with their luggage, a parking area nearby. When they see the spectacle that is Luke's van pull into the parking area they are as split in first impressions as Eric and Lilly were. Indigo has never met Lilly, but they indeed already share common ground in regard to what they consider acceptable artwork to be featured on 1994 Chevy Astro vans.

Lilly opens the rear side door of the van as Eric hops out of the passenger side to greet his family members.

"Clint! Indigo! Where have you been?"

Clint replies as he initiates a hug with Eric. "We've been right here!"

After the brief embrace Eric waves to Indigo, but she is all about hugging as well, holds her arms out, and the gesture reels him right in.

Luke strolls away from the van to join the reunion, but all greetings and hugs seem to have been spent on Eric.

Eric moves the group along toward the van, takes the handle of Indigo's suitcase and wheels it for her. As they approach the van he brings Lilly, who sits at the open door of the van, into conversation.

"You guys remember Lilly?"

Clint responds.

"We do. It has been too long though. We live in the same state, but different countries it seems like."

Indigo goes up to and plants a hug with Lilly while Clint turns to give Luke some delayed attention.

"Luke, how's it going with you?"

"Hardcore."

"Bitchin' van, buddy."

Luke takes the compliment with a smile and doesn't feel inspired to add a punchline. The group is all together, time to pack in and hit some more road.

As they ride Clint flexes his gift for gab. Lots of people know how to talk a lot, but only certain people have the charisma to make their breath always smell refreshing. Clint tells the group about the time he and Indigo rode a Greyhound bus across the country. The story has the central theme of discomfort and turns into a life lessons session when Lilly lets it be known that she is a Greyhound virgin.

"I've never ridden a bus, except for a school bus."

"Let me tell you about riding the bus. You don't want to sit near the toilet because it smells of chemicals. And turd. But, you don't want to sit too far away in case you need to go."

Indigo adds her two cents of experience and eggs her husband on with a question.

"I almost fell into the toilet because the bus was rocking so hard. Did you sit to pee?"

"No. I'm a man. I whipped it all over the walls and myself. That's why you don't wear light colored pants when you ride the bus."

Luke rode a bus once and shares his bad experience.

"Someone tried to steal my luggage when I rode the bus."

Clint one-ups him.

"The driver tried to steal my luggage."

Indigo corrects her husband's lie.

"No she didn't. She made you put it into the storage space under the bus."

"Right where I'd be more likely to "forget" it. When you get off the bus you want to run away, not wait for everyone else to get off and for the driver to open up the luggage hatch."

He continues with more advice for Lilly's future bus riding endeavors.

"Never ride the bus alone. You've got to have someone watching out for you. In fact, it'd be good for one of you to act blind and claim the other needs to sit by you as your nurse or something. Indigo and I got split up after one stop and this fat guy sat next to me straight-up eating out of a bucket of chicken. His ass took half of my seat and I had to lean into the aisle with the armrest jabbing into my side."

Lilly puts all of the tales together and poses a question.

"So, what you're telling me is that the bus is a turd smelling den of fat thieves?"

Clint responds.

"Well, when you put it that way it sounds bad. However, there are guys that will offer you blow jobs at the bus station bathrooms in exchange for bus tickets. The tickets are reasonably priced."

Indigo hits her husband with one of her elbows to punish his lowbrow humor.

The others laugh. The couple has their routines polished.

## 5

Rest stops are haunted by urban legends. Even those who doubt the most fanciful tales of horror tend to sense the danger alive in the air at such locations, a mystical ingredient inhaled with the oxygen, a spiritual spinal tap of dread regardless of how bright the lights or visible the security cameras. These areas are intersections of human characters, interludes from the speed of the highways, where strangers mesh the scents of their lives in progress. Some stop with weariness and full bladders, others with devious intentions and fitful desires.

A man of the road, Luke doesn't shy away from rest stops. The creepiness is a sort of lure to his more noble side. He has bought drugs and gotten laid at rest stops, made friends, and probably smelled the feces of more than one serial killer without even knowing it; all things with a touch of illicit spice. However, when he pulls his big rig into a rest stop he imagines that he is a part of a trucker superhero squad, a familiar comfort to other motorists, watching all from the height of the truck cab with the eyes of a protector. Every now and then a trucker will be the predator, but for the most part he thinks they are the congressional leaders keeping the seedy areas safer than legends will tell. He's going to pitch the idea to his brother for one of his comic books.

Luke, to the chagrin of his passengers, guides Dessi into a rest stop instead of a convenience store situation. Eric calls his brother out on the pit stop.

"Don't take us to a rape hole. Pull into a gas station like a normal person."

"We're almost there, we don't need gas."

"I could use chips and a soda though."

"They've got the credit card vending machines here."

"No way am I swiping my card at a sketchy rest stop."

Luke ignores Eric's protest and parks the van.

As they stretch their legs away from the van Luke is the only one to notice that the parking lot safety lights are all on and draw swarms of nocturnal insects even in broad daylight. At night the insects become a feast for bats, a show of swooping shadows that never fails to enchant Luke when he catches it.

Inside the men's restroom Luke and Clint drain urine at the urinals while Eric uses a stall. Eric finishes up first and then stands behind the other fellows. He doesn't wait for them to finish and zip up before he announces that he has an announcement.

"I've got something to tell you guys."

Luke already knows the answer.

"You didn't flush."

Luke and Clint flush their urinals almost in tandem. Eric waits for the sounds of water to die down before he makes the official announcement.

"I'm going to ask Lilly to marry me."

Clint is supportive.

"Congratulations."

Luke is not.

"Bad idea."

Eric doesn't appreciate Luke's negativity.

"What is your problem with her, Luke?"

"She's kind of mean."

"You're an idiot."

Clint seeks to snuff the fuse on the argument.

"How are you popping the question?"

"At Grandma's house. I'll tell her about how important the place was to me as a kid and then how important to me she is now."

Luke votes against the idea.

"She won't like that."

Clint continues to run argument interference.

"And then a Vegas wedding?"

"She once said Vegas weddings are cool. I have always wanted to be the cool guy."

Luke doesn't think his brother has the right definition of cool.

"She's not going to want to get married the very first time she visits there."

"Jesus tits, Luke, I wasn't asking for your opinion."

"Never mind. You're right. Congratulations."

Luke walks out on the argument and out of the restroom. Clint and Eric linger.

"I see Luke is still weird. Has he been weirder since the arrest?"

"We're just kind of distancing that."

"Indigo was wondering if you guys were still talking."

"I'm trying. I'm sorry if he ruins this trip for you."

"It'll be all good."

Clint gives he cousin a pat on the back and then the men walk to the exit of the restroom. None of them have washed their hands.

In the women's restroom they hover over torn paper coverings above cold plastic seats. It doesn't matter that there is a citrus odor to the air, that most surfaces seem wiped off, that the floor seems mopped, or that the toilet paper is stocked Indigo and Lilly joke about how the cleanliness is a thin film of disguise. The bonding is jovial, not sisterhood stuff, but almost getting them to the social edge beyond small talk.

The hand soap at the sinks is not featured in anchored dispensers. Instead it is in individual pumps, several with broken open tops due to the pump mechanism getting clogged. The soap is the gritty type marketed to mechanics.

Lilly tests the soap and reports her findings to Indigo.

"The soap feels dirty."

Indigo produces some hand wipes from out of her purse. Lilly thanks her.

"Thank you. You're my hero."

Small gestures often hold the world together and as Lilly wipes her hands she dares to think that she might allow herself to have fun on this trip. Her positive outlook lasts as long as the walk takes from the restroom to

the van because inside the van Eric is ready to
take away everyone's cellphones.

He holds out a plastic bag and seems
surprised that no one offers up their device.

"The deal was we'd all put away our
cellphones once we were about to reach
Granny's."

He adds an exclamation of a selling point.

"We're getting away to real life!"

Luke dunks his phone into the bag where
it joins Eric's. Clint and Indigo hand their
phones over as well. Eric holds the bag toward
Lilly and stares at her, not unlike a parent
might their child; it is a look that Eric himself
would not appreciate if he realized in the
moment how it translates.

"Lilly, you're the only holdout."

"You made the deal, I didn't agree to it."

"We'll have them in the van for
emergencies."

"You're a phone hater."

"Proudly, but I love you."

Lilly gives in and places her phone into the
bag.

"I want it back if I get bored."

"I promise you that won't happen."

He turns around and she watches as he
fails to cram the bag of phones into the glove
box. He sets them on the floorboard at his feet.

She wonders if his promise meant that she
would not get bored or that he would not give

her back her phone under any circumstances. The phone is password protected, but it still feels uncomfortable to put it in Eric's control. The phone is her lifeline to a part of her that he's not privy to.

She turns and stares out the window, back to the troubles of her mind, thinking on whether or not he doesn't know her is her fault or his own.

6

The rural highway that leads to the driveway of Grandma Bradbury's house snakes its way through heavy woodlands with scenic views and hairpin turns offering plenty of chances to become one with the roadkill. The driveway itself is a turn that even relatives who recognize her basic mailbox might miss if they are not focused on seeking it out. It does not matter which direction you arrive from; the driveway is a narrow opening after a sharp hill. Once the turn is made you can actually see the house from the road, though to either side of the gravel driveway is more woods. The drive ends in a circle for easy turning around maneuvers with a large two-car garage off to one side of that.

The house is a half basement house with one side aimed toward the end of the driveway. Trees were cleared behind the house to make a back yard upon which grass has always failed to grow. At the front of the house a spacious yard area was cleared leading all the way down to the edge of a man-made pond. Sitting and looking toward the pond is one of the main pastimes to have been enjoyed at the Bradbury residence over the years. One can sit indoors at the kitchen table to look out through the sliding glass front door, or there is a swinging bench on the front porch, or there are lawn chairs on the lawn, or there is a picnic table set up right on a hill at one edge of the pond. There are fish in the pond that cause little ripples when they bob for food, but really the main attraction for those looking pond-ward is the bird feeder in the center of the front yard; the pond is merely a distant backdrop, for the squirrels love to put on acrobatic theater there.

Meta Bradbury's cocker spaniel Cookie Three, son of Cookie Two, generally lives on the front porch of the home. The squirrels and birds used to be for chasing but as he aged he became an avid spectator like the humans. The porch is not where he lives now, however, for he is dead on it.

The trio of Eric, Luke, and Clint stand at the edge of the porch and bear witness to the aftermath of Cookie Three's final battle. The dog is spread across the porch in pieces. The blood still appears sticky and has already been found by the flies and ants. The smell of death is enough to make Clint want to get sick and unintentionally make an inappropriate sound of comment.

"Woof."

Luke calls out to the house.

"Grandma!"

The van Dessi is parked at the end of the driveway. No other vehicles can be seen and the garage doors are both down. Lilly and Indigo walk away from the van to join the men. Clint walks away from the carnage to intercept the women.

"You might want to hang back for a second."

The women stop as Clint joins them. They can see scraps of Cookie Three from their vantage point already. Indigo seeks confirmation for her husband.

"Is that a dead animal?"

He nods.

Luke tiptoes around the death on the porch in order to get to the handle on the sliding glass front door. He pulls on the door and finds it unlocked. He slides it open and yells into the house.

"Grandma!"

No Grandma yodels back.

Luke enters the house with a cautious pace and Eric follows after him.

The layout of the house has the brother's entering the kitchen area, the side that features the kitchen table. Offshoots from this area are the compact laundry room, a bathroom, and then two doors that lead into side by side guest bedrooms. All of the doors to these rooms are open and as the brothers move around the table they peek into them and do not see any signs of a grandmother in distress. They move farther into the quiet house.

The dining side of the kitchen is not separate from the cooking side, but the room is spacious enough that one feels like they have been in two separate areas. Grandma is not at the stove frying bacon; therefore the brothers move on into the living room's dining area. The living room, like the kitchen, is quite spacious and one side of it has been turned into a carpeted dining room. Eating in the kitchen is for casual chit-chat, the second dining area is for special dinners, though the family has not gathered for special dinners on a regular basis since the holidays of Eric and Luke's youth.

Away from the initial dining portion of the living room, the main area features two recliners aimed toward a television, though distanced so far back that one must wonder if Grandma took the "sitting too close will ruin your eyes" lore close to heart. The television is an old school box that sits on the floor and offers no high definition options, though it is still wired to the VCR on top of it. There is a big comfy chair positioned closer to the television at one side, and then a couch across the way from that, with a coffee table of thick wood in-between. Both Luke and Eric have cracked their heads on that coffee table on more than one occasion trying to emulate the ninja moves of action movies. The furniture is not crowded together, the room is indeed spacious, and there is plenty of free space between chairs, coffee table, and couch for lounging around in the floor if one wishes. Grandma is neither in a piece of furniture or lounging on the floor.

Off the living room is the door for the master bedroom. There is a master bathroom off of that and a walk-in closet. Luke and Eric feel a bit weird tiptoeing into Grandma's private quarters, but the door is open. Grandma is not in the made bed.

The closet is the only door that is shut and while Luke goes into the bathroom, Eric checks the interior of the closet. Grandma is not hanging out with her clothes in the closet. Luke calls out from the bathroom.

"Eric, check this out!"

Eric hurries to see what his brother has discovered. Grandma is not in the bathroom; however, someone has scrawled a message across the vanity mirror in lipstick: BEWARE MO.

The phone hangs on the wall in the kitchen, at the edge of where kitchen ends and living room begins. It is a rotary phone designed to appear even more antique than it is. Luke stands by while Eric finishes up talking to their father over the phone.

"Thanks, Dad. You too."

Eric hangs up the phone and Luke pounces after information.

"What's the story?"

"They took Grandma the other day."

"Took?"

"I guess she fell and hurt her leg. When Dad came to take her to the doctor she refused and threw a fit. They had to sedate her."

"Grandma is a rebel."

"Grandma is suffering from dementia."

"What happened to Cookie Three?"

"Dad didn't know anything about that."

Luke references the message left on the mirror.

"Beware Mo. Mo. You remember Mo, right?"

"Yeah."

"We've got the perfect campfire story for later."

Eric is not as thrilled about revisiting the legend of Mo as Luke seems to be.

Blood still stains the concrete and the brothers took on the task of shoveling Cookie Three's remains off the porch and into a garbage bag. After the grisly task is completed they join the rest of the group who sip from cans of beer in the lawn chairs of the front yard. As Eric takes the chair next to Lilly's she lodges a complaint.

"I can still smell it."

Indigo wants to solve the murder mystery.

"What killed the dog?"

Clint offers her the most obvious solution.

"It was probably a coyote."

Eric affirms that a coyote could have easily dispatched the dog.

"Cookie Three was all bark and no bite."

Indigo wants to honor the creature.

"We should give him a proper burial."

Luke disagrees.

"Cookie Three would have wanted to be cremated."

No one laughs at his attempted joke. Luke decides to add on to it.

"When I die I want to be stuffed and set up on a throne. Then everyone can rock out while strippers give me lap dances."

Lilly lets him know what she thinks of his funeral wishes and him in general.

"You're disgusting."

It gets worse.

"And then I want to be cremated and the ashes should be put into bullets. I'll have a list of people that I want the bullets shot into."

As with the paint job on the van, the men are more amused than the ladies. Clint seeks more information from Luke.

"Do you have the list already?"

Indigo is not having it.

"Come on, Lilly, we'll bury the dog ourselves."

When the women get up, Eric hurries up to his feet as well.

"Hold on. I'll find a shovel."

Luke challenges his brother's ability to do such a thing.

"The garage is locked, bro. I checked."

"I'll find something."

Clint gets up to join the burial party. Luke lets the group get a head start, but then follows after.

Gardening spades found in the laundry room get the shallow grave dug. The garbage bag with Cookie Three in it is now planted in the back yard beneath a mound of dirt. The group stands around the fresh grave and Luke takes on the eulogy with a can of beer in hand.

"Here lies Cookie Three. He was a grumpy son of a bitch that wouldn't let anyone else hump grandma's leg. One last dance, ole boy."

He pours some of his beer out on to the dirt.

## 7

The plan of staying the night at Grandma Bradbury's house has not changed. However, while sleeping in the master bedroom seems too creepy for Luke and Eric, Clint has no problem using it for the night with his wife.

Clint sits on the edge of the bed as Indigo walks into the room from out of the master bathroom. She is fresh from the shower and wears a towel around her body. Clint makes conversation as she walks over to one of their bags to get some lotion.

"What do you think of Eric and Lilly together?"

"They're a cute couple."

She rubs lotion on to her arms as he continues with another question.

"What level is cute? Our level?"

"For their sake I hope not."

She chuckles at her own joke.

"They've been together two years-ish I think. You think they should get married?"

"I don't know her that well. She's younger than Eric. Eric is kind of..."

She stops herself from laying out an insult, but Clint pries.

"Eric is kind of what?"

"Eric."

"You think she's out of his league?"

She gets playfully jealous.

"Are you saying that you think she's hot?"

"I don't see others that way. You know I am blinded by my love for you."

Suave save.

"She is hot. Is Eric going to propose or something?"

"Seems so."

"It won't work out."

"Ow. Harsh."

"Don't you dare tell him I said that."

"He'll just have to fool her like I fooled you."

He gets up and walks over to stand closer to her as she drops the lotion back into the bag. He kisses her on a shoulder.

"What is everyone else doing?"

"I don't know, but I locked our door."

"Oh? Are you going to help me put on my jammies?"

Yes he will. He leans in to place kisses on her neck. She tugs on the front of the towel at the fold and the towel drops to the floor at her feet.

A few minutes later Clint and Indigo step out of the master bedroom in the matching pajamas they bought once as a joke that never gets old to them. The red and white pajamas make them seem like a pair of candy canes.

Lilly is alone in the main portion of the living room. She is lounged across the largest chair and a gentle snore escapes her nostrils.

The couple sneak across the room trying not disturb Lilly's slumber. They find that Eric and Luke are at the dining room area and eat sandwiches from paper plates.

Eric holds up what is left of his sandwich.

"Pickle loaf. Do you want one?"

Indigo sticks out her tongue and shakes her head no while Clint vocalizes for them.

"Gross."

His wife decides that it isn't an adequate enough pass on the offer.

"Processed meat is a scary story."

She just lobbed Luke the perfect transition into an activity he has been looking forward to.

"Yes! Scary story time!"

His enthusiasm causes Lilly to wake up in the other portion of the open room.

Luke crams the rest of his sandwich into his mouth. It is too much. Eric, Clint, and Indigo watch to see if he will chew through it all or soon be dead.

A few minutes later and the gang gathers in the main living room area. Lilly remains in her chair, still horizontally lounged with her feet over the arm. Eric sits with his back against the base of her chair. Indigo and Clint sit together on the couch and Luke stands in front of the television set ready to master the ceremony.

Luke has another beer in his hand and as he talks it is obvious that he wavers over the line of sobriety.

"Forget the ghost stories you've heard. Forget that there is a prison just down the road from here that many a chainsaw wielding maniac has escaped from. Forget the werewolf I once saw in these very woods. The story I am going to tell you is about a witch. A grandma witch. True story."

Lilly yawns.

Luke continues.

"On the weekends that we got to stay at Grandma's she would keep us busy with stacks of action movies to watch. Sometimes we'd play in the yard too. What we really wanted though was to explore the woods, but Grandma forbid it. She told us to play with our Barbies and mud pies, but to never, never ever, go into the woods."

Lilly raises her hand as she asks her question.

"You played with Barbies?"

Eric answers with a pivot to make the mud pies the topic of interest.

"I used to make the best mud pies."

Indigo chimes in her love of mud pies.

"I loved making mud pies as a kid."

Eric isn't admitting to playing with dolls, but he doesn't have shame in tasting the sunbaked desserts he used to whip up in the yard.

"I bet you didn't eat them though."

"Uh. No."

"Mine were that good."

Luke gets his story going once again.

"Curiosity got the better of me. I saw that Grandma went into the woods all the time. If it was safe for her, then why not me? So, one day, I made a break for it!"

Eric remembers this part of the story.

"It was in the middle of a game of hide and seek."

"Eric never found me."

"This isn't the right story."

"Shh. There I was, like ten years old, alone in the woods for the first time. I saw a couple of cool rocks, bugs, swung on a vine, but I couldn't shake the feeling that something was watching me. I turned around and that's when I saw it..."

He does his best to raise the tension with a dramatic pause. No one is really all that hooked, but he isn't going to laze out on his showmanship, delivers the reveal in a low, meant to be spooky, voice.

"...the werewolf."

Lilly argues.

"You said forget about the werewolf."

"Oh, it's back in."

Clint urges Luke to continue.

"What did it look like?"

"You know when you sense movement out of the corner of your eye, turn your head real quick, but nothing is there? It looked like that."

Lilly groans.

"You saw nothing."

"My mind screamed: "Werewolf!" Then I ran faster than I have ever ran in my entire life."

Eric ends the story.

"Then I found him."

"Didn't count."

"I found him and told him that he cheated by going into the woods."

Lilly has had enough.

"I'm going to bed."

She climbs out of the chair, pushes around Eric, and Luke warns her.

"You'll miss the best part."

Eric stands up to follow Lilly.

"I'll go with you."

"No. Stay up and hang out. I'm going to zonk right out."

"Okay."

She starts to walk away and he wishes her well in her sleep endeavor.

"Goodnight."

"Night."

She exits the room and Eric takes the chair.

Indigo goes ahead and takes up the criticism where Lilly left off.

"Luke, I thought the story was going to be about a witch."

"There's a witch, but the witch isn't the scary part. The scary part is Mo."

"Like what your grandma wrote on the mirror? You guys said that was gibberish."

"Maybe it is. Maybe it is not."

Eric pushes the story along for Luke.

"We followed Grandma on one of her trips into the woods."

Luke picks the story back up from there, weaves a picture for Clint and Indigo of the event.

The two young boys followed their grandmother, making a spy game out of hiding behind trees and making sure not to step on any branches lest the cracking sound give away their position. Grandma Bradbury never checked to see if she was being trailed. There wasn't a path, but the elderly woman navigated the terrain with the ease of familiarity. She seemed preoccupied with her thoughts and getting to her destination with a burlap sack slung over her shoulder Santa Claus-style.

The boys followed their grandmother until she reached the edge of a creek. They made sure to stay far enough back that any farts or giggles wouldn't attract her attention.

Grandma Bradbury opened the sack that she carried and turned it over to spill its contents into the creek bed. Bloody slop, meat, guts, organs unidentifiable to the children dropped out of the sack.

In the present day living room of the same gut hauling grandmother, adult Luke now leans in closer to his audience of Clint and Indigo. He whispers to try and make the moment more intense.

"We watched as Grandma chanted something over the guts that spilled forth from her sack. And then..."

Clint puts his arm around Indigo as Luke stares at them in dramatic pause. Clint adds what he can to stir suspense into the atmosphere, by literally whispering the word aloud.

"Suspense. Suspense. Suspense."

Luke trains his focus onto Indigo.

"I turned to my brother Eric. The very Eric with you here today. And I whispered into his ear..."

Luke gets too close for indigo's comfort, but she hangs in there and suffers his beer breath with the grand story reveal.

"Eric, it looks like barf-a-roni."

Clint does his best again to help make the story scary. He shakes his wife and yells at her.

"Boo!"

Indigo is not affected. Clint is more afraid of the dirty look that she gives him than she is by the story.

Luke decides to wrap things up.

"Eric laughed like a hyena and gave away our position. Grandma captured us and we didn't see anything else."

Maybe Indigo was drawn in a little bit, because she does have another question.

"What is the Mo?"

Eric answers.

"Grandma told us to stay out of the woods 'cause of the Mo would eat us."

Luke lays out his theory.

"I assume it was a gut eating demon that grandma conjured up."

Clint did not have any similar experiences as a grandchild of Meta Bradbury and has a question of his own.

"Wait. Who told you Grandma was a witch?"

Luke has an answer.

"She did. She always warned me that she'd turn me into a Fig Newton if I didn't behave. Kind lady, but very threatening."

Eric adds more input of his own.

"The scariest part of that story is that mental illness probably runs in our family."

Indigo relates.

"I can see how little kids would have been frightened by all that."

Luke dares her to prove that her nerves are as steely as she acts.

"Little kids? If you're not scared then follow me. We're going into the woods!"

Luke leads the charge, marches across the room and toward one of the exits. However, he stops as he sees that no one moves to follow him out into the night.

Clint speaks on behalf of both he and Indigo.

"No thanks. We're good."

"Chickens."

Luke walks out of the room.

## 8

One last beer sits in a cooler of melted ice. Luke fishes the beer out from the lawn chair that he sits in. He pops the tab open, but doesn't drink, just inhales the aroma. Beer stinks and yet he drinks it. He pouts and doesn't know exactly why.

He tries to recline the back of the chair.

Eric walks out of the house to join his brother. The eldest doesn't sit down. Luke lets loose some of the feelings on his mind.

"I've missed you, Eric."

"Thanks, bro."

"I don't agree with the wedding, but I won't stop it."

Eric isn't reassured.

"Shit. Now I've got to worry about you trying to ruin it, don't I?"

"No. I only ask that I get to be the best man. None of this two best men crap with Clint. Me. Me the best man."

That sound fine to Eric.

"You got it."

He stands there for a second more, watches as Luke brings the can of beer up and guzzles from it. Eric offers his brother some advice.

"You should get some sleep."

Eric turns his back on Luke and walks away to heed his own advice.

When Eric goes into the bedroom that he shares with Lilly he makes sure to be as quiet as possible. The inner horny devil in him wants to crawl into the bed right on top of her. Not really. Really he would rather it play out that she crawls on top of him, waking him in the middle of the night. Spontaneity seems to have gone dormant in the relationship, along with sex altogether. He's going to go down on her tomorrow though, right down on one knee to shake things up.

He strips down to his boxer shorts and crawls into the bed as nimble as his body allows. Lilly is deep in sleep or good at pretending that she is. Eric gets comfortable, fluffs his pillow a few times, nope, has not disturbed her, no kiss goodnight.

As Eric tries to go to sleep he begins to imagine his fantasy of waking up to Lilly mounting him for a ride. He's never going to get to sleep. He tries to think of other things, but there are too many other things as well it seems. But then he falls asleep.

The guest bedroom in which Eric and Lilly reside in slumber is of average size. The queen-sized bed takes up most of the space, with a sliver of walk space on one side. Also fitted into the room, on the other side of the bed, is a long dresser and a short tv stand holding a television with an eight-inch screen. Along the same wall as the dresser and television is a bookcase with framed photos featured on all of the shelves except the bottom one where the Louis L'Amour Western novel collection of the late Grandfather Bradbury are stored.

The entrance door, if one is standing within the room, is to the far right of the front wall and then the largest portion of that wall extending over to the bookcase is a closet with folding doors. The door to the bedroom is open a tiny bit as are the folding doors of the closet. In fact, the doors to the closet have not been capable of fully shutting since shortly after they were installed, just a kink that no one cared enough about to grease out. And now a loud creak comes from the direction of the closet, the sound the doors make when they move.

The sound startles Lilly awake. The room is strange to her and the room is dark; she could use a second set of eyes.

"Eric."

He is not quick to respond.

"Eric, I heard something."

He comes to and responds.

"What?"

"I heard a noise by the closet."

"Those doors make noise."

"Something moved in the closet."

"It's an old house. It makes sounds."

"Eric, get up."

He sits up. He doesn't grumble, but he doesn't throw off the blankets and rush to be a hero.

"The closet is full of junk. It falls."

"Turn on the light."

Men often make the boyish mistake of teasing a woman in the wrong moment, not that there is often ever a right moment.

"There's nothing to be scared of. Do you think it's the werewolf?"

"You're an ass."

He has pissed her off into being brave. Lilly pushes off the blankets and gets out of the bed to go and investigate for herself. She doesn't even bother switching on the light.

Lilly grabs one of the creaky closet doors and yanks it open.

Luke lunges out with a growl!

217

"Rawwrrr!"

"Ahh!"

Lilly's scream is impressive as she scrambles backward and trips back against the bed. She ends up half-sitting on the foot of the bed.

Luke stumbles the rest of the way out of the closet and hits the floor laughing.

Lilly's mind catches up to the action and registers the prank that occurred. She steps up and kicks Luke as hard as she can, which hurts her foot and stokes the fires of rage.

Clint flips on the kitchen light. His wife is right behind him and they witness Luke stagger out of one of the bedrooms. Lilly follows him out and slaps at him, but Eric grabs her from behind and deadens the power of the blows.

Luke scuttles over to lean against a counter near where Clint and Indigo stand.

"Let go of me!"

Eric is now a victim to one of her slaps and he does as she demands. She storms over toward Luke but as furious as she is at the dumb grin on his face pulls up short and doesn't try to hit him again.

"You're a degenerate pervert! Wipe that smile off your face!"

Luke doesn't care if she is angry; it makes him chuckle along with the smile. Lilly turns her rage back to Eric.

"Why did you invite him?"

"He's driving us."

"We don't need him."

"He's my brother."

Luke is touched to hear his brother say that. Lilly is irate.

"That's your burden! The rest of us don't want to get raped in our sleep!"

She turns back to Luke.

"You're a creep. We all know you're a creep. Go to Hell."

She is finished and walks back toward the bedroom. Eric reaches a hand out to her as she passes him and she pushes it away. He doesn't watch her to go into the room, hears the door slam, as he apologizes to Clint and Indigo.

"I'm sorry, guys. Luke hid in our closet and jumped out."

Indigo holds an expression of concern on her face. Clint is understanding in tone.

"Drunk people make bad jokes. Look at him, he won't even remember this later."

Clint and Indigo mosey out of the drama and off to bed. They hold hands as they go. Indigo doesn't just feel the warmth of her husband's hand, she hones in on his pulse. The rhythm of his heartbeat always takes her back to the first night of their honeymoon. There had been plenty of romance before then, but that night she learned to savor the details even deeper, to share into his pulse. It's a poetic thought she has shared with Clint and he knows exactly what is in her mind when they are linked by hands.

Eric on the other hand finds that his romantic partner has locked the bedroom door. He isn't going to argue with the decision. He will bunk with his drunken brother.

The brothers reach the doorway of the second guest room at the same time and Luke is polite enough to belch rancid beer breath into Eric's face as he allows him to enter first. Luke has sense enough to leave his brother alone after that.

The bedroom is almost identical to the one Eric shared with Lilly, only no television or bookcase. When he opens the closet to find spare blankets he notices that the toys of their youth are still stored on the floor. He can see a deflated kickball, off-brand action figures, and naked Barbie dolls; relics of the good ole days when the spare blankets at the top of the closet were of no concern.

Eric makes himself an uncomfortable pallet on the floor. Later he wraps a pillow around his head because it sounds like Luke is having a chainsaw orgy with the booger gnomes in his sleep.

Clint and Indigo are the first to rise the next morning. However, it doesn't take long for them to rustle everyone else up for a group investigation.

Previously on the front porch the gang had cleaned up the remains of Cookie Three, but no search was conducted for a water hose; a mop had been ruined to swath away some of the excess blood. As Clint looked out of the sliding glass door at the remaining blood stains he decided it would be nice to try and clean some more of those off. He went outside to see if there might be a garden hose to assist in that task. He found something else instead and now Luke, Eric, Indigo, and Lilly have joined him in the back yard.

The grave of Cookie Three is a shallow, empty hole. The garbage bag coffin is shredded across the yard, and the remains it contained are spread out again as well. Something seems to have truly hated Cookie Three.

Luke nudges some of the displaced dirt back into the hole. He feels guilt from his behavior last night and feels the eyes of the others on him even though they are not.

"Why is everyone looking at me?"

Eric responds.

"No one said you did this."

Indigo lets her displeasure be known.

"This isn't funny."

Clint agrees, no "bad joke," understanding this time.

"This is messed up."

Luke defends himself.

"I didn't do it."

Lilly isn't shy about laying the blame on him now.

"You were the only one creeping around in the night."

"It's not like we dug it six feet. Critters probably came back to finish off their meal."

Eric reasons with the group, believes Luke.

"None of us would have done this."

"Finally you defend me."

Luke's memory of the previous night doesn't actually include the moment when Eric vouched for his inclusion on the trip. Eric's memory is still clear.

"I'm always defending you. You don't make it easy."

Luke looks around at the somber faces that do indeed look back at him now.

"I thought you guys were my friends."

Lilly hasn't been hiding her dislike for him.

"What gave you that idea? I don't friend pedophiles."

The major issue that has been simmering below the surface can now break free. Luke points his finger at Lilly and defends himself once again.

"I was arrested NOT guilty. I bought some weed on the dark net. The guy I bought from also sold kiddie porn. I didn't know that. I didn't buy any."

"That's not what it said in the newspaper."

"The newspaper people lied! I got in trouble for weed."

"Why were you sneaking into my bedroom last night?"

"I was drunk."

"That's an excuse not an apology."

"I don't owe you an apology."

Eric steps into the argument.

"Okay. Let's shut up."

Lilly redirects her anger to Eric.

"Did you just tell me to shut up?"

"No."

She scowls at him, shakes her head, and then walks away. The only thing missing from her sour departure was a flippant "whatever."

Luke takes a shot at her behind her back.

"How old were you when your girlfriend was born, Eric?"

Eric ignores his brother and walks after Lilly.

Luke turns to Clint and Indigo.

"I'm not going to apologize to you guys either."

Indigo accepts this with sarcasm.

"Gee. Thanks."

Clint also accepts.

"Apology accepted I guess."

Inside the house Lilly goes right to shoving her dirty clothes into her luggage. The bedroom door is open and Eric appears there to watch her make a show out of trying to zip up her bag.

"Are you okay?"

She stops what she is doing to embrace confrontation.

"I can't believe you let him talk to me like that."

"I'm going to have a talk with him."

"Pfft. As if that'll do any good."

She grabs hold of her piece of luggage and drops it from the bed to the floor in Eric's general direction. Eric eyes the luggage, a terrible bellhop.

"Your grandma isn't home. Why are we still here?"

He's going to turn the mood around, salvage the trip, change their lives for happily ever after, he's got plans.

"We'll go soon. I've got a surprise for you."

"I don't want a surprise."

Eric can tell that she means it, but he smiles because it's not about her, it's about them together, and a good surprise can sometimes turn even the sourest frown upside down.

Outside, Clint and Indigo have decided to take in the view at the side of the pond. Luke remains in the back yard area doing his best Sherlock Holmes impersonation trying to add up the bits of gore and fur that trail away from Cookie Three's grave and to the edge of the woods.

Eric approaches Luke to have their talk. Luke goes first, points out a patch of fur clumped against the base of a tree. His detective skills are blunt, his conclusions obvious.

"Dog fur."

Eric lobs back some sarcasm.

"Shocking. Woodland coyotes. Who would have thunk it?"

"Did you settle things with your wench?"

"Watch what you say."

The shift in tone is serious. Luke and Eric have a staring contest. Luke doesn't doubt that his brother might physically attack him over Lilly. Luke blinks first, goes back to the open case file at hand.

"No paw prints. Coyotes would leave paw prints. There's something bad out there in the woods. You feel it?"

The brothers gaze off into the woods, listen to the choir of insects that sing of the glory of Mother Nature. Luke shrugs off his premonition of evil in the woods.

"But, I don't ever know what I'm talking about. I'll quit drinking and behave. When we get to Vegas I'll try to go my own way, leave you guys alone."

It's a type of apology and it is awkward for both of them. Luke walks away. Eric doesn't say anything to let his brother know that he doesn't think he should have to wander around alone in Vegas; they can all have a good time together somehow. He doesn't say it though, best to let Luke wallow in his social outcast status and possibly self-pity.

9

The moment has arrived. Eric leads Lilly to the picnic bench down by the pond.

Clint and Indigo watch the event from inside the house. Clint speaks about love as they peer through the sliding glass door.

"Love is like a box of chocolates. Sometimes it gets hot and the chocolate melts. It gets sticky, but it still tastes yummy licking it off of your fingers. It's better than frozen love. Frozen love chips your teeth."

Indigo pats her husband on the back.

"You missed your calling. You could have been the Forrest Gump of the greeting card industry."

Down by the pond Lilly is already tired of silently taking in the view of the murky water.

"What are we doing?"

"As weird as granny could be she, and this place, had a big impact on me. There's something wondrous about this place. It's inspirational."

She doesn't get it.

"Okay."

"I'm nervous."

226

He leaves his bench seat and goes down on one knee.

She suddenly gets its. Panic sets in. He continues to talk.

"I'm in a new place in life. It's the right place."

She needs to stop him. All she can get out is his name.

"Eric."

He pulls a ring box out of one pocket, pops it open, and presents a dainty diamond ring to her.

"You're the woman of my dreams. Lilly, will you marry me?"

She is at first speechless. Tears arrive and then drip from her eyes. Eric thinks that the long pause works in his favor. She devastates him.

"No."

She jumps up and runs away with her tears.

Eric remains on his knee for a moment longer with the wind out of his sails and a pain in his back.

Lilly paces in the living room, weeping within the grips of a panic attack. Indigo tries to keep pace with her and calm her.

"Breathe. You can handle this."

Eric enters the room. His appearance stops Lilly in her tracks and they connect their eyes in a gaze across the room.

Indigo decides that being the referee won't be fruitful. She walks over to join Clint by the doorway of the master bedroom. The couple back into the room and out of sight.

Eric walks toward Lilly and as he does the sorrowful expression on her face hardens. If looks could kill hers is a tractor beam that draws Eric closer as a willing sacrifice. She unleashes some thoughts.

"You don't propose at your grandma's scary house in the woods. How is that romantic?"

"It's a lot of pressure on a guy. I thought that it'd be unique, like, like giving you my childhood or something."

"What does that even mean?"

"I'm sorry. I screwed it up. I meant for it to be sweet and it went silly. Let's forget it."

"I don't know, Eric."

"Don't know what?"

"About us."

"Us what?"

"Us at all!"

Her anger breaks out a new wave of her tears. Eric might cry himself, does his best to pull that back by the slippery leash as he asks a heartbreaking question.

"Are you breaking up with me?"

"I don't know."

"When did you plan on telling me?"

"I don't know."

He's losing her.

"Let me know what I need to do. I love you, Lilly."

"I don't."

Her legs take the order of evacuation from her brain, take her sprinting away from Eric once again. He lets her get by without trying to touch her, but this time he gives chase.

As she rushes out of the living room and into the kitchen Lilly slips, the transfer from carpet to linoleum takes the lack of emotional control to a new level of humiliation. Her feet go out from under her and she lands with a hard crack on her tailbone.

Eric reaches her and reaches for her. It scares him, it hurts him to see her on the floor. However, she isn't there for long and pulls away from his hands. She slides some on the ground and then scrambles up to her feet, finishes the journey across the kitchen in a hobbled gallop. She goes into the bedroom and slams the door.

Eric reaches the door, knocks on it, doesn't bother to check and see if it is locked. He thumps the door once with the palm of his hand.

"Hey! Lilly, are you okay?"

"I want you to leave me alone."

"This doesn't make sense."

She wants to get past the embarrassment of busting down on her ass, keeps them on the topic of dismantling their relationship.

"We argue, you work, we watch movies, that's all we do. That's our relationship. I don't even like movies."

"Okay. We won't watch movies."

It's not that simple.

"We get married, then what? We start a family? There's more that I want. I don't know what yet, but I know what all you have to offer, Eric."

"You wanted us. When did you become unhappy? A day ago you were fine."

"I was pretending."

She wants it all to be over with that confession. On her side of the door she backs away. Her butt hurts, but it will be okay, she doesn't suspect any new cracks. She sits her butt down on the foot of the bed. She can still hear Eric through the door.

"Did you ever love me?"

He can still hear Lilly, but can tell that she has pulled farther away.

"I don't know. I want to be alone."

"Lilly, we should..."

She erupts in a scream at him.

"Go away! Leave me alone! Leave me alone!"

Eric backs away from the door. He considers another response, but fails to grasp whatever magic words might heal the situation. He hesitates for another second just in case Lilly has those magic words to deliver from her side of the door. And then he walks away and leaves the silence standing between them.

## 10

Eric sits on the couch in the living room. Luke lies on his back on the floor while Clint and Indigo have smooshed themselves together in the chair that Lilly lounged in the previous night.

Lilly won't talk to him, but Eric feels the need for talk.

"That did not go well."

Indigo offers some advice and hope.

"Give her space, maybe it will work out."

"Tell me how you do it. You and Clint are the perfect couple."

"I don't know about that. We're just really freaky I guess."

"I'm trying to figure out what to do. Maybe I'm not ambitious enough for her. I can find a more exciting job. Lose some weight. Lease a sports car. Buy myself a sexy wig."

Clint throws out some more advice.

"You find a woman that lets you be you, Cuz. That's it. No secret."

Luke chimes in with his observation.

"She's too young to get married."

Eric doesn't appreciate it.

"Too young seems to be your area of expertise."

"Whatever. She's too cute. You're too old. You knew it. She knew it. You ignored it because you're a great guy, but deep down you weren't comfortable. You wanted it to end too."

"You're way off, Dr. Luke."

"One day she'll feel like a moron for letting you go, but that's the way it goes. You were always doomed and you only want her because you never should have been able to have her."

"You sound jealous. When is the last time you had a real relationship?"

Eric had his brother's card on that question. The answer wasn't a simple one. Matty Owens had been the love of Luke's life as far as Luke was concerned. He was a young man that he met at an open mic poetry reading night at a bar. Luke had gone to the bar for a drink not poetry, but Matty had taken the stage and his words on self-punishment and shame had struck a powerful note with him.

Luke bought Matty a drink and they spent the rest of the night hanging out together. After the bar closed they snuck into a park and laid in the grass talking about the stars over their heads and everything below them. Eventually they parted, with a long hug. The next day Matty was killed when a drunk driver swerved into his lane. The loss resonated with Luke making the love he felt in their brief connection all the stronger. He has never felt anything like that again. Therefore no "real" relationships have seemed to elude him or he them.

He tries to keep his reply simple.

"Maybe you'd know if you paid more attention to the people that actually care about you."

Heads turn as Lilly arrives in the room.

"I'm here. You can talk shit to my face now."

Luke sits up and sees the demented hope on his brother's face as he reacts to Lilly's voice. Lilly states her wants.

"The van is locked. I want my phone."

Luke quickly tries to take charge before his brother can cave in and be led farther down the pathetic road. He does this with a question, a drawing out of suspicion against her.

"Who are you calling?"

Eric answers for her against his brother.

"Luke, it's none of your business."

"It's my van and I think it's your business. You need to understand. I bet she's calling another guy."

She can stand up for herself.

"You keep me from my phone and that's unlawful imprisonment."

Eric looks from her over to his brother. It is a plot twist to himself as he feels his emotions swing to his brother's side of the brewing debate. Eric stands up and seeks some brutal enlightenment.

"Is Luke right? Are you calling another guy?"

"I don't have to answer that."

"It's true then."

He turns to the others of the room, drama court is in session.

"She cheated and kissed a guy at a party once. I forgave her."

Then he is back to direct questioning Lilly.

"I forgave you. What do I need to do now?"

She is confused by his stance, his voice, she has never heard him speak with the energy that she senses now. It is as though he perhaps balances on the edge of begging her again and wanting to commence with the stoning. If it is Pandora's box between them, she will help him pry open the lid in order to get it all over with.

"There were other guys that I didn't tell you about. There are others right now. I don't need forgiveness. I need to find myself."

The hurt shifts into gear; it is obvious on his face.

"Why are you acting like this?"

"Like what? Like a cold bitch? I don't know how else to say it, Eric. You forced it out."

He's grasping for straws, a lifeline, a soothing mint, something, anger. He takes the hand of anger.

"I'm just a loser who's in your way. You want a phone call? Come on."

He walks past her and she follows him thinking she is getting her phone.

Eric leads her into the kitchen and over to the landline telephone that hangs on the wall. He grabs hold of the phone and rips it free. He makes sure that all wires are severed from plugs and then he smashes the phone on to the floor, breaks it.

"Go ahead and use the house phone!"

He kicks the broken phone. He seethes. He glares at her, his outburst perhaps a shot at masculine dominance. However, he can see her absolute terror. He regrets the outburst.

"That was ugly. I'm sorry."

The others of the group decide they will not be bystanders. Clint offers to help bring a calm.

"Eric, buddy, you want to take a walk?"

Eric ignores his cousin's offer. He keeps his eyes locked on Lilly, issues words somewhere between request and demand.

"Look me in the eyes."

She does.

"Nothing else exists. It's just you and me. Now tell me you don't love me. You can't fake how we felt."

"I don't love you. I don't want to be with you."

Eric goes down in desperation to one knee.

"Marry me."

Lilly weeps and shakes her head: "No."

Eric pleads.

"Don't do this to me. Lilly, don't do this."

Luke has seen enough. He pushes through and grabs his brother under the arms and heaves him up to his feet. Eric doesn't fight against his handler as he is pushed toward one of the guest bedrooms.

Lilly retreats in the opposite direction. She crosses the living room and goes to the master bedroom. She shuts the door behind her, clicks the lock into place.

Clint and Indigo are left standing in the middle. Clint makes an observation to his wife.

"I don't think we'll be leaving soon."

"Viva Las Vegas."

Luke exits the guest bedroom where he has placed Eric, shuts the door, and joins Clint and Indigo.

"You can walk me if you want, Clint."

It all seems like a babysitting nightmare of many sharp angles for Clint and Indigo. They hold hands and think about the fulfillment they have in each other and the goals they will reach together: the dog shelter they will open (shoveling dog poop seems more appealing than changing diapers; one has only to see what children grow up to become not to trust themselves with watering them during the stages of supposed innocence).

In the bedroom Eric yells with his face pressed into a pillow. It is a muffled sound, but the trio in the kitchen still hear it.

Luke has a joint in his pocket. He'll go off on his own to smoke it by the pond.

## 11

"Time heals all wounds," rings false to Luke, but he figures a person should give time a chance until they run out of it. Night has fallen. It dawns on Luke that he has left his brother alone too long. He worries that the mental anguish might lead to damage of the physical nature.

He knocks on the bedroom door and Eric opens it right away. Luke doesn't give him gentle concern.

"We appreciate your mid-life crisis, but the rest of us are finished vacationing in it."

Eric does seem to have found a level of peace.

"I'm okay."

"Have you been in there thinking about all of the new titties you're going to chase?"

"Lilly and I don't have to marry. Breaking up seems drastic though, right? Maybe we could start over. I could ask her out on a first date."

"Oh Christ, dude. No. No. You need to go to a strip club and get grimy."

"I'd rather go back to bed and pretend I don't exist."

The brothers walk across the house together and into the living room. Eric is somewhat surprised to see that Clint and Indigo hang out with Lilly in the room. In fact, as they enter Lilly shares in a laugh with the couple.

"I see you're all best friends now."

Clint takes the blame for the cheery mood.

"I was sharing my fart quota theory with them."

Eric doesn't want to be left out of THAT. "Tell me."

"In a relationship all of the farts add up. Every fart is a tally mark against you in your partner's book of grievances. We all have our limits, sometimes people just get farted out."

"Cute."

Luke moves to stand near the television area where the front windows are located with the curtains still open, the panes of glass dark from the night beyond them. He crosses his arms like a bouncer waiting to be called into action.

Lilly raises her hand up from her side in the chair in which she sits. Eric can see that she has her cellphone.

"You've got your phone. I hope you haven't been giving my grandma's address to strange men."

She hits back at him sarcasm.

"Yeah, Eric. I've got men in all parts of the state that will pick me up at a moment's notice."

She waves the phone.

"There's no signal here."

Indigo tries to be the adult and lead their party.

"It's dark and we were supposed to leave a long time ago. I think we should all head home."

Eric counters that proposal.

"Why head home? Vegas is waiting."

Luke likes his brother's stance and seconds the motion.

"I still want Vegas."

Lilly votes in the negative toward Vegas.

"I want to go home."

Luke reminds her of who owns the wheels.

"You better start walking then."

The adult Indigo isn't having it.

"Luke, take us home."

"I will after Vegas."

"Then drop us off at a bus station. Lilly, I'll buy you a ticket if you need."

Eric keeps the argument alive.

"No. We should take a vote. Luke?"

"Vegas."

"Clint?"

"This trip seems busted. I need to go home with my wife."

Indigo votes.

"Home."

Eric looks to Lilly. She takes a moment in his gaze. Then she decides to play his game.

"Fine. I vote Vegas too."

Indigo is disappointed.

"Oh for crapsake."

Luke is quite amused.

"You're the tie-breaker vote, Eric."

Indigo continues to voice her displeasure.

"This is stupid. I'm tired of the drama."

Eric reads the room. Indigo's stern expression paired next to Clint's sympathetic one seems like the direction in which he should cast his vote. The expression on Lilly's face is as best as he can read one of smugness and then the beacon of support that is Luke is not what Eric sees when he looks toward him.

At the window glass behind his brother Eric catches a quick glimpse of a pale face twisted in agony. A brief flash, the face presses to the glass, and then is gone.

"Whoa! What was that?"

Eric points his finger and everyone looks in the direction of the window. Luke turns around and dares to go closer to the glass as he questions what he is supposed to be seeing there.

"What?"

"Someone looked in the window."

Everyone buys into the seriousness with which Eric makes this claim, the bud of his own fear evident in his voice. Lilly, however, doesn't want to buy into it.

"Quit trying to scare us."

Eric has never been the guy who tries to scare people. However, all bets are uncertain when it comes to the stability of a personality in emotional crisis. No one could tell which way Eric was about to vote in regard to the Vegas trip.

Eric announces the start of the investigation.

"Grandma keeps a flashlight in the kitchen drawer."

Eric leads the way to get the tool of illumination and the rest of the group follow him. Moments later he leads them right out onto the front porch.

Eric sweeps the weak beam from the flashlight across the front yard in search of the trespasser. Nothing.

He turns the beam in the direction of the wooded area off to one side of the driveway.

"There! See that?"

No one saw it and Clint answers for them. "No."

Maybe Luke saw something, movement, or movement of shadow caused by the flashlight. He disagrees with Clint's assessment of the group and what they have or have not seen.

"I saw it."

Luke is the leader off the porch, though he is glad that Eric follows right after and keeps to his side with the flashlight. Clint goes with them as Indigo and Lilly hang back on the porch with the glow of the porch light to protect them. The men walk toward the wooded area in search of what might have been seen.

As they near a certain tree it becomes evident that there is a figure huddled on the opposite side of it. Eric aims the flashlight and the figure shuffles forward out of being an outline of shape in the darkness and into being a pale nightmare walking erect.

Eric's mind immediately dials into the horror hotline and reports: zombie!

The zombie is a man, drained of color, flesh caked in mud, maybe blood, there are open wounds. If the men knew their grandmother's neighbor better they might recognize Gilbert Ryan as the monster before them.

Zombie Gilbert sloshes toward the trio, but then pulls up to a stop, huddles over again as if to pose for the beam of the flashlight to inspect. His eyeballs are glazed over in murky whiteness.

Eric, Luke, and Clint are stupefied by their discovery.

Gilbert turns as if maybe he listens to the gathered breathing of the men. Eric tries to communicate.

"Hello."

Clint wipes the fantastical first impressions from his mind. There is an explanation for this man's appearance and it is one that involves some sort of normal malady or injury.

"He's hurt. You okay, buddy?"

Gilbert staggers in place, no forward momentum. His appearance in that moment is frightening to behold, but he level of threat he poses does not seem strong. Clint moves toward him as an ambassador of assistance.

"We can get you some help."

Luke warns Clint off of his bravery.

"He could be contagious."

Clint leaves a gap of space between himself and the wounded man-creature.

"Sir?"

The zombie lunges with a growl, a sudden burst of strength and speed. Gilbert is on Clint before he can flee, grabs on to him and they fall to the ground. Clint yells out.

"Ahh!"

They struggle on the ground and the brothers watch, spellbound, doing a terrible job at acting to help their downed cousin.

The zombie straddles Clint, pins him, but Clint is able to push upward with his arms and keep the zombie's swiping fingers from clawing into his flesh.

"Help me!"

Zombie Gilbert leans downward and belches. A foul stench floods into Clint's nostrils.

"Yack!"

A watery, muddy substance plops out of the zombie's mouth and spatters on to Clint's face. Chunks of the goo drop right into his open mouth.

Eric and Luke spur themselves into action.

Luke grabs hold of the zombie, heaves him back and off of Clint. As the creature struggles in Luke's arms Eric helps Clint get up to his feet.

Luke swings and shoves the zombie away from him and it rolls on to the ground. However, the switch has been flipped and it seems to have a primal need to continue attacking. The zombie scrambles across the ground and grabs Luke by the leg as he attempts to run away with Eric and Clint.

Eric turns to see Luke trying to shake the zombie off of his leg. He lets go of Clint, who staggers along well enough on his own toward the two screaming women on the porch.

Eric runs back to help Luke.

The zombie humps its way up Luke's leg and Luke does his best to shove the head pushed back, keep the snapping teeth from biting into him.

Eric runs in and swings the flashlight, conks it into the side of Gilbert's head. The blow is powerful enough in combination with Luke's kick that the zombie loses his hold and tumbles to the ground. Eric lost his grip on the flashlight and it too falls to the ground.

The flashlight and any attempt to aid the freakish man are abandoned. Clint stands on the front porch with the women and they form the finish line in the mad sprint that the brother's make together.

Lilly jumps the gun and decides to flee into the house before the others. She slams the sliding glass door shut behind her and locks it.

As they near the porch, Eric slows up to turn and see if the monster is pursuit.

Zombie Gilbert is back on his feet, twitches and convulses in place, does not hunt for the escaped prey. However, a new battle cry growls from out of the darkness in the direction of the pond.

The four still outside look to see another zombie figure shuffling out of the darkness toward them. As Nianna hits the edge of the porch light's reach she is revealed to be in the same eroded state as her grandfather Gilbert.

No one is going to bother asking her if she needs any help. They turn to find the front door locked. Clint has his hand on the handle.

"Open the door!"

Lilly did not retreat far into the house, still stands in the dining area of the kitchen in sight of the door with a chair in front of her like a shield. She is quick to rush over and correct the mistake that she made in her panic. She unlocks the door.

She gets a bump on the head when the others push through the door, but she only notices for the one flash of light in her skull and then she is working the vertical blinds shut as if they will provide some extra seal of protection across the sliding glass door that Eric slams and locks.

A feral yowl sounds off in the front yard. The group linger for a moment. They can see peeks of glass and the night beyond via the porch light; however, no creature comes into view.

They decide not to stick around any longer. Before they exit the area Luke flips the switch to turn off the porch light, just in case it is an attractive lure for the things outside.

The group gathers in the living room, which features the second exit door for the house. As Eric checks the lock on that door, solid wood not sliding glass, Clint pulls the curtains shut on the bank of windows where they got their first tease from the freaks outside.

The group then gathers in a panning circle, on their feet and ready to run every person for themselves if they have to. Lilly wants some direction.

"What do we do?"

Eric does his best to take charge.

"We block the windows and find weapons."

Clint leans on Indigo for support.

"I'm dizzy."

She shoulders some of his weight with severe concern.

Luke offers an alternative plan to barricading themselves in.

"We need to fight our way out."

Eric debates.

"We don't know what we're dealing with."

"They're not attacking now. It's time we run to van."

"We're safer in here. We can wait for daylight."

Indigo helps her husband over to a chair and helps him sit down in it. He updates his status.

"I'm fine."

She can tell that he is not. She doesn't want to leave his side but decides that the risk of a few seconds is worth the warm towel she can get to wipe some of the zombie sludge off his face.

Eric continues to hash out their situation.

"If zombies exist, those things out there are zombies."

Lilly throws in a dose of reality as she understands it.

"They don't exist."

Her plan now involves her cellphone. She pulls it out and holds it in the air, seeks a signal.

Indigo rushes back to Clint with the towel. He opens his eyes, appears to have nodded off, as she wipes at him.

Luke debates Eric's assessment of the enemy.

"Zombies require a master to control them."

"The undead don't need a master."

"You've been brainwashed by monster movies."

"Don't start the voodoo argument again! Animated corpses can be called zombies! Period."

"There is a world of difference between ghouls and zombies!"

Indigo can't believe that they are going to argue creature feature semantics at a time like this.

"Guys! Really?"

Eric's attention is drawn to the chair and he steps over to check on his cousin.

"Clint, are you still fine?"

Clint grimaces, pain evident.

"No."

Lilly gives up on her phone and joins the conversation about Clint's well-being.

"If he's sick we need to quarantine him."

She covers her mouth and nose with a hand. Luke actually agrees with her for once.

"It could be a viral outbreak."

Eric sees that as support for his plan.

"Which means going back out into it would be bad."

Indigo is done listening and makes the decision for the group.

"We're leaving. We're taking Clint to the hospital."

No one argues with her command. Luke votes anyway.

"We kick ass and hit the gas."

Clint gives him a thumbs up.

## 12

The group gathers in the kitchen armed with what weaponry they could find. Luke has an aluminum baseball bat, a relic from their childhood that they used for hitting rocks out of the driveway. The bat is dented up from all of the homeruns.

Eric wields a large kitchen knife. It may or may not be the same one they used as children to try and saw to the center of the giant jawbreakers grandma bought them at the mall candy store. Eric hopes that it isn't, hopes that it is sharp enough to cut through any trouble.

Lilly has traded her cellphone for a hammer. She stands to the side of Indigo and has her shirt pulled up to cover her mouth and nose. Meanwhile, Indigo is armed with her determination to help Clint maneuver and stay on his feet.

Eric slides the blinds back and then side by side he and Luke try to peer through the door glass and into the night beyond. The kitchen light shows them their reflections and Luke questions their next move.

"If I turn on the porch light it might draw their attention. Porch light, yay or nay?"

His hand is at the switch.

Eric feels that they are sitting ducks at the moment, illuminated with the kitchen light backdrop, framed by the glass of the door for anything outside that wishes to see what they are up to.

"Might as well."

Luke flips the switch and the porch light goes on. There are not any monsters visible on the porch. Eric slides the door open and Luke steps outside in the lead.

The night seems still. The night seems quiet. Luke signals the others.

"The coast is clear."

Nianna screeches and charges from beyond the reach of the porch light!

The distance the zombie must travel gives Luke the chance to raise his weapon; batter up. However, he was never all that good at sports. His swing misses his target as she ducks.

Lucky for him she isn't able to latch on to him as he sidesteps and gears up for another swing. Unlucky for him she grabs hold of the bat with both of her rotten looking hands. Luke and Nianna twirl off of the porch as they struggle with the bat between them. The step to the ground causes them both to lose their footing and tumble down.

Eric sees his brother crash down to the ground with the zombie girl flailing on top of him. He starts to step out to help, but then the zombie man lurches into the light.

Lilly screams.

"Shut the door!"

Eric instinctually aims to please Lilly. As the zombie man steps up on to the porch, Eric slams the door in its face. The zombie man stands at the glass door, poses for the group in all of his decaying glory, but does not try to pound his way through the glass.

In the front yard Luke bench presses the crazed freak girl off of him with a mighty thrust. He is able to knock his attacker away, but also loses the baseball bat in the process.

He gets up to his feet and runs for his life. He does not go toward the house, chooses instead to make a beeline for Dessi and the warrior angel women in the driveway.

He gets to the van and opens the unlocked driver's side door. He gets inside and shuts the door. Then he looks out the window to see that the zombie girl, calling them zombies is fine, who cares, is en route to the driveway. She does not sprint, but her pace is quick and the abnormal barking sound she makes is unsettling, sounds as if she might transform into a demon of a sea lion.

Luke pats himself down, searches for the keys to van.

"Ah butt."

He has lost the keys.

Zombie Nianna slams herself against the van.

Inside the house Eric keeps an eye on the zombie that remains on the porch. It stays in place, brain perhaps not firing on all cylinders. Eric cannot see what has become of his brother, debates with himself as to whether or not going back outside with the knife will help anyone.

Clint can see the tight squeeze Eric applies to the handle of the knife in his hand. He gives a weak offer of support.

"I'll help. We can kill it, Eric."

Eric turns to see that Clint has become quite the weight for Indigo to hold up. Lilly is petrified, holds her hammer with both hands apparently ready to lash out with it as if it is a *Star Wars* lightsaber should the creature break into the house.

"Indigo, get him to Grandma's room. I'll be there in a minute."

Indigo likes that plan and she looks to Lilly for help. Lilly doesn't want to touch Clint. She instead hurries off ahead of the married couple without a word.

Indigo doesn't have time to be offended. She takes a deep breath and pulls Clint along.

In the van Luke has his own staring match with the female zombie. She stops slapping her hands against the side of the van and presses up against the driver's side door window. Luke gets a very close look into her glazed over eyes and can see only flecks of humanity behind the milky whites. Her eyeballs tremble, rapid eye movements that may signify she is caught up in a dream.

Her hair is coated in mud and there appears to be a wetness to her skin. Droplets of water roll down her cheek and Luke wonder if it is a tear secreted from an eye. Now that she is not hitting his van in madness he feels compassion for this tortured being.

As she presses her face to the glass of the window a blob of goo pushes past her lips and out of her mouth. She smears this muddy substance across the surface of the glass.

Luke's fixation on the girl is broken by movement. He senses that a dark hulk of something just walked between some of the trees off to the side of the driveway. Luke looks beyond the girl, thinks that the movement was behind her and went farther down the side of the driveway to where it would be positioned behind the van.

The zombie woman loses interest in him. Her shoulders slumped, she turns away and walks off toward the woods in the same direction that Luke suspects another being is located. He doesn't know what to make of this.

At the front door the zombie man turns away and shambles off the porch. Eric watches the thing disappear from sight. His nerve is relived, his curiosity stoked, as he finds the courage now to open the door.

Right as he pulls the door open Luke races up to it.

"Let me in!"

Eric is startled, the scare causes him to jump back and let Luke enter the house. Luke can't stop his forward momentum, doesn't slow as he enters the house, speeds right through the kitchen and out the other side into the living room.

Eric shuts the front door and locks it.

The master bedroom is positioned at the back side of the half-basement house; therefore, the windows are just above ground

254

level and small. The curtains were already drawn. This detail makes the bedroom feel like the most secure place in the house when Eric arrives and shuts the door behind him.

Eric surveys the room, takes a head count.

Clint shivers on the bed as Indigo tucks him under the blanket.

"So cold."

Luke is doubled over and tries to catch his breath. Lilly is not present.

"Where is Lilly?"

The closet door and the master bathroom door are both shut. Logically she could be behind one of those doors, or under the bed, or not in the room at all.

Indigo saves Eric the trouble of playing hide and seek.

"She locked herself in the bathroom."

The master bathroom is at the front of the house. Therefore, the window in there is a bit larger and of more normal placement in regard to windows and walls of houses. It doesn't seem as secure a place as the bedroom and Eric wants Lilly at his side. But before he can seek her out Luke instigates a discussion over what he witnessed outside.

"There's something else out there. I sensed it was bigger than those other two things."

"Sensed? Is that like a magic power you've got?"

"I saw it from the van. Sort of. Something big walking around in the dark."

"You got to the van? Why didn't you bring the other phones? We could try for signals."

"I didn't think of it."

"You never think."

"I lost the van keys too."

Eric points the kitchen knife at him.

"You always screw everything up. You're an idiot."

"Thanks for having my back out there. Brother."

Indigo is still over the petty squabbles.

"Stop fighting!"

The men halt their argument. Luke tries to convince them of what he saw and concedes to his brother's preference to call the creatures zombies; a little victory of words that Eric will never notice he won.

"Whatever else was out there, it might have been a taller zombie. I don't know, but the girl zombie had me trapped and then she just walked away. It was like she was either scared of the other one or going to join it."

Eric explains what he saw at the front door.

"The zombie on the porch walked away all of a sudden too."

Indigo wants less speculation and more of a plan.

"If I walk out of here, how far is it to the closest neighbor?"

Eric estimates.

"Far."

She looks back to Clint on the bed. He continues to tremble with a vicious chill under his skin.

"Will one of you go with me? The other one stay here with Clint."

A suspicion dawns on Eric and he directs it at Luke.

"You weren't bitten or anything were you?"

"No."

"I saw you fall. Someone always lies about being bitten."

"Stupid movies and comic books again, Eric."

"I don't think we can trust you."

Before Indigo can scold the brothers once again and redirect the focus on to her husband's dire condition, Clint jolts upright and flings the blanket away from him with a yell.

"Ahh!"

All eyes jump to Clint as he yells out again.

"It hurts!"

Indigo tries to pull the blanket back around him, but he pushes it away. He stands up off of the bed. He hones in on Eric and the knife in Eric's hand. He issues an urgent plea.

"Cut me."

Indigo questions her husband's request.

"What? Clint, what?"

"The pressure is too much. Cut me."

He is obviously in excruciating pain; however, no one wants to do anything drastic.

"Cut me!"

A spasm rocks Clint's body.

Eric ignores the demand.

"Maybe Grandma has some medicine in the bathroom."

Eric goes to the bathroom door and knocks on it.

"Lilly, open the door."

Clint yells again.

"Cut me!"

Indigo tries to hold her husband, to soothe him.

"Clint, look at me."

Lilly does not open the bathroom door. Eric pounds on it.

"Open the door!"

Clint begins to gag, to choke. Luke searches his mental folders for whether or not he still remembers how to properly perform the Heimlich maneuver.

Indigo pats Clint hard on the back. She says his name, wants him to reassure her that he is hanging tough and everything is going to be fine again.

Clint jerks around and projectile vomits a dark, muddy substance right into Indigo's face!

She screams out in surprise, gets a taste of the substance as she also reels away from Clint.

"Ahh!"

Clint shudders and flops over, hits down on to the bed, but bounces off it and drops into the floor.

Indigo screams for help as she wipes goo from her eyes.

"Clint! Someone do something!"

She spits, needs the substance off her tongue.

Eric rushes over to Indigo's side, but is hesitant to touch her with the goop on her. He looks down at Clint on the floor. Clint shakes in a violent seizure for a moment, but then suddenly ceases to move at all.

A silence comes over the room. Indigo and Eric stare down at Clint and Luke stares at Eric and Indigo. Eric breaks the silence.

"Clint. Buddy."

Indigo sobs.

Eric steps over to Clint's still form. His cousin lies there with his fingers stuck in the gnarled formation of someone grasping on to unbearable pain.

"Clint."

He sets his knife down on the side of the bed. Then he stoops down to check Clint for a pulse.

Indigo already knows the answer. She weeps and backs her way against a wall. She uses the wall for support, slides down it to sit on the floor with her tears.

Luke asks Eric for an update.

"Eric, is he..."

Sorrow wails out of Indigo.

Eric stands up and looks over to Paul, doesn't say anything as he pronounces Clint deceased.

## 13

The master bathroom is an "L" shaped room. A long dual sink area with one long vanity mirror leads to the shower and then a right turn takes one to the toilet and the door to a shallow closet. The single window of the room is behind the toilet. Lilly needs to pee, but doesn't like the dark portal of glass, even with the curtains drawn, that would be at her back if she were to sit in the usual place people sit when peeing in the bathroom.

Currently there is too much commotion for her to execute her sink or tub urination plan and she stands a couple of feet back from the locked bathroom door. Eric bangs on the door and yells from the other side.

"Don't make me break the door down."

Lilly caves, goes over to the door and unlocks it.

Eric pushes past her and goes right to the sink area. He opens cabinets and drawers. He removes a pill bottle from one drawer and sets it on the countertop and the search continues.

Luke then hustles into the room with Indigo leaning on him for support. Lilly backs away, places herself at the edge of the tub with shower.

Indigo now uses the sink countertop to keep her balance and Eric holds up a bottle of mouthwash.

"Maybe this?"

Indigo nods, updates them on her state of queasiness.

"I feel sick already. The dizziness."

Eric removes the cap from the mouthwash and she takes the bottle. She pours a healthy dose into her mouth, swishes, gargles, spits into the sink. Then she puts the bottle back to her lips and guzzles mouthwash down her throat.

After she swallows she looks at her reflection in the mirror. She speaks to herself and to the reflections of Luke and Eric.

"I want to get Clint out of here."

Eric agrees, but does not come forth with a gung-ho plan to fulfill that request.

"Okay."

Indigo weeps for her lost husband.

"Oh, Clint, baby."

She staggers away from the sink and when Luke tries to catch her she waves him off. She walks out of the room to return to her husband's side.

Eric instructs Luke.

"Watch her."

Luke takes on the duty, leaves Eric and Lilly alone in the bathroom.

His emotions swell up in his throat as Eric turns to Lilly and speaks to her.

"Thank you for opening the door. Clint is dead."

If he seeks consoling from her she doesn't have it to give. She is mortified.

"I can't handle that."

Eric reaches out to touch and console her instead. She pulls away.

"Leave me alone."

"We've got to stick together."

"I'm not getting sick. Leave me alone."

He makes a vow to her.

"I will get you out of here safe. This will be over and we can talk about us again."

"What? There's nothing to talk about."

"I can fix it. If it's because I'm a fast food manager, hey, that can change."

She can't believe that in spite of everything going on Eric is still hung up on winning her affection.

"Your cousin is dead and there are monsters outside."

"Give me something I can work with. Give me a chance."

"Clue in to reality, Eric. Everything about you annoys me. I annoy myself by being with you."

"Why were you going to Vegas then? Why not break up with me before? You were using me for a free trip."

Eric got into the room by yelling and Lilly decides to try and get him out of the room by yelling.

"It's over! Leave me alone! Leave me alone! Leave me alone!"

Eric lashes out, smacks the pill bottle that he set on to the counter. The pill bottle smashes against the mirror and careens across the counter to land in one of the sinks. Eric turns his back on Lilly and walks out per her wishes.

As Eric enters the bedroom he sees that Luke stands watch as Indigo hunkers down by where Clint fell. At first the bed hides her activity from Eric, but he positions himself for a better view. Indigo holds one of Clint's arms and uses the kitchen knife to cut into it. It appears that she has already cut him in a few other spots on the same arm, fat splits are visible in the flesh, though the wounds seem bloodless.

Eric calls his brother out on dereliction of duty.

"Luke, what the hell?"

"I'm watching her like you asked."

Indigo speaks to her beloved Clint.

"Wake up, Clint. Wake up."

She cuts another deep score into the dead man's arm. This time there is plasma seepage. He doesn't wake up. Eric decides that he needs to help Indigo pick up all of her marbles before she loses any of them.

"Indigo."

She acknowledges him.

"He wanted you to cut him. I can feel the pressure now. It's cold. It burns. It's like my blood wants to burst out of my body."

Eric doesn't know what to say to that.

Indigo gets up to her feet. She cries as she confirms the sad fact that they had already realized.

"Clint is dead."

She put the sharp edge of the knife to one of her own arms. Luke tries to stop her.

"Don't do it."

She slices into the skin, releases a thin stream of blood that is darker than anyone in the room expected.

Eric steps to her, ready to wrestle the knife away if he needs to.

"Indigo, give me the knife."

Luke edges closer to her from the other side.

Lilly arrives at the open bathroom door and watches the showdown from there.

Indigo does not offer Eric the blade.

"I'm going to need it. It's going to get worse."

He offers an alternative.

"We're getting out of here.

He glances to Luke for some backup on that claim. Luke obliges.

"The keys probably fell out of my pocket when I hit the ground. They're right off the porch. I'm sure we can find them."

Eric extends his hand out as a target for the knife to be placed into; preferably handle first.

"Let me have the knife. We'll all go together right now."

Lilly voices an objection.

"It's safer in here. I'm staying."

Eric turns to give Lilly a stab of stank eye. She doubles down on her stance.

"I'm not standing around out there while you search for keys."

Eric yields his stank eye to her logic.

"She's right. Luke and I will get the keys. Lilly you can watch over Indigo."

Lilly shuts the bathroom door and locks herself inside.

Eric curses.

"Damn it."

Luke has always wanted to try his foot at kicking down a door. He strides right over to the bathroom door and without calling out any warning to Lilly kicks the door as hard as he can.

Pain shoots up Luke's leg and the door frame cracks; however, the door still hangs. Luke isn't discouraged and shoulders into it and this blow breaks the hold of the lock, cracks the door open.

Lilly is quite disappointed to see Luke step inside the bathroom with a smile and word of celebration.

"There."

He flashes a winning smile at Lilly and her fury rewards him with a flash of her middle finger.

Indigo hands Eric the knife.

"Hurry, Eric. I'll keep an eye on your girl for you."

She places a hand against the wound that she opened in her arm. A visible shiver courses through her.

Indigo walks toward the bathroom as Eric pairs up with Luke at the exit of the bedroom. The men don't want to take the time to work up their nerve because they know that the longer they wait the more unnerved they will become. They do want to define their plan, however.

Luke is the key man. He tries to convince himself in his key finding skills.

"I can find the keys."

"I'll have your back with the knife."

Solid.

Luke opens the door and away they go.

# 14

In the bathroom Lilly eyes Indigo. It is clear that she wants to keep her distance from the sickly woman.

Indigo places a hand against the sink countertop for balance as pain swirls through her. She overcomes the moment without swooning and then informs Lilly of her plan.

"I'll get in the tub. I'm so cold."

Lilly acts against her want for self-preservation and grabs a bath towel from a rack. She walks the towel over and wraps it around Indigo. Then she guides the woman toward the tub.

At the front door Eric and Luke discover a new obstacle in the path of their mission. On the front porch, placed against the front door, is the body of zombie Gilbert. No longer is the man animated, now a husk that has been split open to reveal that his innards have been harvested. There are patches of dark blood as well as chucks of guts chewed and dropped. Stringy, white, worm-like entities twist around the mess, in and out of the remains. Luke seeks knowledge from his elder.

"What are those worm things? Long maggots?"

"They look like worms."

"What kind of weird worms?"

Eric has a graver concern.

"What tore him apart and put him there?"

Indigo sits in the tub with the towel still around her, but she has not run any warming water. She is in the throes of the same sick decline her husband endured.

As for Lilly she can't hold in her piss anymore. She makes the uncomfortable choice to sit on the toilet for some relief.

The brothers Bradbury are stuck between a rock of concern and a hard place of concern. Their concern for Indigo is of the utmost concern and they tap into their inner most wells of honor and courage. Luke reaches for the handle of the sliding glass door and Eric prepares to be the first man out with the knife for protection.

The door opens and Eric gets a shoe out on to the porch. He plots the best path for circumnavigating the wormy corpse. He keeps a wary eye on the carnage because misery loves company and that pile of death looks very miserable.

Glass shatters! It sounds as though a window farther down the front wall of the house has exploded. This sound causes Eric to retreat.

Luke catches an elbow to the nose as Eric backpedals into the house. However, he is able to see through the tears well enough to slam the door shut behind his brother.

A scream, a Lilly scream rips through the moment before either brother can recover from their shock. She keeps screaming.

Eric takes off and runs fast with his sharp object.

Indigo is helplessly ill in the tub, twitches as she tries to hold herself, hold the warm spirit of life to her body.

Lilly screams and flails as she is drug out of the window that is over the toilet. Broken glass pierces her side, but her brain worries over that fact that she is going out with her pants still down. Then she is out into the night and her brain shuts off for a spell.

Eric rushes into the bathroom in time to see the last kick of Lilly's foot as she disappears. He goes to the toilet and stands over it. He stares at the broken window. He is lost.

Something outside issues a valiant roar. The roar trails off as if the thing moves away from the yard and into the woods.

Indigo lets out a roar of her own.

"Ahh."

Eric turns his attention to her agony. Luke arrives and stands at the ready if he can figure out how to help.

Indigo leans over the side of the tub and groans her words past grinding teeth.

"I love."

Then she spews vomit of dark matter on to the floor.

Luke hops backward and Eric shies off to the side to avoid the spray.

Indigo goes into a seizure, thumps hard against the sides of the tub. She flops about for a few seconds and then goes rigid. She is beyond life and never coming back.

Lilly's brain sparks and she realizes that she is being carried through the woods. It is chilly and smells of dead animals. Her mind fails to make the necessary adjustment for further comprehension and clicks off once again.

Moments later it is a harsh jerk on her legs that revives her. Something tears her pants away from her. She mutters an explanation that is nonsense to herself.

"It escaped from the zoo."

The beast is upon her. The furry mass blocks out the world for Lilly. Hot, sour breath replaces her oxygen supply. The beast opens wide and covers Lilly's mouth and nose with its own mouth. Her lips are nicked by the fangs and her mouth is forced open by a meaty probe of a tongue. A thick muddy substance is regurgitated into her. The last sensation that Lilly registers is of a writhing ball within the mud. It hangs in her mouth, like a ball of worms that separates. She feels them travel down her throat, feels them slither into her sinuses.

The Bradbury brothers moved Clint's body into the bathroom to be with Indigo. It had seemed like a romantic gesture, but once realized it just seemed morbid.

They blocked off the broken bathroom door by shoving their grandmother's chest of drawers in front of it. A blockade in case whatever broke through the window decides to return and add entering to the breaking. The dresser of Grandpa Bradbury blocks the main door of the room. As they shoved it into place they thought it romantic that Grandma held on to Grandpa's furniture. However, once they saw that it still held all of his clothes that notion too seemed morbid.

Luke and Eric now hide in the walk-in closet. Eric questions his bravery.

"I should have gone after her."

"It would be useless in the dark. We don't know what we're dealing with."

"Don't we?"

Luke gives it a name.

"Mo."

Eric repeats the warning that was left on the mirror.

"Beware Mo."

"Grandma has some explaining to do."

"What do you think it is doing with Lilly?"

"Best not to think about that."

"It might be turning her into one of those zombie things."

"Doctors and scientists will have a cure."

Their conversation ends. Eric dozes off with the word cure as a hope. Despite all the danger and tragedy the human systems of Eric and Luke are exhausted enough to power down into deep sleep. The dreams are fragmented nightmares. The kind of dreams that you don't remember the details of the next day, but you wake up weighted down by an extra layer of gloom.

Eric awakens and his movement in the closet wakes Luke. Specifically the waking blow is Eric's knee connecting to the side of Luke's head when he trips trying to walk to the closet door. Up and at 'em! Eric gets the closet door open and even with the curtains drawn they can tell that they have snoozed to the return of daylight.

Outside they find that the corpse that was on the porch is no longer there. There is still evidence that it was there and there is a brief drag trail of remnants that suggest it did not get up and walk off on its own. The missing body makes Eric ponder whether or not they should check in on the bodies of Clint and Indigo in the master bathroom. He decides that he can ignore that curiosity.

Luke stands by his van. He gets a bar of cellphone service, but isn't sure how to proceed.

"Do we call the police? The army? Dad? How do we explain this without sounding nuts? Dad grew up here. Shit. You think he already knows?"

Eric has a different priority at the top of his list.

"I'm going after Lilly."

Luke watches his brother shove up against one of the garage doors. The doors are all locked tight and too stout to kick down. Luke offers up a better course of action.

"We'll drive out of here. Get help."

Eric moves away from the locked garage and back over to stand near Luke and Dessi. The kitchen knife is on the roof of the van and Eric retrieves it. For a moment he finds himself with a knife in his hand and face to face with a painting of an angel holding a flaming sword. In dark times dark humor threatens to let unbridled laughter slip, but Eric is able to maintain his composure. Luke opens the passenger side door for Eric and tries to persuade him to enter it.

"It's stupid to go hunting that thing ourselves."

"I love her. Love is relentless."

"It's demented. You'll get yourself killed. She wouldn't come for you, Eric. I'm not going to watch my brother die over a girl. If you go you go alone."

His mind is made up.

"Go get help. I'm going into the woods."

Luke watches his brother walk away to hunt monsters with a kitchen knife. As Eric nears the edge of the woods Luke yells out to him.

"Last chance! Dessi and I are driving out of here! You're on your own!"

Eric doesn't acknowledge the "last chance" and enters the woods.

He navigates down a steep hill. He doesn't know how he will find Lilly, but he tries to imagine his way back behind the eyes of himself as a child following Grandma to the creek. He thinks he can pick up Lilly's trail there. Alternatively he considers yelling out her name at the top of his lungs as he goes.

The deeper into the woods that Eric goes the more serene and ominous the environment seems. Surrounded by nature's beauty, he is conflicted between feeling exposed by the openness and suffocated by it.

He finds the creek. He adheres to it as a trail. The first body that he discovers is the female zombie that attacked them the night before. She lies in a shallow puddle within the creek with her limbs all broken and in wrong directions. On a broken neck, her head appears to have been twisted around in a full circle.

Her belly is split open, guts strung out in a pile. Whatever cruel life that animated her on the previous night seems to have vanished.

The condition of the body is unsettling, but the most disturbing detail to Eric is in the water around the spillage of her guts. The odd worms are there; some float, some swim.

Eric moves on in his search. He throws up a prayer that the creek will help him find Lilly, but that he won't find Lilly in the creek.

Lilly is in the creek. Her body is mostly submerged in water, with her head propped up out of it thanks to the gnarled roots of a tree growing right at the edge. Aside from the root, a large branch was placed down as if to help keep her pinned in place, body soaked in water.

Eric is on the opposite side of the creek from the tree and sets his knife on the ground there. Then he hops right into the water and sloshes over to his beloved. She is pale, face smeared with mud, and there is a wide gash in one of her cheeks.

Eric hefts the branch away and shoves it aside. Then he lifts Lilly up and cradles her in his arms.

"I'm going to get you out of here."

Lilly's eyes open at the sound of his voice. However, the eyeballs are clouded over similar to the eyes of the other zombies. Eric convinces himself that her eyes are less cloudy, he can see some color. She is still in there.

At first she doesn't help her own cause as he tries to drag her to the shore. His efforts seem to work some energy into her eventually and she uses her own limbs to climb up. She is unsteady and Eric is a needed support to get her up and to keep her on her feet. He finds that this does involve groping her bare nether regions for she has lost her clothing from the waist down.

It is not her mud spattered nude bits that Eric ogles, however, as he stands next to her and scans her body. He is concerned about the open wounds gashed here and there similar to the one on her cheek. He saw those wounds on the zombies and he has not forgotten the pleas from Clint and Indigo to be sliced open. The meaning of it all is a mystery not at the forefront of his mysteries to be solved caseload.

Lilly stands in place and slowly moves her lips in a silent conversation. Eric places a hand on her shoulder and tries to motivate her into moving.

"Lilly, we've got to go. It's Eric. Lilly. Lilly."

She takes a single step forward. Then she pivots and ambles a few more steps away from Eric before she stops again. A growl rumbles up from her throat and then she tongues a muddy blob out of her mouth and allows it to plop down her front.

Eric takes his eyes off her and looks over to where he left the kitchen knife. He measures the distance: not too far. He gauges the willingness of his legs to carry him swiftly: not too far. Time seems to slow down. He recognizes it as an action movie moment, but he doesn't feel cool or confident in it as the hero. He feels the urge to cry, not only over the condition of Lilly, but over the fact that he knows that something is stalking him from behind.

Eric doesn't go for the knife. He turns around to face whatever approaches.

The Mo roars and pounds its fists, fists that end in hands of five fingers graced with bear-like claws, against its chest not unlike a gorilla might do. It stands more erect, not as bulky a mass as a gorilla, more in the shape of a very muscular man of eight feet in height. Its body is carpeted in wild fur that is brown with mud, blood, sticks, and leaves.

The creature is a cyclops, one large eye centered in the facial area. Below that eye are two holes that have fur sucked into them by inhalation and bubble with mucous. The mouth on the beast is expansive and the fangs lined within it are impressive.

Mo charges toward its prey. "His" prey, Eric's eyes drift downward as his emergency preparedness wires cross and he sees a floppy sausage and swinging sack. Already stopped,

Eric now drops, and rolls. He rolls his body toward the creek, but he isn't on fire and the Mo is not fooled. It pounces, grabs him, lifts him up off of the ground, and slings him over the creek.

Eric hits against the fat nest of tree roots that extend into the creek. The wind is knocked out of him and he splashes down into the water.

The Mo roars and jumps down into the creek to grab hold of Eric once again. It lifts him and body slams him on to dry land.

Then the beast hops up and grabs Eric by a shoe. It drags him a few feet away and then decides that it is time to straddle him and squat down over him.

Eric is able to suck in a breath as he stares up into the menacing eye of the Mo. The beast births a warm splat of malformed turds on to Eric's legs.

Feces expulsion complete, it now leans down and Eric is sure that his face is about to get eaten.

Luke rushes onto the scene with a battle cry!

"Ay-yi-yi-yi-yiii!"

The battle cry isn't all that he brings to the fight: he has a large ax and he is able to control it, rear it back as he skids to a stop by Mo and Eric. He swings the ax, chops it right down into the head of the hostile creature as it turns to face him.

The ax blow doesn't kill the Mo. But its skull is split and its single eyeball is destroyed. Enraged, eyeball pus oozing out with spurts of pink fluid, it swipes in the direction of Luke and tries to hook him with its sharp claws.

Luke may not be a track star, but he is able to belly dance himself out of harm's way when his dance partner is blind. The Mo steps away from Eric, but does not stand tall, it remains hunched over, perhaps as it sorts through the pain that has been afflicted upon it. It is vulnerable and Luke aims to take advantage.

He raises the ax once again and chops it down into the neck of the beast. The ax sticks tight into the furry stump. Luke chokes up on the handle and rips the blade forward. This motion causes the blade to tear through and then out of the Mo's throat.

Dark fluids gush out as the Mo collapses. Masses of squirming worms surf the gory spray.

Luke chops the ax down against the felled beast, once, twice, three, four times for good measure. The ax drips with Mo goo and Luke drops the weapon as if he is suddenly squeamish. He glances down at himself and sees that the splashing on to his person was kept at a minimum.

Eric is thankful on his feet.

"You came back for me."

"Let's get, bro."

"Where's Lilly?"

She is not where he left her.

Luke points off into the woods. Eric repositions himself to see beyond the trees in the direction of note. He sees that zombie Lilly walks away from them.

Eric runs after her. Luke doesn't yell after him this time: he follows.

When Eric reaches Lilly he touches a hand to her shoulder.

"Lilly."

She whips around on him with a grabby hands and a snarl!

Eric is able to shake free from the groping attack, but she gnashes her teeth and pursues a bite.

The feral behavior, the blank eyes, Eric recognizes all of the symptoms and he runs for his life.

Luke knows the way out of the woods and is more than happy to give his lungs the extra dose of stress to lead his brother in escape.

Lilly yowls and gives chase. However, the things that drive her lack grace and she careens into a tree. The blow causes her to stumble off course, then she trips over a branch and plants into the ground face down and bare ass up.

Luke and Eric hit the bottom of a steep incline and Eric looks back. He sees that they have put some distance between themselves and Lilly, sees her prone on the ground, and he stops. Luke pulls up as well.

Eric's heart is in his throat. He feels humiliation for Lilly, wants to run to her, wants to make everything "okay." It would be death.

Eric watches as Lilly gets back up to her feet. She appears to have forgotten the thrill of the chase and turns her back on the brothers. She ambles away in the opposite direction.

Eric watches Lilly walk deeper into the woods, watches until she is out of sight. Luke gives his brother a thought to consider.

"She wanted you to leave her alone. Give her some space."

If it's meant to be, set it free, and all that bummer jazz.

The brothers turn and walk. Eventually they reach the hill that will lead them back to Granny's. The incline causes them both to sweat profusely.

Once they arrive in Grandma's driveway, Eric sees where Luke got the ax. He reversed Dessi and the angels at ramming speed into one of the garage doors for access to the tools inside. The door is smashed down and the rear end of the Grandma's old Buick Regal is crunched. Dessi's rear has suffered dents, but the engine purrs with the turn of a key and Luke brags about her.

"Dessi is a tank."

They change into fresh clothes before they go, leave the blood and shit stained articles on the ground for crime scene technicians to process.

As they travel down the highway the brothers do not find themselves in want of conversation with each other. Eric watches the trees that whiz by and worries about Lilly.

Luke wonders if Mo is a singular creature or if Grandma Bradbury meant "Mo" as the plural, like how moose is what a person says instead of meese.

# A Trip to the Convenience Store

The Texas morning sun came with a sweltering vengeance over the Crawford ass farm. The hell-heat is not centrally located on this specific farm, but the parched landscape does seem like the perfect snapshot for a postcard: HOTTER THAN AN ASS-A-SAURUS IN TEXAS!

There was a large ass auction in Mexico the week before last; therefore, the farm is not stocked with asses, but of those that do reside there, most seek shade in a large barn. Of course, there is Peabrain, an ass seemingly born to snort dirt, who enjoys the scorching sun rays as he rolls a thorny tumbleweed to and fro in the grassless pasture.

Hank Crawford currently bares the heat inside of the ranch house on his property. A cowboy by trade sounds better than an assboy; his under arms are wet before even working to work up a sweat. A white t-shirt and blue jeans

283

are his outfit, though his overalls await on the floor.

He sits in a chair at the kitchen table, contemplates his breakfast on the plate before him. Nausea swells within his early to rise belly, an odd feeling that feels less like a sickness and more like a premonition. He does not know what is to come, but considering the fart that woke him this morning also stained his underwear, it is surely a premonition of ill things.

On the breakfast plate for Hank lie bacon and eggs. Hank is quite carnivorous, but today the bacon seems like grizzled strips of fat void of meat. He looks down on the bacon and imagines it being fresh sliced from a squealing pig, the disconnecting goopy strings as it is pulled from the innards. The eggs are greasy. It's all cold, having been prepared for him by his wife Jess, she left early to see a man about an ass, unknowing that her husband would be slow to the table and so grotesquely imaginative. Hank decides to skip breakfast and get to working up a better appetite for lunch.

Overalls on, Hank takes his cowboy hat off of its peg by the back door. His manure powdered work boots sit on a rubber mat, ready to be pulled on and get to blister forming. Hank mutters through some spinal soreness as he shoves his feet into the boots.

The crusty boot laces make him wish for the Velcro of youth and once both feet are planted he decides he won't even bother tying them. He won't be running, no chasing, no matter how stubborn and elusive Peabrain is today, Hank is going to shuffle walk, no tripping.

And then the entire house violently shakes. "Whoa."

Hank tries to steady himself by placing the palm of a hand against the wall. However, the wall is not steady itself and Hank goes down to one knee, hears a pop in his back just as loud as the sound of all the glass that rattles in the home. A bottle of laundry detergent falls off a shelf, bangs off the top of the washing machine, and then thumps to the floor near Hank. The cowboy studies the detergent bottle, focuses on it to try and navigate the seasickness and wait out the bucking bronco that the world has become. He stares into the soft eyes of a cartoon bear.

The tremor ends.

Hank remains on his knee, wishes Jess were there to help him back up. He is a man who endured open heart surgery, bones broken by kicking hooves, flesh cut via slipped blade and barbed wire entanglements. There was the time he split his head wide open in a car accident. In all of those events he had the grit to overcome without complaint, shooing away most assistance. However, when it comes to little things like cooking chicken noodle soup during a bout of the sniffles or getting erect after going down on bad back and bended knee, a man needs the strength of his wife. He would even whimper out for her now, assuming she would already be up on her own feet, if only she were home. He hopes she is safe.

And then the balance of the Earth goes mad and Hank's thoughts are all shaken out of his head. This tremor is far more intense and there is a loud explosion followed by a sonorous hum. Hank doubles over on to the floor, covers his head in his hands, and momentarily ceases to exist, his mind is the hum, the vibrations, with backing vocals of breaking wood and glass. The room twists and collapses in on the cowboy.

The searing heat is a Texas event; however, the earthquake is an ass farm anomaly. When the second round of shaking ends, a portion of the ranch house has crumbled, the few trees that were in the yard have been felled, the fences are all broken, and the main barn full of asses appears to have imploded. Beyond the barn and broken fences the desert ground has ruptured into a gigantic, perfectly symmetrical crater.

Hank crawls out from under the section of home that fell on his head. The creaks and groans of aged bone are forgotten as the man scurries up to his feet quicker than a pretend paraplegic in a televangelist's audience. His upward mobility is a shock of instinctual need to confirm his survival as well being driven by the pain of crude acupuncture, hundreds of splinters embedded into his flesh.

The cowboy staggers away from his wounded home and takes in the sight of his wounded land, the destruction swaying his attention away from the fiery pricks in his wounded epidermis. The devastation is a sight that brings Hank serenity in his awe. His ears pop and the sense of hearing rushes in with a sense of relief to be free from the invading hum that had accompanied the quake. One of Hank's boots is gone. He trips over the untied lace of the remaining boot.

The stumble step is the first of many that take Hank closer to the rubble that was once the barn. He does not see animal fur mixed in with the collapsed building materials, but he doesn't hear any pleas either. He figures that the asses that took shelter within the barn have not survived. Asses in collapsed barns are not known for their silence. Hank knows this from an experience with a tornado event once upon a time in Oklahoma. Then again, who knows anything? The dice might roll different each time you wager on the vocal habits of asses in barn collapses.

Beyond the barn the crater draws Hank toward it, shuffle step, limp through the dirt, no tripping. On approach he takes mental note that there aren't any signs of blasting, the dig work is perfect, no discarded piles of soil are to be seen, and there isn't obvious evidence of a meteor. *The Blob*, Hank remembers seeing the movie *The Blob*, and when he reaches the edge of the crater he thinks: *The Blob*.

The depth of the crater from top ridge to center floor can be easily seen. It is an uncomfortable depth for Hank's vertigo, but stare into it he does with the nausea of premonition. There comes a sound, a quick poot, and Hank is not sure at first whether or not he has just sharted into his underwear again. However, the first sound of escaping air is followed by a louder rush, a blast, and a geyser of soil spews from out of the center of the crater.

The geyser spirals out of the crater with increasing ferocity and Hank is forced to retreat as stones strike him. Again he trips over his boot laces, and this time he falls down because of it. An elbow takes the brunt of the rough landing, a new scrape in his collection is better than the pummeling the storm of rocks and dirt offered if he had remained at the side of the crater.

Hank turns as the spray of earthen materials ceases. The man decides that for the time being he is comfortable enough to stay on the ground right where he is. Two seconds later the rays of the sun have changed his mind, too hot to sit outside, better to find some shade on the good side of the house. Three seconds later he forgets most everything that occurred in his life up until this very second as Satan crawls out of the crater.

Satan, Beelzebub, Abaddon, Apollyon, The Deceiver, Angel of the Bottomless Pit, Father Of Lies, The Evil One, King of Babylon, Lawless One, Wicked One, Ruler of Demons, Lucifer, the Goddamned Devil steps away from the crater and walks right over to Hank.

The Evil One is his fanciful storybook image, but grittier on this side of reality. The classic anatomy is all there, curved horns akin to Halloween costume style and length, slim, not bulky headgear, wings are folded upon his back, a barbed tail snakes away from his rear, and dull red is definitely his color. His bulbous yellow eyes glow like nothing under the sun should be capable of and the red skin pulsates with a multitude of scars oozing pus. Eight feet tall, Satan's smile is a killer one with thick, needle fangs. However, it's hard for Hank not to focus on the grapefruit testicles and throbbing eggplant cock that loom over him from Satan's crotch region.

Satan's voice is a polite tone, the genial sound of a smooth operator.

"Get on your feet, Sir."

Hank's compliance to the request is not of his own doing. An unseen force scoops under him and levitates him into a standing position. A melodic purr begins inside of Hank's ears, the strange music going from feline to human wails, the rhythm of suffering, spiraling knots of pain and flashes of tortured meat and flames overcome the cowboy's mind. The images of slaughter in dark caverns via talon and blades, carcasses of roasting spits, entrails wrapped around entrails wrapped around decapitated torsos only include one last thought from Hank, the bacon from his breakfast plate, but that is quickly washed away by the bubbling flesh of a stranger in Hell crucified. An acidic vomit streams out from between Hank's lips, as blood trickles from his nostrils.

Satan grasps Hank by the neck with one of his clawed hands. His other hand goes to the cowboy's mouth, pries open the lips farther, and crams his long finger into the oral cavity. The Evil One's hand contorts to slide deeper into the man, down his throat, gagging Hank up to his demonic elbow.

Hank's eyeballs roll into pure white as his life leaves him, though his body remains erect.

Then, with a sickening jerk, Satan retreats his arm. In his hand is an orb of light. However, the illumination quickly winks out and what remains is a milky colored orb accented with veiny networks of blood red. The orb is squishy and appears to be slathered in a film of clear mucus.

Satan takes a bite from the orb, savors it, oh, it has been a long time since he has tasted such a treat. The remainder of the orb is then popped into his mouth, chewed, swallowed. As the treat goes down into him, Satan rubs one of his own breasts, titillated by the ingested protein.

Meanwhile, Peabrain the ass ran away from the farm the moment the shaking ended and the fences fell; being alert for weaknesses in the farm fencing was always one of his top priorities. His story if one were to follow it might make a solid children's book, what with his enthusiasm for carefree romping, his befriending of a lizard that would become his traveling mate until as a duo they are rescued and spoiled by a teenage girl sent to live on her grandparents' horse farm due to some fallout over mischief in school. Milly is the name of the girl and she renames Peabrain as Mr. Bray Stevens, dubs the lizard Seymour, and the trio find love and adventure around every corner as well as mischief, but of the adorable nature.

Love is in the air, love and the smell of ass. It is with that love that Satan rewinds the devastation wrought to the Crawford farm. The house rebuilds, the barn returns to barn status, the fences rise, the field levels out, all returns to shape as the Crawford's loved it. Perverting love is an amusement Satan would never pass up; catastrophic masterpieces can be built on a foundation of abused love.

The asses in the barn will never be the same, extra cantankerous, and Hank will never be the same either. Jess Crawford returns home to find her husband sprawled out in the driveway the victim of a massive stroke; no evidence of foul play, no massive craters, naturally unfortunate causes are to blame.

Satan roars down the highway on the partially rebuilt motorcycle he found buried in one of the Crawford's garages. Jess will never notice that the bike is missing, a long forgotten project. The orb that Satan pulled from Hank helped him link power into the machine, brings the speed of tortured souls into the rusty engine, the screeching power of bats out of Hell.

The nibble of human soul won't be enough to keep Satan on this plane of existence and he doesn't dare push his luck at harvesting more. His escape will be short-lived and he won't make it much farther, he knows. It is a race against time that he will lose, but he has to take every chance he can get with his only goal right now to get down the road, to find a store that contains the nectar he seeks to indulge in, then it's back to Hell. All he wants is a Pepsi.

# Blood and Nuts

Wendy and Bubba, lady and dude, for better or worse married to each another, sit side by side in lawn chairs on their lawn. A hard working couple, they met at the same factory that still employs them and helps them afford their country home that sits on twenty acres with some surrounding woods.

On this Friday night in an attempt to wind down from the week of monotonous labor, the couple decided to do some hand holding and romantic star gazing. Mostly they've been sitting in the chairs whining about bug bites and how they can't see anything beyond the thick cloud cover, and if Bubba smacks the flashlight one more time Wendy may smack him.

"Quit it, Bubba! Put new batteries in the dang thing!"

Bubba shakes the flashlight, perturbed by the blinking weak light that emits from it.

"I don't know where the batteries are. They were in the ottoman, but somebody moved them."

"I didn't move them."

"I didn't say you did. They probably moved themselves."

"Did you look in the tool thing under the sink? That's where they always are."

"No. They were inside the ottoman last I saw them."

"Well, go look under the sink."

"Who put them under the sink? Whoa, what was that?!"

Bubba's attention is diverted from the important debate over battery location by a sudden movement at the edge of the woods. He points the flashlight with its mediocre beam of light in the direction of said wooded area.

"What was what?"

"I thought I saw something move over there."

"A tree?"

"No."

Bubba yells out toward the woods.

"Hey, who's there?! Come out! This is private property!"

Wendy is confused and unsettled by the alertness she can see in Bubba's rigid staring at the woods.

"Who are you yelling at? There's no one there."

"I swear I saw something. I think it was a man."

"Stop it. You're scaring me."

Bubba waves the flashlight from side to side, is able to get some illumination on a few low to the ground plants and weeds.

A twig is snapped and there is the sound of something moving through the woods again.

Bubba pivots the flashlight to try and see what makes the noise. He makes sure to get out his "I told you so."

"See! Did you hear that?"

Wendy DID hear that and she might have seen something. Bubba reiterates his guess as to what has come to visit them.

"I think there's a man walking around over there."

"No it's not. You're being a jerk. It's just a squirrel or raccoon."

"I'm not trying to scare you."

"All I saw was like a flash of fur. Little. It's probably a squirrel bouncing around."

"Do squirrels even come out at night?"

"The cool ones probably do."

"It's not a squirrel. There's somebody out there."

"I'm going back inside. You've always got to get worked up over nothing."

"You've always got to argue with everything I say! I saw a man, no, it was a squirrel. If I said I saw a squirrel you'd probably argue that I saw a man!"

"Now you're really being ridiculous."

And then a six-foot-tall, two-hundred and fifty pound, foaming at the mouth with glowing red eyes, squirrel-man-monster, rushes out of the woods toward the couple, screaming with its hunger for blood and nuts.

# Wretch

"**M**eep. Mahp. Ahhrp. Do you think I'm sexy? Am I sexy? Huh?"

Kate Rollins is an attractive young woman who does her best to impersonate Pee-Wee Herman. She has lifted her nose up into a snout with lots of clear tape and presents this face to the webcam next to her computer.

She perches in a comfy office chair before a computer desk that is in the living room area of an apartment. The computer on the desk is an all-in-one rig with a built in webcam but Kate splurged for an external device with more HD bells and whistles.

The webcam model makes sure to show off her taped up nose in side profile before she snorts and then stands up out of the chair. She wheels the chair out of the way to give herself performance space.

Kate poses and makes weird sounds, struts from side to side with her hands held out to mimic the puny appendages of a mighty T-Rex. She adds some screech quality to her voice as she speaks words again.

"Sexy. Sexy. Rah. Sexy. Sexy. I sexy, sexy."

A few goofy roars later and she is bored with that random routine and tears the tape from her face.

"Ouch."

She sits down in the chair to host discussions with her webcam audience. The conversation steers toward the topic of diet.

"Every time I've tried to quit eating meat I get headaches. I know planting crops hurt the environment and animals too. And I'm not sure plants don't have more consciousness than we give them credit for."

She reads the words that scroll in the chatroom to the left of her video feed on the computer screen. She responds to some of the responses.

"Right. Show me all of the vegetarians and vegans that live longer than all other humans. People live to what they live to. Genetics and stuff. I've seen old people that say they ate greasy bacon and drank soda all their lives."

She reads some more and chuckles as a regular viewer, going by the handle of Charmy, tells a mean-spirited vegan joke.

"Good one. No, Charmy, no more vegan jokes. I like the idea of it. I don't want animals crammed into cages waiting to die or the impact the industry has on our planet. But, then, like, other animals would probably do like we do if they could. Like bears, they always wait for all the fish to migrate into certain spots to scoop them out easy. Bears would totally open slaughterhouses."

Kate's attention drifts again. She rocks in her seat, puckers her lips, and waves her hands over the keyboard as she reads the chatter sent to her.

"Predators and prey and plants and people preach this and that and then they're that and this when it comes to this and that that someone else preaches. I don't know what I'm talking about anymore. Let's talk about music."

A tiny ukulele is nearby and Kate bounds out of her seat to retrieve it. When she returns to her chair she right away starts strumming the instrument. Strum, strum, she croons.

*"I can't play the ukulele, but I have a ukulele. I can't really sing! I'm getting bored, you can pay me to stop. Stop, drop, drop out my boobies."*

Down low for the low notes.

*"Booooooob. Beeeeeees."*

Ca-ching. A nickel tip is digitally sent, but that is not enough for boobs. A typist with a specific fetish requests some one on one time and while Kate wanted to ignore it, changes her tune because she's got to earn the rent money. She sets the ukulele aside and types out a private message to green-light the private session.

The private session initiates seconds later and Kate doesn't stall, aims to please. She holds her arms up to give the pay by the minute lover a view of her armpits. She sniffs a pit, then flicks her tongue out, gives it a lick.

"Mmm. You like that? I want you to put your fat cock in there big boy."

She can tell that the session isn't going to last long by the silence that passes as she continues to flirt with her armpit flesh. Single words are typed to urge her on for the viewer is typing with one hand, yep, yep, oh, yep, he's going to blow.

After a from ten countdown in which she only gets to six the user logs out of the session and Kate is left alone in the buffer time before the return to the live feed chat. What will she feed them next?

The audience, those who hung around and those surfing through, get to watch an empty chair while their sex dream pours herself some red wine in the kitchen. She returns to her chair with her glass of wine. Cheers.

"If you have to drink to be comfortable on camera then you shouldn't be a webcam model, I say."

She takes a big drink from the glass. She closes her eyes and when she slowly reopens them, blink, blink, makes an announcement.

"My eyes hurt."

She closes a single eye and quotes the Bible.

"The light of the body is the eye, if therefore thine eye be single, thy whole body shall be full of light."

No need to state the gospel or elaborate, no need for a proper goodbye, a click of the mouse ends her transmission.

Water pours from the faucet, plunges into the tub, and churns the bubble bath. To Kate's ears it sounds like an epic waterfall accompanied by kettle drums. Sometimes you get to drop the needle for your soundtrack, sometimes it is dropped for you.

Candles illuminate the bathroom causing shadows to dance in rhythm to their flames. Kate, in a robe, meditates on the flame that is positioned on the tank of the toilet.

She turns to the percussion of the tub and pushes back on the robe, allows it to drop down below her shoulders, but hang on. Then the tie is pulled at the front and the robe is allowed to pile down at Kate's feet. She steps away from the cloth and walks to the tub, steps into the hot water. It hurts for a flash, but then it is a comfort once she gets all of her delicate bits submerged.

Her hand turns the knob and cuts off the epic waterfall; silence ensues. She soaks, relaxes, closes her eyes.

Flashback.

There is a clearing in a wooded area. A storm rolled through at some point and the exposed dirt in this clearing is still thick with moisture.

Kate is thrown to the ground and mud splatters her joyful print dress of suns and powder blue. She is distraught, terrified against the earth. She scrambles to turn around, to sit up and face the direction from which she fell.

Bree, a young woman who is luscious and tough with curves, looms over Kate. She holds a large knife that gently shakes with the tightness of her grip on it. It will calm, thy will be done.

Kate holds one of her own hands up, a defensive stop sign, a plea for mercy.

In the tub Kate's bath water transforms into mud. She sinks below the mud, deeper into the fragment of memory.

Bree looks away from Kate, pathetic on the ground, and looks over toward the nearest tree not chopped down for the clearing. Hannah is a young woman bound to that tree by rope. There is fight left in Hannah, she screams and twists against the bindings, but they keep her uncomfortably snug against the bark.

Kate splashes out of her muddy memory, out of the water, and gasps for air as she grabs on to the sides of the tub for support. Now she wipes water from her eyes and looks down to see that the bubbles have dissipated; however, she is in water not water.

The plug is pulled and as the water drains Kate kneels at the side of the tub, legs crossed at the ankles, naked before her God, prays for some divine guidance.

Up to her feet, Kate dries her body with a towel. Then she puts on some pajamas, scrubs the towel against her hair, and drops the towel to the floor when she finishes. She steps over to the sink and looks into the mirror above it. The reflection disturbs her with its engorged, pitch black eyes.

Kate leans in closer, snarls to see that her reflection has a mouth full of fangs. She tests these new teeth with her tongue and gets the meat of that organ nicked by the sharp edges.

Kate averts her eyes and counts to three in her head. When she looks at the mirror again the demon Kate is still there. The vision worries her, yet she studies it for another minute before walking away in a calm state.

The bulb of a lamp keeps the deepest shade of shadows away from the bed in Kate's bedroom. She is on the bed, sound asleep, a woman not a demon twisted in the sheets.

Kate is a light heavy sleeper, aware of being in her bed even as she snores. The jukebox in her head plays a lullaby of jarring industrial music, which helps her find some peace in slumber, though if actually audible might be scarier to others than the shadows held at bay.

It's a new dawn, it's a new day, it's the ca-ching, ca-ching grind. Kate stands in front of her computer and listens to the sound effects of tips being tipped. The audience has coaxed her into lifting her tight shirt and revealing her belly. She traces her fingers around the bellybutton, flirts with winks to the camera, however, it is all mechanical not sensual.

After netting some earnings on the day, Kate finds herself drawn to the bathroom mirror. Once again her reflection is demonic. Cue the music, 80s synths, a playful sitcom theme song style to try and lessen impact of the horror within the ridiculousness.

Demonic Kate in the mirror makes a few silly faces as directed by Kate outside of the mirror. It is a brave front that the woman cannot hold. The music ends and Kate runs out of the room in tears.

She crosses the living room and dries her eyes as she sits on to the loveseat. It's hard to feel safe when crying. And then she realizes that safety is no longer a feature of her apartment. In her office chair, positioned away from the desk and catty-corner to the loveseat, sits Kate with the demon eyes.

Demon Kate speaks in a voice befitting something evil from a pit.

"I am not a reflection you can leave behind."

Kate on the loveseat fears this, speaks to this in her own weak plea of a voice.

"What do you want from me?"

The demon has more to say.

"You can't lie to me child."

Kate fights off the fresh urge to weep. She shuts her eyes and throws a wish out to the universe, wishes for a divine exorcism. Instead she gets to visit a bad memory again.

Kate on the ground, Hannah tied to the tree, and Bree paces between them with the knife. Hannah screams on Kate's behalf.

"Let her go, Bree!"

Bree stomps over to Hannah and feigns as if to stab her with the knife. Hannah cringes and screams.

"No!"

Tears leak from behind Kate's eyelids. She opens her tearful eyes, finds that she is on the loveseat and that the office chair across from her is void of demons.

The same 80s sitcom tune that she composed for herself in the bathroom conjures again to help her transition in reverse: from tears to silly face making. She laughs. It is not joyful laughter, it's an attempt to again cope with absurd, a doubting of her sanity.

A webcam model can't sit around talking to demons and expect to stay in the shape of lust that she prefers. Kate goes to her bedroom to work out. She has developed her own specialized exercise routine.

She kicks and punches the air as if in battle with invisible ninjas. However, the violent gestures then flow into freestyle dance moves. It is obvious that she is neither a trained fighter nor dancer, but she commits with vigor and works up a sweat.

When it is time to clock back in, Kate doesn't dress in a seductive manner. She sits in front of her computer wearing pajamas and some goofy elephant slippers. She gives the webcam audience more insight into her life.

"I don't own a cellphone. I don't need another bill to pay. I don't go out either. I'm a homebody. A home girl. I go out shopping, but really you guys are my friends."

Regular visitor Charmy types something to which Kate responds.

"Aww. I'd miss you too, Charmy. My apartment can seem like a prison. I go a little crazy, but I'm so anti-social. You go out and around people and everyone is starring in their own soap opera. It's exhausting."

Someone mentions family.

"Yeah, family too. I call my mom on holidays when I remember."

She pivots to answer a question from another user on a different topic.

"No, Hardfarard, I won't flash my bobs. What are bobs? Tip me if you want something. Quit begging. Ugh."

She grunts in frustration and then mimes the pulling out of her hair.

"It's been slow on here, Charmy. I like hanging out, but too many people want to type their fantasy fiction or beg me to wink my butthole for free. It's like, dude, I've got a tip menu. There's a link off to the side if you want to buy me a gift. Why are you here?"

She pauses to read some reactions. Then she continues on.

"I know, Charmy, I'm not talking about you. It's cool that you're hanging out. Maybe I'll do a special show tonight. I need to burn off some anxiety."

The loud whoosh of a ventilation fan violates the sound spectrum. Harsh, unharmonious, yet if one listens long enough one might find a pattern in the chaos, hear sounds, maybe voices within it.

Kate shows an expression of strain on her face. Perhaps the fan hurts her ears. Perhaps she poops. She poops. Positioned on the toilet without reading material, she touches her hands to her face, taps, rubs downward from her eyes. As she removes her hands from her face her head does a slow turn to bring the mirror over the sink from peripheral vision into full view.

No reading material and a pooper just might imagine that they are in a horror movie about a haunted mirror or hear those imaginary things in the whoosh of the fan.

And the poop stinks.

Bowels clear and mind needing to be, Kate plots out and commences with her "special show." Thumping, bumping electronic music fuels a rave atmosphere. The living room is illuminated by blacklight and Kate dances with glow sticks in her hands. Her outfit is a bikini and paint glows neon where it has been smeared on the exposed skin.

After pushing herself to exhaustion Kate ends the show, doesn't bother to read the applause, forgetting the audience after all of the tickets to the show had been sold and the routine begun. Now she needs to wash off the paint, but there is a problem, she doesn't want to go into the bathroom and accidentally provoke her reflection into returning.

Kate goes into the kitchen and fills a couple of mixing bowls with water, sets them on the counter. She strips off her swimsuit and then uses a dish towel as a wash cloth to scrub the paint from her skin. It is not a tender bath, a job to get done, and she doesn't bother to worry about all of the water that slops down the cabinet doors and to the floor.

From the kitchen to her bed, Kate crashes down into the industrial grind of sleep. She sleeps with both of her knees bent, raised up in the air, ready for a quick escape, maybe, gently she snores.

Hot coffee is in a coffee mug. The mug sits on the kitchen counter. Kate leans over, brings her mouth close to the brim of the mug. Her tongue extends down and the tip of it tests the temperature of the coffee. Dip, dip, she laps up some coffee in this manner for a few weird moments.

Next she takes her coffee into the living room where sits in the office chair and sips down the rest of the beverage using a straw. Recommended cat, dog, and bird videos entertain her from the computer screen.

Once her system is charged up with caffeine, Kate goes into her bedroom for some exercise. She launches a barrage of haymakers and uppercuts that transition into some shoulder shimmy dance moves. The day is on! But she is not going to bother washing or combing her hair.

Kate sits in her office chair with her bare feet propped up to where the webcam is sure to capture them in frame with the rest of her while she chats.

"People try to shame me all the time, probably while jerking off. I think I do a lot of good helping lonely people."

Off of that positive note her energy begins to wane.

"Sometimes I wonder how many underage kids have seen me naked on here though. Or if a terrorist is somewhere getting off to me."

She dwells on her thoughts, forgets the chat scroll for a bit. When she returns from her daze she notices that someone notices her feet.

"My feet? Oh, someone paid me to keep them up."

She chuckles and waves a foot, wiggles her toes at the camera.

"If you think that's weird, one time a guy paid me to…never mind. Nothing's weird anymore."

Later Kate kneels on her bed, hands clasped together, face tilted upward, desperation evident in her prayer.

"I've turned myself into a piece of meat. I've thrown myself on the altar. What do I have to do to make everything okay again?"

No answer beams down through the ceiling.

Kate throws her frustration face down into a pillow muffled tantrum. Eventually this leads to sleep but Kate doesn't remember sleeping the next day when she finds herself in the living room tapping the palm of her hand against an arm of the loveseat; tapping to the tune of a ticking clock that she doesn't literally hear.

Once upon a time Kate's hand clicked open the lock on her front door to let her friend Hannah enter the apartment. At this time the ladies were wearing the same outfits from Kate's traumatic memory involving the clearing in the woods.

Hannah and Kate go into her bedroom and sit on the edge of the bed. Hannah's hand trembles and she holds it out to show the tremors to her friend. Kate takes hold of the hand, reels it in against her to hold it and to try and soothe Hannah's nerves. She gives some advice.

"You need to tell the cops. You need to file a restraining order."

Hannah disagrees.

"After everything we went through together, I was too cold."

"Hannah, you did nothing wrong."

Fast forward that day in the past and wrong gets did. Bree points the knife down at Hannah, who shifts and whimpers, but has nowhere to go, tight against the tree.

Bree presses a hand across Hannah's mouth, smothers her lips as she works the blade of the knife against the skin of the throat. She is going to cut.

Demon Kate perches on the office chair, head tilted, hands balanced under its chin, a gleeful, wicked smile formed by its lips, and it poses a question.

"What had they been through together?"

Kate, on the loveseat, is baffled by the need for such clarification.

"It doesn't matter. Bree went crazy and killed my friend."

Kate tries to take charge and sum up the situation as she now reads it.

"I summoned you. That's why you're here."

She swallows, conceives the way forward with her demon.

"You can bring my friend Hannah back."

Demon Kate is amused and strokes its chin as if there is an invisible little beard there for stroking. It offers a different read on the situation.

"Maybe you have gone crazy. Have you ever seen someone brought back from the dead?"

"You wouldn't be here if it wasn't possible. What do I have to do?"

The demon considers the question for a dramatic moment and then manifests the price.

"A trade."

It holds up a hand, five fingers extended.
"Five souls."

It raises its other hand with only one finger up.

"For one."

Kate understands.

Understanding is a dark comfort and she has the nerve to return to the bathroom. Comfort does not unclothe her or coax her into sliding her body into the womb of the tub. Instead Kate leans over the side of the tub and dunks her head into the collected water to baptize herself and wash her hair.

Into pajamas and on to her bed, hair still wet, Kate holds a hand up and focuses on the five fingers. The fingers bend. She scrunches the five down, inspects their nails, extends them out again. Then she wiggles them in random patterns and speaks to herself: reassurance.

"This is the kind of stuff people do when they are alone and contemplating matters of soul collection."

From reassurance to motivation, a bad memory is always just a thought away.

Muddy in her dress, Kate is on the ground, her hand grips as tight as it can to the Earth, but she doesn't have the arm strength to stop and reverse the rotation.

Slumped against the tree that she is bound to, Hannah is dead, her heart works to catch up to that, blood drains from her slit throat.

Bree steps away from the murder and turns to face Kate.

"Remember: you did this."

She takes another step toward Kate and raises the knife. Bree doesn't bring the knife to Kate, she points the blade at herself, lines up her aim, and slowly reels the hand outward into a starting position. One last look shared with Kate and then she stabs, slams the blade into her chest. Her aim is lethal and true.

The day comes after the night once again for Kate. Sleep was unsteady, but she leaves the bed without yawns and gets right to the exercise. Her attempt at enthusiasm is brief, mind drifts to the preparation ahead. Lackluster punches connect with air, but she tries out a new theme song.

"Bum. Bum. Bum. Bum. Bum. Bum. Bum."

Punch. Punch. Punch.

Bum. Bum. Bum. It throbs in her mind.

She gets dressed and goes to the front door. She's got her purse and reusable shopping bags, however, hesitates in opening the door.

Bum. Bum. Bum.

Time to go.

Kate exits her house and hurries away from the apartment complex; someone leaving the scene of a crime, trying to act normal, walk don't run, and then speed walking with an abnormal gait. Down the sidewalk she goes, paranoid that she is being watched and followed. No one watches, no one follows, and by the time she gets to the first store she remembers how to act natural enough.

Bum. Bum. Bum.

Kate bustles through her front door with her shopping bags full. She kicks the door shut behind her and hefts the bags across the living room.

The shopping bags are set down on to the loveseat along with Kate's purse. She speaks aloud as she looks down at her purchases.

"I got all this stuff and no one said a thing. The army surplus store I found was cheapo."

She turns away from the loveseat and walks to the computer desk. She continues to talk as if to the webcam.

"I watched people and weighed their lives in my hands. No one noticed."

The conversation goes from Kate being impressed with herself to realizing that she talks to herself.

"Who the hell am I talking to?"

The computer is not on. A push of a button remedies that, but Kate decided to visit some of her purchases rather than observe the boot-up process.

There are five clean, glass, sealed, vintage style jars that Kate places on to the kitchen counter in a row. One jar for each soul to be collected.

A sick feeling swishes in the woman's stomach as she counts the jars, measures the lengths to which she has already gone.

The computer is on, the webcam website is open, the woman is engaged in the chat flow, much better for her than talking to herself of counting jars.

"I want world peace. You want to love everyone, but then you have a bad day and hate everyone."

She scolds herself.

"You shouldn't take things out on others just because you've had a bad day."

Potatodick makes her smile through the computer.

"I agree. Dogs are better than people. I don't know about your screen name though, Mr. Potatodick."

She mocks Potatodick with a playful facial expression of disgust before continuing on with the topic of dogs and people.

"Every time I see a dog I have to point and go: doggie! I can't ever own a dog because they're too great. So strong, loyal, and they make people seem crappy. If you gave me a puppy I'd probably hate all people and turn into a serial killer."

The smile is dead.

"Loyalty is hard to come by. It really is."

Ca-ching.

Kate reacts to the sound effect with gratitude.

"Thank you, Potatodick."

She cuts off the broadcast soon after that.

Heavy on thoughts, the clockwork gears of the world grind in her head, Kate tosses and turns in bed where screeching death metal infiltrates and warps the customary nocturnal record. As she lifts up from the attempt to sleep she punishes a pillow with several blows.

Into the bathroom she goes and into the mirror she stares. She questions her normal reflection not the demon.

"Who deserves to die?"

She mulls it over then produces an answer.

"The bullies."

On goes the sink faucet, under the water goes her hands, wet hands go to her face, pitty-pat-pat. Kate turns the water off and speaks to the mirror again.

"No one. No ones."

She leans in to intimidate her reflection.

"Who? Who? You gotta get away with it."

She slaps her face.

"The no ones."

More slaps to the face.

"Who? Who?"

One more smack for good measure. The blow changes her answer.

"Everybody."

Kate bows her head, whimpers, whines like an animal.

When Kate awakens the next day, wipes drool from the corner of her mouth, she discovers that she fell asleep with her head on the computer desk. Her eyes register that the computer screen in front of her features a live feed from her webcam to the Internet.

"Oh. Whoa. Oops. Hi, guys. I, uh, night, night."

She clicks her way off of the world wide web and steps away from the computer desk. The show today will be different and the show must go on, the life of her friend depends on it.

A herky-jerky jumble of jazz music with thriller movie tempo crashes about in Kate's skull. She stands outside, neatly dressed for the day with new accessories. She has her hair tucked into a trucker cap and wears glasses that are not prescription—a disguise. She does not have her purse, not going shopping in the traditional sense. A brave next/first step is taken and she jazzes on her way.

The Kate that wears a hat and glasses returns home with a guest. Skylar is a young woman and the fashion statement she makes is "homeless," rumpled from top to stained pants to ratty flip-flops that show off dirty toes. Skylar slides off her flip-flops and leaves them against the baseboard of the wall off to the side of the door that Kate shuts. It seems like proper etiquette even if her feet appear just as dirty as the shoes.

Kate leads the way across the living room and Skylar accepts the invite to sit on the loveseat. She sits with one leg crossed over the other as lady-like as she can pose. Kate offers refreshments.

"I'll get drinks. I have some soda, but I also bought some nice wine."

Skylar purses her lips, seems undecided. Kate adds to the menu.

"Or there's water."

Skylar reacts to that, points a finger and then gives a thumbs up. Kate returns the thumb gesture and walks out of the room.

Kate pours two glasses of water in the kitchen and sets them right in the row with her five jars awaiting souls. Then she opens the cabinet below the sink and pulls out a jug of chemical drain declogger. She opens the lid of the cleaning fluid and takes a whiff of the contents, potent stuff, yet she yells out and tries to sell her guest on taking the red wine.

"Are you sure that you wouldn't prefer wine?!"

No answer.

"It's red! Just bought it!"

Skylar still doesn't reply. Therefore, Kate stores the drain cleaner under the sink, declogging a human probably would have gotten too nasty anyway.

Kate returns to the living room and serves her guest a glass of water. Skylar accepts the drink with a gracious smile.

Kate's own glass of water gets set down on to her computer desk, no coaster, and left there as she wheels the desk chair away and positions it so that she can sit across from Skylar. Kate breaks the silence by noticing the silence.

"You sure haven't said much since we met. Wait. Do you talk at all?"

Skylar shakes her head from side to side for "no."

"You can hear me though?"

Skylar nods.

"Do you keep a pencil and paper to write on? To communicate?"

Skylar replies in sign language, describes herself as "shy."

Kate continues on with the conversation without a translator.

"It must be tough."

Skylar doesn't respond to this even though Kate gives her a few seconds to do so before she again carries onward with the gab.

"I never realized that there are so many homeless people in my neighborhood. It's like a different world in the alleyways."

Skylar signs: "same world."

"It must be a living hell. People probably take advantage of you a lot."

No words are signed by Skylar.

"So many forgotten people. Do you have family that I can get you in touch with? Someone must be missing you."

Another side to side shake of the head comes from Skylar.

"I look at you and I think in another world we could have been friends."

It's a confusing statement to Skylar and she signs the question: "Do you want to be friends?"

Kate moves along.

"We'll have a girl's day. I'll treat you to a meal and get you a new outfit. First, I'm sure you'd love a bath. Cleanliness is next to godliness, right?"

Kate starts the bath water, but then leaves Skylar to it and takes herself into her bedroom. Under the pretense, not entirely false, of finding her guest some fresh clothes, Kate raids her shopping bags and inspects some of her purchases. Tools are lined up for inspection on the bed: hatchet, screwdriver, hammer, and a knife in a sheath.

Pulse throbbing Allegretto, Kate chooses to pick up the knife and slide it from its outer casing. She touches the steel of the blade to her own throat and contemplates how easy it may be to slit open the skin and ravage the jugular. As dramatic as cutting one's own throat seems, in the intensity of the moment, release the pressure, let the blood out to play, Kate considers that the procedure could be such a shock as to be painless.

Instead of suicide she puts the knife down and goes to her closet to see what she can bear to part with and donate to Skylar.

After she has made some fashion choices, Kate carries the clothing folded in her arms to the bathroom. She pushes the door open and sees that Skylar soaks in the tub.

"Knock, knock."

Skylar signs along: "who's there?"

"I brought some clothes for you to try on."

She sets the outfit on to the closed toilet lid. The outfit that Skylar arrived in lies in a disheveled pile at the base of the toilet.

Delivery made, Kate backs toward the exit to give Skylar some privacy, but then changes her route and walks forward to the side of the tub instead. She moves one hand behind her back, holds it there, suspiciously if one were suspicious, however, Skylar is relaxed enough to not read into the posture as an indication of sinister intentions.

"A good bath changes the day don't you think?"

Kate's question leads them into an awkward silence with the women gazing at one another. Kate breaks the silence with an apology.

"I'm sorry. I'm ruining your time. Let me know if the clothes fit. If you need anything else just holler."

Skylar watches Kate stride in reverse out of the room and wonders what voice she is expected to holler with.

A flustered Kate returns to her bedroom. It isn't clear in her mind whether she is upset that she did not execute Skylar or that she planned to in the first place. She reaches behind her, under her shirt, and pulls out the sheathed knife hidden in the waistband of her pants. She tosses the knife on to the bed and then heads to the living room to find distractions at her computer.

Car crashes, road rage, and the comedic timing of karma's wrath are the subjects of the video flow that swallows a bite of time for Kate, a small cookie. She swivels in her office chair as the bathed Skylar enters the room with wet and wild hair. Skylar wears the outfit that Kate picked out and poses in it for approval.

"They fit. Do you like them?"

Skylar curtsies.

"Cool. You know, you could make a lot of money as a webcam model."

Kate gestures toward her computer.

"It's what I do. People are into a lot of different things and you've got a nice body."

Skylar takes this as a cue for action having read Kate's awkward vibe in the bathroom as a crush. She moves closer to Kate and goes down on her knees before her. She makes purposeful eye contact as she touches her hands to Kate's legs and rubs them along the outer side.

Kate is mesmerized by the face of the woman at her lap. Skylar moves her hands to the inner portions of Kate's legs and rubs them toward her crotch. At the edge of letting the moment go full erotic Kate snaps out of the seduction.

"Stop!"

She grabs, flings, slaps Skylar's hands away from her at the same time that she shoves the chair back. Skylar almost topples over on to her face in the floor, but manages to find balance.

"I don't want that."

Both women stand.

"You need to go. Get out of here. Go!"

Skylar is irritated and lets loose a series of signs for "whatever, "you're crazy," and the punctuation mark of an extended middle finger. Kate doesn't need a translator for those.

Skylar stomps over to the front door, collects her flips-flops, and then shows herself out of the apartment. The door is left swinging open.

Kate hustles across the room and slams the front door shut. Once the lock is in place, she turns and presses her back against the door, slides down it until her bottom is against the floor.

The office chair is propelled across the room by the feet of the demon, which are not unlike Kate's own feet. The Kate demon stops the chair in front of Kate and then leans forward to stare and get the scoop.

"I failed. I can't do it."

The demon claps its hands in sarcastic applause. It wants more from the performance, however.

"Now sing us a song."

Kate doesn't appreciate being mocked by a Hell-thing.

"I didn't summon you."

"Maybe I summoned you."

This notion disturbs the young woman. She presses against the door and uses it to slide herself upward to her feet. She turns her head to one side and closes her eyes in order to pretend that the demon is no longer there. The demon vanishes, but Kate feels oddly compelled to fulfill its request. Her singing voice is very soft.

*"I know I'm crazy, I know you hate me, it's true. But, I'd walk, I'd walk on blood for you."*

It is not for the demon's entertainment; it is a declaration to her friend.

*"I'd walk on blood for you. Yeah."*

A breath.

*"Yeah. Yeah."*

The towel that Skylar dried off with is thrown into a garbage bag along with the dirty clothing the homeless woman left behind. Kate then takes the garbage bag into her bedroom and drops it on the floor.

A boxed roll of painter's plastic sticks out one of the shopping bags on the bed and this item draws Kate's attention. She pulls the box out, pries it open, and frees the plastic.

The plastic unfurls across the bedroom floor and Kate lies down on to it while gripping one edge. She rolls herself and pulls the plastic along to turn herself into a plastic burrito stuffed with human woman, anxiety, and thoughts of asphyxiation.

Oxygen stifled, Kate starts to see through the blur of plastic once again into clear memory. Bree lies on the ground across from her with the knife protruding from her chest. Anger is set on the dying woman's face and Kate gets to watch Bree seethe her last breath.

Kate doesn't want to time travel anymore, doesn't want to sleep just yet, wants to breathe, and rolls herself out of the plastic.

A bent hip-hop beat puts a groove into Kate as she chugs red wine from the bottle. Slippers, panties, and a hoodie are the attire worn by her as she drinks and sways in front of the webcam.

Heavy knocks at the front door revive her awareness, sober her up out of the music and alcohol. She moves to the desk, sets her wine down, and shuts off the music.

The knocking is loud and clear and Kate theorizes on it for her computer audience.

"I've probably pissed off the neighbors. I don't complain about their vuvuzelas, but I'm always too loud."

She walks away from the computer, but leaves her live stream running. At the front door she uses the security peephole to scope out the late night visitor. Skyal stands outside of the door.

Kate opens the door and Skylar greets her with a one finger up to her lips for "shh."

Skylar steps aside and a man dressed low-key pimp, he goes out to clubs, but not the classy ones, steps out from where he hid to one side. This man, as Kate will soon find out, goes by the name of Cupid. Cupid isn't physically imposing, however, the handgun he holds is very intimidating.

Kate raises her hands and back away giving Cupid and Skylar clearance to enter the apartment. Skylar shuts the door and clicks the locks into place while Kate makes a plea to the man with the gun.

"Please don't hurt me."

"Stay smooth, baby. I'm Cupid the great lover come to collect my arrows."

His name and words are terrifying nonsense to her.

"Please no. Please don't do this."

"Bitch, shut up and listen. You had a date with my girl Skylar here. You didn't pay her my money AND you stole her clothes. That's just cold-hearted perverse."

He makes a show out of eye-balling Kate up and down. He leans in to get a better peek at her booty. He directs her with the gun.

"Pull that hoodie off and let me see what you're working with."

Kate complies and pulls the hoodie off, however, she holds it in her hands to provide some extra coverage over her bra as Cupid inspects. A twirl of the gun inspires her to turn in a slow circle for the man. He likes what he sees.

"Mmm mmm. I'd like to dip my nuggets in that sauce."

Kate looks to Skylar and Skylar averts her eyes away; no sympathy there. Cupid lays out more of the story as he heard it.

"Skylar tells me you make a lot of money with your webcam. Says you tried to recruit her away from me for some girl-girl shows."

"I didn't."

"Bitch, what did I say about shut up?"

She doesn't dare respond, lesson learned. He continues and she listens.

"I'm a business man. I think you and Skylar together is a hot idea. It's your lucky night.

Take us to the bedroom, I want to see what I'm investing in."

Kate moves to survive.

Skylar, ever so polite, removes her flip-flops and leaves them by the front door.

In the bedroom Kate, Skylar, and Cupid stand on the plastic covered floor. Cupid is curious.

"You doing some painting?"

Kate agrees to that guess with a nod.

"Don't lie to me. This is for squirt shows."

She shakes her head "no."

"Golden showers?"

Skylar pushes past Cupid and wrinkles her nose at him, makes sure he understands that she wants to get the show going and that she thinks him to be juvenile and gross. He grins, always loves it when she flirts with doling out her opinions because she knows where the boundaries are drawn and he never has to sock her.

Skylar crawls on to the bed and sits up on her knees. Kate's shopping bags and tools are still on the bed but pushed over on to the opposite side from where Skylar poses. Neither Skylar nor Cupid pay any mind to the bags of items tucked against them. Kate glances at the bags and specifically takes notice of the hatchet handle that pokes out next to one. Cupid directs.

"Go on. Join her."

He licks his lips and watches as Kate crawls up to position herself across from Skylar. On their knees the women face each another. Cupid moves closer to the edge of the bed, front row seat, eyes fixated on the two women.

Skylar removes her shirt at the exact speed that she knows her pimp enjoys. She smiles for him and then one at a time sucks, lubes up two of her fingers. Cupid provides some commentary.

"Skylar can't talk, but she sure knows how to use her mouth."

Next she slides those wet fingers underneath a strap of her bra. She teases the strap slowly down her shoulder.

Kate snatches up the hatchet from between the shopping bags and swings it at Cupid. Thwack!

The head of the tool cleaves open the temple of Cupid's noggin. The blow is devastating to his system. First he drops his gun, but then his entire body drops to the floor behind it.

Kate doesn't make a sound, not a whimper, as she hops off of the bed to finish the job.

Skylar remains on the bed, in awe as Kate chops the hatchet down again and again against Cupid. Whack. Whack. Whack. Cupid is fatally mutilated.

Kate rises up, spattered in pimp blood, and looks to Skylar. The mute woman offers up an apology and excuse as she steps off the bed, signs them as fast as possible: "I'm sorry. He made me do it."

Kate steps aside, clears a lane for Skylar. Skylar takes the route toward the exit, steps through Cupid's blood with a wary eye kept on his killer. A stride away from the door, however, she dares to turn her eyes from Kate and toward the future.

Kate steps after Skylar and viciously chops the hatchet down into the back of her skull. Thwack. Skylar is dispatched.

Murders complete, Kate leaves her weapon and the death behind, switches gears, races into the living room.

"Oh my God oh my God oh my God."

She runs to the computer and shrieks at the screen.

"Help! Call the police! Ahh!"

Once her scream tails off, her energy level sags, hysteria fades, and Kate becomes more aware and in control.

"I'm logging off now."

Click.

Pain flares between her ribs as she dry heaves into the toilet bowl. Out of vomit, but not nausea, Kate lifts her head from the commode and wipes acidic spittle from her chin.

A wash cloth awaits her at the sink and she uses it with some water to wipe at the dried blood on her skin; another special performance, another paint.

Kate changes into a clean outfit and then goes into the living room expecting the Calvary to come to the rescue or to come arrest her. She positions the office chair to where she can sit in it and stare at the front door. She waits with Cupid's handgun in her hands. Looking over the weapon, she considers how different events would have played out if she had such a weapon on the day that Bree barged in to claim Hannah.

Kate and Hannah had been sitting on the loveseat when Bree let herself into the apartment wielding a knife. The shock of that moment is a splinter in the festering wound of memory and it triggers a reaction in present day Kate. She jumps up from the office chair and points the gun at the front door. Her finger pulls the trigger: click. She exhales a deep breath and then pulls the trigger some more. Click. Click. Click. No bullets.

Kate is disappointed, lets the past flood her again as she drops into the chair.

Bree has her knife and channels her rage toward Kate. However, Hannah is quick to her feet to intervene. It plays out wordless this time, but the hatred in Bree's eyes is louder than ever and it pins Kate to her seat as she watches Hannah lead the threat willingly out of the door.

Kate gets off of the loveseat and follows after them, catches up to them, and complicates the diffusing of the bomb. It is not a hero's journey and the ending as she experienced it is not acceptable. This is why she quits waiting for the cops to bust down the door and returns to the original plan, the original, new deal. She needs to get two of her jars to collect the souls of Skylar and Cupid.

Soul collecting is not an exact science and Kate doesn't have the stomach for advanced surgery or exploration. No demons whisper the answer into her ears, unless it is a sweet nothing that guides her cupped hands into the blood.

A twangy frolic of blues rock made with the devil at a crossroads sparks a confidence in instinct, carries Kate musically from the harvest in the bedroom to the placement of the jars back in the row on the kitchen counter. There stands the row of five, two of them with splashes of plasma in them as evidence of commitment, maybe it can still turn out to be a hero's journey.

Tired, Kate lets the corpses have the bedroom and she makes a bed on the loveseat. Pillow to one side, blanket wrapped around her, Kate meditates on the sleep to come. However, it is a night void of repose.

The following day does not bring any detectives to the door and Kate uses her morning to tidy up the crime scene. Towels are ruined, bleach is spread, and Kate works her muscles rolling Skylar and Cupid up into crude bundles of painter's plastic.

When she goes to collect Skylar's flip-flops instead of picking them up she slides her own feet into the dirty pair. She shuffles across the room in someone else's shoes and picks up someone else's gun from where she left it. She doesn't find the shoes or gun very comfortable and takes them into the bedroom to store them inside a garbage bag. The bag is dropped next to the corpse of Skylar. Kate has some stern words for the dead woman.

"You made me do this. You got what you deserved. Hannah was my best friend and she deserved better. Bree was like you. You're sick animals."

Kate spends hours more of the day pacing and contemplating concepts such as "strong love is pre-meditation for murder." She saw the heart carved into the tree upon which Hannah perished. The letters H and B were carved into that heart. Had Bree carved it before or after the relationship went sour? Or had Hannah carved it once upon a time when the place held some special meaning for the women, unaware that it was her own headstone she carved?

Kate spends some time in the bathroom trying to call upon her demon.

"Where are you? Huh?"

Tough girl.

"You don't summon me. I summon you."

Kate is the only Kate that appears in the mirror.

"Yeah. I'll handle this."

The night finds her in tears at the computer desk. She blubbers her woes to her Internet audience.

"I'm sorry guys. I had a rough night and it's been a long day. Yes, Mack45, I'll check my private messages later."

She perks up and sucks back some snot as she recognizes an arrival in the chat scroll.

"Charmy! Hi, Charmy. I missed you!"

Ca-ching, a donation is made, a question posed, and the services of a knight offered.

"No. No worries. No one said anything mean. It's me. I was on last night and didn't recognize anyone, no one cared. If someone wanted to break right in to my apartment and kill me I could scream and not even my neighbors would care."

Ca-ching. Ca-ching. Charmy tries to sweeten her tears and Mack45 competes.

"Thank you, Charmy. Thank you, Mack45."

Ca-ching. It's a gratuity gang-bang.

"Thank you, Durpdurp. It was a lonely day and I'm a big baby."

Kate pulls off her t-shirt and uses it to wipe away her tears before she tosses it away. She squeezes her breasts together in front of the camera to reward the donors. Wiping away the tears did nothing to block new ones from forming. She continues to weep out her gratitude and sadness.

"Thank you. I know you guys care about me."

Ca-ching. Ca-ching.

Tonight Kate finds the industrial soundtrack of dreams, blasts herself into sleep on the loveseat. At times she hangs off of the piece of furniture upside down but this positioning doesn't disturb the rhythm of her snoring.

The smell of air freshener doesn't help a good morning headache; however, Kate sprays out an entire can of the chemical into her bedroom as perfume for the dead.

In the living room she finds that exercise does help ease the groggy pain. There is a new prop added to the usual randomness of her fight and dance routine: the knife. It slices, dices, and stabs the air. She will handle this. Two down, one to go.

Kate dresses herself for a public excursion but keeps the swimsuit on beneath the other articles as a precaution, knowing that she plots going off the deep end. The hat and glasses disguise return to her cranium, but there isn't any hesitation in her departure this time. It is upon her return to the apartment, shopping hunt completed, that Kate's adrenaline swirls her around doubt and threatens her composure.

The front door of the apartment opens and Kate hurries inside alone, shuts the door, and pins herself against it as if to prevent the portal from being opened. She takes this moment to catch her breath and remind herself that she is capable of great and horrible things.

She opens the door and as a part of the ruse in motion she greets her guest in what she thinks is an Irish accent.

"Please come in. Welcome."

The person that Kate has lured in this time is Joe Till. Joe is disheveled, reeks of "fallen on hard times," yet within the outline of his present state one can sense the shape of a man who was once "put together" physically and mentally.

Joe steps into the apartment far enough to let Kate seal him in but he eyeballs the place, cautious.

Kate smiles as she walks ahead of him, hopes the silence isn't too awkward and that her pleasant demeanor is strong enough to pull him along.

Joe breaks the silence without taking another step.

"You said that you, you, where you family at?"

Kate shrugs off the question in her fake accent.

"Do you want something to eat?"

Joe isn't comfortable, but he is hungry.

Kate removes her hat and glasses, sets them down, and suggests that Joe make use of the loveseat.

"Please sit and I'll whip up something in the kitchen."

Joe gives in and takes a seat. Moments later he scarfs down reheated spaghetti out of a Tupperware container as Kate watches on from the office chair she has pulled over. Her gaze falls to his crusty boots and the clots of dirt that she will have to clean up later along with everything else.

Joe sets the dish down to exhibit his dine and dash manners.

"Thank you for the meal. I should get out of here."

Kate can't allow that.

"You said your name is Joe?"

"Joe Till."

She repeats her lie of a name to go with her lie of an accent.

"My name is Elouise."

"You mentioned that. You lied about your family being here though. You shouldn't be inviting street folk to your spot, Elouise."

He lingered on the pronunciation of her false name as if he is aware of the deceit. Kate realizes that he is not a man whose trust can be seduced simply through his stomach.

"I trust you."

He's not buying it.

"What's your game about?"

She diverts with a question of her own to find conversational footing.

"What made you homeless?"

"Why do you care about that?"

"Shouldn't more people?"

"I should get out of here."

"No. No. On the street you were yelling about how the government and the army stole your soul. I want to understand."

He shifts in his seat and she continues to talk in order to keep him in that seat.

"I was drawn to you, Joe. I will listen."

Joe decides to tell his story.

"I was in the army. There's a lot of anger. Sometimes I've got to yell at the world."

Kate nods to signal that she is right there on that page with him. Joe sees a teaching opportunity.

"This country was founded by rich folks running the colonies. The poor and the working man were in revolt, so the rich folk redirected that anger at the British. They convinced their slaves to do all the fighting so they could extend their power. The constitution, that's your slave papers. Pledge of allegiance to the American dream, they call it a dream for a reason, to keep the slaves thinking that they're free."

"I can't say that I've read that in a history book."

"You young people got the Internet and just get smarter in the dumbest ways."

She doesn't really know what he means by that, but consents to almost agreeing with the statement.

"Maybe."

"I fought in Afghanistan. The slaves here, they hide under a blanket. I went out in the world and seen things. When I came home I couldn't pretend to be comfortable with pulling the blanket back up. I risked my life for the elitists that own this country. I'm on the street because I can't get back in line and punch their clock."

"Joe, I'll be honest, you smell like booze."

He cops to that.

"Yeah. We're all full of shit."

Now he has a war story to share.

"I had an army sergeant that called himself Gravedigga. He had a shovel and he sharpened its edges. He'd have us hold people down, prisoners, civilians, men, women, children..."

He trails off as the confession strikes a nerve of conscience. He finds himself willing to continue.

"We held them down and he'd put the shovel against their necks and stomp it. We took their heads off and laughed about it. Real American heroes."

The sharing has been too heavy and now the two are buried under the intimate revelations of the conversation, the awkward silence is something Joe might use as an escape from the apartment. Before he can excuse himself Kate finds the voice to tell him what she wants.

"I want you to take a bath."

Joe did not know that he wants that too, but it now seems right.

Once again Kate takes on the duty of starting the water flow, but then leaves her guest with a moment of privacy. While Joe transitions from his dingy attire into the tub, Kate strips down to her swimming suit in the living room. In line with the military theme of Joe's story, as she peels off clothing Kate imagines that she hears the dramatic roll of a snare drum. Perhaps she is not Rambo, but as part of her preparation she does get her knife.

The bathroom door nudges open slowly and Kate creeps into the room. She tiptoes toward the tub without Joe taking deliberate notice. The man relaxes in the water with his face turned away from the direction of his visitor.

Kate holds the knife behind her back. As she lowers to her knees at the side of the tub she brings the knife around, crosses it from one hand to the other. The blade stays out of view, not that Joe turns his head to take in any immediate views.

Kate doesn't slouch, stays raised on the knees, and Joe chooses to acknowledge her presence by opening his eyes and turning his head with a question.

"Why are you here?"

He glances at his nether region, self-conscious. She speaks to his face.

"You hurt people. How do you live with what you did?"

Joe is dramatic, yet casual.

"I'm not alive."

This answer clicks for Kate, she doesn't need to say anything in return. Joe, however, is curious about her intentions in the bathing suit.

"Did you want in with me?"

He wants her inside of the tub with him. It is not a lusty plea; in the moment it seems like it might be comforting. He tries to relate that.

"I just want peace."

Kate extends herself forward. She keeps the knife hidden against the side while she reaches her other hand into the tub. She dips her fingers into the water. Then she brings the wet fingers up and touches them to Joe's face.

"I want peace too."

Her gentle touch becomes a gentle push, coaxes Joe to turn his head, to close his eyes and rest to one side again. The gentle hand retreats and the knife is transferred into it.

Joe remains relaxed and exposed.

The knife is brought up and over the side of the tub. It trembles; however, Kate maintains her grip and brings the sharp edge to the man's throat.

She doesn't cut, it is a slow poke that pierces into a jab of a stab. Joe thrashes and this causes Kate to shove the blade deeper, widens the damage before she has to jerk the blade free.

After the initial flinch of surprise Joe's splashing is timid. He gargles and keeps his eyes fixed on nothing that Kate can see. The moment is surreal and Kate panics that the simplicity of it is a sign of failure. The wound is nasty and gushes with suffering. Kate spurs herself to be brave and brutal and leans into the tub to stab into the gore already rendered. The violence is more cathartic and gets Joe to close his eyes.

Kate rotates out of the act and still on her knees, braces an arm against the side of the tub to keep herself from keeling over into the floor. Her mind flashes to the day when she held

Hannah's hand as they sat on her bedside. She assured her friend of her innocence.

"Hannah, you did nothing wrong. Bree did you wrong."

Hannah shrugs and Kate battles to inspire.

"Look at me."

Hannah meets her eyes.

"You deserve to be loved. I'm always here for you. Forever or worse."

An amused smile comes to Hannah's lips as she repeats Kate's words, enjoys the turn of phrase.

"Forever or worse."

Kate makes her move. She leans in and plants her lips against Hannah's. Astonished, Hannah terminates the kiss, pulls away just enough to get a virtuous read into Kate's eyes. Kate holds her gaze.

Hannah pledges her lips to Kate's, who accepts, and they share a romantic kiss.

No one will kiss Joe Till again—not that he had any prospective suitors. His life vacates through his gashed open throat. Before it all purges into the water, Kate turns and places her hand into the warm plasma, clenches her fist to capture some essence. She stands up with a fistful of blood, plenty more of it spattered on her swimsuit, and exits the crime scene to go deposit Joe Till into one of the jars in the kitchen.

She returns to the bathroom and doesn't want to peel off her layer of protective swimwear in front of dead Joe, but his face is sunk in the other direction; therefore, she strips down quick and uses a wash cloth to clean herself at the sink. She doesn't have any plans for Joe, he will soak.

Once the visible blood is wiped from her, Kate rifles through Joe's discarded pants. Wads of folded up papers are crammed inside of the pockets and unfolded they reveal rambling paragraphs of words.

Kate takes Joe's papers with her to the computer desk, after a quick pit stop to don a t-shirt and some sweatpants from her bedroom. She logs into the camming website to share Joe's words with her audience.

"Consumers buy boxes to put themselves in and then pay someone to ship them to them. To break this cycle they need to get it all or get rid of it all. Square one, square box, triangulate the circle, seek and destroy the outside from within. Zig-zag in a straight line."

Kate sets that paper down.

"Is that poetry? There's a lot of it. I can't read most of the handwriting."

She lifts another piece of paper from the collection and reads a line off it.

"We tried to digitize our souls, but digitized our demons instead."

She critiques that line for her audience.

"I like that one."

She peruses the chat responses and then explains some context.

"These came from a guy that lives down the street, ON the street. He rambles a lot of crazy stuff. He's kind of scary interesting."

She observes the computer screen and then uses a finger to outline the square of the chat box featured on it. She does the same for the video feed window.

"We're in boxes here. When you pick out a girl on the website we're in boxes."

Now she chooses to realize that her computer monitor itself is a square. She traces the square in the air with her finger and it disturbs her that she has found a way to connect with a portion of a lunatic's manifesto.

Kate decides that she wants to get away from the boxes and talk to someone else. She relocates to the loveseat.

Skylar was easy enough to talk to and so Kate imagines that Skylar sits next to her and listens.

"I get lonely and wish that I had someone to talk to in person. Not just someone to listen, a co-conspirator."

She chuckles with herself.

"Hannah wouldn't approve of what I am doing, but once she's here, I know she'll help me hide the bodies. I didn't know I could go through with it. Once you pull the Band-aid off though, you know?"

Skylar waves her hands in a flurry of nonsensical gestures that represent Kate's utter lack of understanding when it comes to sign language. Kate responds with a repeat of sentiment that she shared when Skylar was alive.

"In another world I really think we could be friends. That's why I'm imagining you. It's unforgivable how you set me up, but it did give me a needed push. You can haunt me if you want."

Skylar flips her "the bird." Kate appreciates it, imagines it is a token of Skylar's sense of humor. She continues to talk about her own life.

"Being a cam girl helped at first. It was freeing. It's acting though. Maybe I can become an actress. I figure that's what they want in Hollywood, people to show some skin and make funny faces."

Skylar makes a "funny face" at Kate, inflates her cheeks out with air and wrinkles her brow. This makes Kate grin and she expands her grin and shakes her head from side to side to make it as manic looking as possible. In turn Skylar sucks in her cheeks to make a "fish face." Kate counters with a thumb to the nose, four fingers waving, tongue out maneuver. Skylar keeps with the animal theme and goes "duck face."

Kate snort laughs.

"Hannah and I used to play this game when we were kids."

Kate goes for the grand finale of face making by crossing her eyes and opening her mouth as wide as possible with tongue waggles. Game over.

Earlier Kate dared to take off her swimming suit in the presence of Joe's corpse; however, now she enters the bathroom in need of using the toilet and cannot find the nerve to do such. So she steals into the room and gets herself a roll of toilet paper.

The roll of toilet paper is taken into the kitchen and set down on the counter. Kate drops her pants and panties and climbs up to hover her ass over the kitchen sink. She pees into the sink. It is a tricky balancing act, but relief is achieved. After she hops down, Kate flushes by letting the sink faucet run for an extended period of time, more time to dwell on things done done.

Hannah had walked out of the bedroom after the kiss. Kate followed her, sensed that she was chasing her friend.

"Hannah."

She remembers the conversation as clear as the day of. Hannah turns and states her state of flux.

"I'm confused."

"I'm not."

"Kate, you're not even gay."

"Why do I have to be gay to love you? We're best friends, perfect friends. I love you. I'm attracted to you."

"You've never said anything."

"Haven't I? I tell you you're sexy."

"As a friend."

"Remember when we kissed in senior year?"

"That was a game."

"It was special to me."

"Aren't you dating Steve?"

"We were and we aren't."

Hannah goes quiet, bites her lip. It causes an ache, a discomfort within Kate.

"What are you thinking now?"

Hannah steps to Kate and goes in for a kiss. Kate accepts and reciprocates. The young women share tongues and tingles and when they pull apart Hannah vocalizes an answer to Kate's last question.

"This is still a lot to process."

Hand in hand they walked to the loveseat and that is where Bree found them.

After Kate finishes pissing down the sink and memory lane she wipes and exits the kitchen. She decides to lie down on the loveseat with low hopes of sleeping herself away from all the murders and memories. A state of sleep is indeed reached, a transition into a dream influenced by the brutal past and present.

A knee to the ground, superhero landing pose, Kate is in the place where she was a captive audience to a slayer-suicider's swan song. She is not going down for the count, she is ready for the countdown at the starting line. Ahead of Kate is a gauntlet of troubles: cupid with his gun, Joe with a shovel, and Bree stands at the end with Hannah held hostage by the point of her blade against soft neck skin.

Kate's mind seeks inspiration from answers not torture from terrors, thus she launches herself toward the first obstacle, bounds to her feet and toward Cupid. She waves her arms as an erratic distraction, presents herself as a moving target of chaos.

She reaches the pimp before he can cement a destination to send a bullet. Kate grabs the gun and forces it to one side as she strikes Cupid in the face with the heel of her other palm. The blow buckles Cupid at the knees and Kate retains the gun as the pimp crumples to the ground.

Easy-peasy. She flings the gun away, doesn't need it as she sets her sights on Joe. The soldier shows off his shovel twirling skills. The obvious and confident protagonist of the dream, Kate is not impressed. She charges straight toward Joe and he takes on this challenge by doing the same in her direction.

When the combatants reach each another the woman of her dreams once again is quick enough to lay hands on her opponent's weapon. Joe has the size advantage; however, Kate is stronger. She spins Joe around with her hold on the shovel and he trips over his own feet. He falls and the shovel is now firm in Kate's possession. She swings the shovel down at Joe to put out his fight.

Threat number two out of commission, Kate tosses the shovel aside before she faces Bree. Bree steps away from Hannah and beckons with the knife for Kate to come get skewered.

By reverie magic Kate suddenly holds a knife of her own. She takes a page out of Joe's playbook and shows off her knife skills. They are amateur slashes but Bree is impressed enough to doubt her own chance at domination. Bree turns tail and runs away leaving Kate and Hannah alone. Kate's knife sheathes back to invisibility.

The women move closer to each another. Hannah reaches a hand out, touches Kate's hair, and makes a comment.

"An angel sent to rescue me."

"I'm not an angel."

Hannah points beyond Kate.

"No. See."

Kate turns around to see an angelic man, radiant in his handsomeness behind her—fit, topless in rugged cowboy jeans, barefoot, his feathered, white wings extend upward from his shoulders. Kate asks him for his name.

"Who are you?"

His voice is the type of pop singer smooth that makes a cat purr.

"It's me. Charmy. I'm your number one fan."

Hannah presses up to Kate from behind and delivers kisses to her neck. Charmy moves in from the front and goes to his knees before Kate.

As Charmy works his hands up under the hem of Kate's dress, Hannah continues to massage Kate with her lips. The nightmare works toward a happy ending.

Kate is asleep on the loveseat. She rubs herself with a hand down the front of her pajama pants. Her legs are spread, one balanced over the back of the furniture as she lightly moans a step outside the dream world. This is a walk she will take to the end of the path. As she climaxes Kate clenches her legs together, rolls over to one side and, instead of waking, drops into a perfect, blank void of sleep.

Kate tries to remain out of conscious existence late into the next day. Her mother knocks at the front door and spoils this. The elder announces herself through the sealed door.

"Kate, it's your mother."

Kate considers ignoring her visitor, but then the lock at the front door clicks and she becomes horrified, wide awake. She hurries to confront the intruder.

Kate's mother lets herself in through the front door, drops the key she used into the enormous purse she hauls, and steps into the confrontation.

"Why do you have a key to my apartment?"

"Everyone needs a spare key."

"I didn't give you one."

"I've been phoning you. Your number is disconnected."

"You know I don't like phones."

Mother comes closer to her daughter and sniffs her.

"Do you like baths? It smells like you haven't bathed in days. This whole apartment stinks. There's rodents."

Kate demands an explanation.

"What are you doing here?"

Her mother sidesteps the question.

"I'm going to use the bathroom."

Kate is quick to shoot down this idea.

"No! The toilet is broken."

"I'll take a look at it."

Kate moves to cut her mother off.

"No. The handyman is fixing it. He went to get a new stopper thing."

"He's fixing it today?"

"Yes."

"I can hold it for a bit. Invite me to sit down."

She doesn't wait for the invitation; she walks over to the loveseat and plops down with her giant purse on her lap.

"I'm worried about you, Kate. Are you paying your bills?"

"I work. I'm paying my bills."

"You're whoring on the computer again."

That pushes a button: red.

"I'm not a whore."

"You're sliding back into your old ways. I don't see how you can live here after all that happened. I want you to live at the house with me."

"You can shove your house up your ass."

"That's nice, Kate."

"You called me a whore!"

"After all the counseling, all the money and time I've invested in you, I thought you might want to do better for yourself. It's embarrassing."

"I'm not embarrassed."

"Then maybe you need to go back on medication."

Kate is too pissed off to formulate words. Instead, she grumbles and turns her back on her mother. She walks over to the computer desk as her mother asks her a question.

"When you were a baby do you know what your first words were?"

Kate doesn't answer as she eyes the knife that is on the computer desk. Mom answers for her.

"'I good.' Your first words were 'I Good.'"

Eyes still on the knife, Kate has a reply.

"Apologize for calling me a whore."

"I'm here to help you."

"I'm tired of owing you. I didn't ask for your help."

"You can't choose the help you want to take, you take the help you can get."

Kate's mother stands up.

Kate's hand goes for the knife; however, she doesn't grab and stab. She covers the blade with a piece of paper to prevent her mother from seeing it as she walk closer.

"I'm sorry. I didn't come here to argue. I brought you a gift."

Her mother digs into the mammoth purse and pulls out an electric clothes iron. Kate accepts the gift as it is handed to her, but allows the cord to fall loose and dangle.

"You wore a wrinkly shirt the last time I saw you. I told you I'd bring you one of my irons. We can get you an ironing board too."

"Thanks."

"I want good things for my good girl."

"I know."

"Can I get a hug before I leave?"

Kate holds one arm out. "Are you kidding me," is the look she gets from her mother.

Kate slides her hand down the cord of the iron and then dangles the device down by the cord, sets the iron to the floor, gentle, and then drops the cord, allows the plug to crack down. Then she presents herself to her mother with both arms out and the parent comes forward and hugs her daughter. Her mother brings a message into the hug.

"Come home, Sweetie."

"Bye, Mom."

Her mother leaves with her life and thinking that she made a positive impression on her daughter.

Kate goes to her room. She doesn't bother picking the clothes iron out of the floor.

In the bedroom a lively version of Skylar sits on the bed while a much deader one decomposes in plastic on the floor. The Skylar on the bed sits cross-legged while Kate sits on the edge of the bed with the hatchet that dispatched the mute woman in her hands.

"I'm going to quit pretending that I'm talking to you."

She gestures to the body in the floor.

"You stink and you're leaking on the floor. I'm going to have to chop you up and put you in garbage bags."

Skylar listens as she is disposed to do.

"I'll have to cut up the guy in the tub first. I don't know if I can do it. Chopping someone up seems worse than killing them."

Dispirited, Kate lies the hatchet down, not up to the task just yet.

"First thing is first, finish what is started. The end of the beginning."

A sheet has been draped over the tub to hide the water, the blood, the rot, and the homicide.

Kate stands at the sink and has already brushed her hair and cleaned up some. Now she applies bold, purple lipstick to her lips. She checks her teeth in the mirror, no fangs, no lipstick on the enamel. She is ready for some computing.

Gussied up, Kate is at her computer. She has a lollipop and makes a show out of licking it, mouth too open, tongue too extended, she's not after flavor, she's a vixen, powerful, has her audience salivating, oops, she salivates on herself. Someone who she has been waiting for arrives in the chat room and Kate beams a smile at the computer screen.

"Charmy! There you are! I was hoping that you would log in. Tonight is your lucky night. You win!"

She gives him a moment to probe for details of his prize.

"Clear your schedule for tomorrow. We're going to meet and do some of the things we've talked about. IF you're still interested."

Ca-ching. Ca-ching.

She slides the lollipop into her mouth, turns it in slow circles as she sucks. An epic tune sweeps into her optimistic mind, real "when a man loves a woman" type of material. For the rest of the night she cams, goofing around while sexually stimulating people.

Once she logs off for the night Kate decides to let loose and get into serial killer character. She goes into her bedroom and spreads Joe's collection of writings over the bed. Then she lies down amongst them and reads until she cannot keep her eyes open. She dials right in to the slumber station that plays her sleep song.

The next day is date-day, sorta-kinda, and Kate feels cute in a dress and has an exceptional temperament as she opens the front door. Charmy has arrived and the wind is knocked right out of Kate's zip-a-dee-doo-dah sails as she discovers that he has brought along another man. She had counted on Charmy not fitting the sole picture of himself that he shared, but the second male was never a part of the arrangement. Charmy was supposed to bring along a lady named Liza for the concocted threesome.

Charmy isn't as unnaturally handsome as the angel from Kate's inspirational nightmare.

He appears older than the picture that he shared over the computer, nose far more crooked than what was discernible from the photographed angle. The other stranger danger is a chubby hulk that looms behind the invited.

Charmy plays off the surprise as best he can, voice nothing like that of a popstar angel.

"Hey. It's me. Charmy. My friend Liza that I told you about couldn't make it. This is my friend Pieman. That okay?"

It's not okay, but she allows them to enter.

"You guys can come in."

When Charmy moves it reveals that Pieman holds a dress box. He carries it over to the loveseat and then hands the box over to Charmy as the duo squeeze down together on the loveseat. Kate wheels her office chair over and sits down in it across from the buddies. Charmy hands over the gift box.

"It's something you can put on when you're ready."

"Gracias."

The wink that she catches from Pieman creeps her out.

Charmy leads the conversation with naughty observational humor.

"How about this weather? Perfect for a threesome."

Kate doesn't chuckle with the guys.

"I wish you had warned me you were bringing another man. I had a different idea about today."

"Yeah. Liza bailed and I wanted to meet you so bad. I figured I'd being another option. Pieman is cool with just watching if you're cool with that."

She's not, however, she consents.

"I'm cool with that."

"He does have a neat dick."

Pieman tries to help sell himself.

"It's pierced."

Kate isn't wooed, but gives room for horny hopefulness.

"We'll see how it goes."

She stands up and goes about her hosting duties.

"Let's get down to business. You boys stay right there."

She shakes the dress box.

"I'll slip into something a little more comfortable."

As the men watch Kate walk away, Pieman pats an excited hand against one of Charmy's knees. Charmy's friend makes Charmy cringe.

Kate opens her gift box in the bathroom, has to sit down, does so on the toilet.

"Jesus Christ."

Her knife is on the sink but it is not what she is after when she gets up and seeks out something to help with the content of the box.

She sets the box down and opens the cabinet beneath the sink to withdraw talcum powder.

Powder pours into Kate's palms and then she prays as she claps the hands together.

"Oh God let me pull this off."

The powder and prayer are to help her pull on the latex fetish outfit that is in the box.

Charmy and Pieman stayed on the loveseat as they were instructed. They did remove their shirts, as they assumed they should.

Kate walks into the room with her body hermetically sealed in the latex. Her hands and feet are free from the material, but her face is masked with openings for the eyes, holes for breathing through the nose, and an unzipped zippered rift for the mouth. She does her best to walk sexy; squeak, squeak.

Kate goes to a spot and points to the floor at her bare feet.

"Here."

She whistles and Charmy hops up, eager as a dog to go to where Kate directs. He lies down on his back below her.

Kate lowers herself and manages to straddle Charmy, sits across his chest.

Pieman is revved up and wants to play as well. He proposes a deal.

"I've got one hundred dollars. Can I lie next to him?"

Kate's covered face turns toward Pieman. She sees that he is on the edge of his seat but she doesn't give him permission to rise.

"I do what I want, not what people with money tell me to do. I'm not a whore. Stay."

Pieman accepts this.

"Yes, mistress."

She turns her attention back to Charmy. Charmy offers her a command.

"Choke me."

She puts her hands around his throat and squeezes. Charmy urges her on.

"Harder."

She squeezes harder.

His veins bulge at his temples and his fierce stare says "harder."

Kate goes full bore into it, intends to strangle him to death. Charmy closes his eyes to enjoy it.

Pieman fondles one of his own breasts as he watches the show.

Kate squeezes with all of her might, harder, die, die, die, she groans out.

"Arrahh."

Charmy shudders and then goes still as if the lack of air has finished him. Kate believes that the task is completed and relinquishes her grip on his throat. She speaks his name as a way to check his pulse.

"Charmy."

He remains still.

She pats his cheek and still doesn't get a reaction.

She glances over to check on Pieman behind her. He likes the action.

"Oh, mistress, please, kill me next."

Charmy gags, coughs back to life with a deep inhale riddled with giggles.

"Ha ha."

He draws Kate's focus to him.

"You really thought I was dead didn't you?"

He can see it on her face and is amused that she is such a silly girl.

"It takes a lot longer than that to kill somebody. Ha ha. You made me hard, baby. I want my pants off."

Kate attacks!

"Grahh!"

Her hands go to Charmy's face and she presses her thumbs into his eyes.

Charmy screams as Kate gouges her thumbs deep into his eye sockets. She screams along with him; killing and being killed can both be quite traumatic.

Pieman rises and rushes to the rescue. He grabs Kate by her hair and yanks her off his pal. He lifts and twists her away, sends Kate crashing hard against the floor.

Charmy bawls with his eyes out. Pieman isn't a paramedic though, he is a destroyer and pounces on to Kate to get his beefy hands around her throat. He squeezes with insult.

"You fucking whore."

Pinned, Kate struggles to breathe, senses that Pieman has the strength and just might break her neck before strangulation ends her, squeak, squeak goes the latex.

The clothes iron that Kate's mother brought her is still in the floor where Kate left it. Kate flails an arm out in panic and the fingers on her outstretched hand find the plug at the end of the iron cord. A tug slides the iron closer. She grabs the iron by the handle and swings it for survival. The point end of the iron's metal surface connects with Pieman's temple; his church bell has been rung, it's funeral services today.

Stunned, Pieman tips over and off of Kate. The woman sucks in air as she wiggles her legs free from the disoriented bulk of man. She pops up to her knees, squeaky wedgie, and shuffles over to swing the iron down against Pieman's head again. Thunk.

"I'm not a whore."

Blood slings with the subsequent blows, as Kate irons out what is left of Pieman's filling. He will never call another person a whore. More whimpers out of Charmy disengage Kate from overkill mode and she stands up, walks away from Pieman.

Charmy pleads.

"Help me. Help me."

She regurgitates one of his lines as she stands over him.

"You made me hard, baby."

She holds the iron out over his head, aims for his face, and lets the appliance drop. The iron strikes and splits open Charmy's upper lip at one corner of his mouth, a wound that registers fresh pain against the numb shock of having already lost his eyeballs.

"Ow!"

Kate peels off the portion of latex that covers her face, doesn't exclaim "ow," even though it hurts. Wild hair, sweaty, Kate is ready to end this date. She strides out of the room to get her knife that was left behind in the bathroom.

Knife in hand she returns to the living room to find that while Pieman is still an immobile hunk of death, Charmy has flopped over and slithers on his belly across the floor. He slithers too cockeyed to ever reach the front door.

Kate stomps a foot down against Charmy's spine to halt his escape. Then she lowers down and lifts his head in order to tuck her knife under the chin and against the flesh of his throat. She softly whispers her first words.

"I good."

She cuts Charmy's throat. Murder is easier the fifth time but the way he squirms in the expanding puddle of blood as she continues to saw with the knife does make her feel a tad ill. The blood does sort of flood toward the front door. It won't make it there either.

A shot of adrenaline hits Kate's system, lingers, pulsates as she collects souls number four and five and deposits them into their jars.

The adrenaline carries over into the bedroom where she struggles to remove the latex outfit. She kicks and bucks around on the bed until she achieves freedom.

Five jars, one demon, a best friend, a tremendous deal, Kate considers going into the final stage of the pact in her birthday suit; however, that might seem odd to Hannah if her return is an instant out of a puff of smoke sort of arrival. Kate puts on one of her favorite blouses and a pair of jeans that make her feel sexy while covered.

In the kitchen Kate finds her demon. It observes the row of jars, taps the lid, each jar sealed with a splash of blood within, as it counts to five.

The demon picks up the last jar in the row and holds it out in the direction of Kate. It asks a question.

"What are these?"

"Souls. I got you five souls for one. You'll bring Hannah back to me now."

The demon is amused enough to let half a cackle slip out before commenting.

"These are just empty jars."

Now the demon laughs like it's the funniest thing it has heard on any side of damnation.

Kate pushes past the demon, goes to the counter, and picks out one of the other jars from the row. She turns to show the jar to the hell-thing as if by being in her own hand the point will be proven.

"See."

There is nothing to see. The demon is gone.

"No! We had a deal!"

The jar in her hand appears empty to her. She looks at the counter and sees that the other four jars are there in a row and all of them are empty as well.

"You tricked me! We had a deal!"

She smashes the jar to the floor. It breaks, but not in a satisfying shatter.

In the living room Kate discovers that the corpses, the messes of Charmy and Pieman, aren't where she left them. The room spins.

"This isn't happening."

Kate runs sideways to the bathroom. Again she doesn't find the death that she left behind, not even a blood stain around the drain.

In the bedroom it is the same story: no dead bodies, no evidence of slaughter beyond the shopping bags and tools seemingly unused. Kate yells out to her demon.

"Demon, where are you? We had a deal!"

She continues to rage as she returns in stomp-step to the living room. The thud of her bare feet against the floor cease the spinning of the room for her.

"Rahh! You tricked me! Tricked me!"

Anger cracks into an apologetic sorrow.

"Hannah, I'm sorry. Hannah. Hannah!"

She is about to fall to her knees to wail some more but another tenant of the building, Mr. Grimes, bangs his fists against the front door. Kate freezes in a pathetic state, half-bent at the knees, and listens.

"What's going on in there? Open up! This is your neighbor Mr. Grimes!"

Kate composes herself and decides to answer the door. Before she opens it she does a double-checks to make sure Charmy doesn't ooze in the floor behind her.

Mr. Grimes is an elderly man, animated and spry even with a walking cane. He is ready to use the cane if it is needed as a club.

"Are you okay?"

She is honest.

"No."

"Do you need me to call the police or an ambulance?"

"No."

His concern for her safety erupts into irritation over her inconsiderate dispensing of noise.

"Then shut up! People are trying to sleep! I can't stand it anymore!"

He calms himself, but extends his complaint, delivered with heavy stank-eye.

"Between your hootin' and hollarin' and those damn vuvuzelas in 4B, it's intolerable. Shut. It. Up."

She nods in a display of understanding. Satisfied, he bids her good night.

"Good night."

He scoots away and Kate shuts her door.

Kates takes a seat at her computer desk and fires up the system on it. She watches the computer screen. On it she spies on a couple who are aware of the voyeurs to their broadcast even if not of the personalities behind those eyes. The couple appears to be Cupid and Skylar. They pose and chat while in their underwear, the topic lost on Kate as she keeps the speakers on mute.

When the new day alights on the world outside Kate is still at her computer. She kept vigil all through the night without falling asleep. Sound now emits from the computer speakers, however, as she has moved on to the joyful barks of puppies at play.

Eventually Kate escapes the mindless soaking of her mind and heads to the bathroom for a bath. The tub fills without fanfare and she climbs into the water, soon stares off into memory.

It is that same special place in Hell where Kate goes. Bree stands watch with her knife as Kate works to tie Hannah to the tree. Kate tries to slip a whisper into Hannah's ear unnoticed.

"Is that too tight?"

It is noticed.

"No more whispery secret birds behind my back. Get up."

Kate stands up straight and Hannah appeals to Bree's sanity.

"You don't want to do this. Bree, if you want to talk let's go get coffee, let's do talk."

Bree counters with a viewpoint from "it's too late."

"I was on my knees for you and you wouldn't listen. No. You only listen to lies."

She points her knife at Kate. Hannah defends Kate.

"This is between you and me. Let Kate go."

"She's between us! Always was jealous. Her lies did this. Today is the truth."

Bree puts her attention fully on to Kate.

"This is all your fault. Tell the truth."

Hannah interjects.

"Run, Kate! Run!"

Hannah makes a strong effort to tear free from the ropes; stuck tight.

Kate doesn't move; scared tight. Bree presses.

"Tell Hannah that you lied. You never saw me making out with Angie at that party. I never cheated."

Bree turns again to Hannah, disgusted by the urgency with which her former wants to save Kate.

"But, who did you believe? She got your trust."

She snaps back to Kate.

"Tell her! You did this. Tell her you lied! This is your last chance."

Kate doesn't budge, doesn't speak.

Bree lunges at Kate to grab her. Hannah screams out in defense once again.

"Bree, no!"

Bree swings Kate away from the tree and shoves her, an action that sends Kate in a falling spiral down to the ground. This is where she hits the mud.

Kate is in her bathroom. Kate is in her tub. The water is no longer water, it is thick blood. Kate sinks below the red.

Outside the apartment building the day remains bright. Kate walks out into this illumination, nude, coated from head to toe in the blood from her bath. She walks down the sidewalk leaving wet footprints on the concrete as she goes.

# Pizza On The Brain

Pete Lawson had the distinction of being the fastest kid in our school. When he ran it was always in first place from start to finish as long as it was a structured race. Now, you take him away from that structure, you smack some rules aside, and no one could beat my speed. I was the king of playing tag at recess, no one bested me, no one caught up to my wild free-form running skills.

It's too bad they took recess away from us after the fourth grade. No one will remember how quick on my feet I was or probably even remember playing with me. Pete though, he went on to be a track and field super-athlete in the school history books.

My speed diminished the older I got, but the memory of it never left me. Even after I plumped up, if I were to take off in a run, my mind told me I could move as quick as the wind. I realized that my mind was playing tricks on me though after an incident in high school.

One day I entered the gymnasium at the same time as Pete Lawson. I did not make the decision to race him, my mind did that without me. When Pete Lawson took off in a run to reach his pals on the other side of the gym, I am told that I too took off right beside him. The school nurse had to tell me what witnesses reported because I couldn't remember. Apparently I ran straight across the gym and then, without slowing, ran straight into the wall on the other side. And Pete beat me by so much that he was gone and never even noticed me racing after him or my hitting the wall.

I awoke on the floor of the gym in a baffled state of mind. The goose egg on my forehead and the concussion symptoms I had to suffer through were my prize for letting my imagination try and tap into skills of former playground glory. Yet, even after that event, that lesson, I still know that somewhere inside of me is that speed. It is a part of the drive that has me diet time and time again after periods of weight gain. Of course, it is a back and forth battle, because I have a great weakness for pizza.

Pete Lawson also had the distinction of being the smartest kid in our school. He got straight A's all the way to valedictorian. I made passing grades. Honestly, I found schoolwork really boring. I bet Pete and I had that in common.

Pete Lawson was very popular and dated the girl of my dreams: Lindsey Perry. They started as an item all the way back in Kindergarten. How the heck did they know how awesome they were even back then? In Kindergarten I was doing my best not to glue my fingers together or poop my pants.

Lindsey Perry never spoke to me. Even in my fantasies she never spoke to me. Pete never spoke to me either. In my youth I stewed in jealousy quite thick.

When I was in my early twenties and trying to lose some extra pounds a therapist gave me a free consultation. She listened to some of my woes of youth and then implied that I was eating my feelings. But that's not true, I eat food because I like food. Again, pizza, it is my thing, all the different varieties one can make, truly the catch-all food, truly enjoyable for the sake of being pizza.

However, I'm not going to pretend I ever became a snob for gourmet pizza. Classic pepperoni with extra cheese kept my face greasy through high school and community college. The best part is when the edges of the pepperoni are slightly upturned, crispy as the meat reached the edge of being too burnt before being pulled from the oven.

After high-school graduation Pete went off to a prestigious college on a full scholarship, both academic and athletic I'd wager. Aside from that I did not keep up with the movements of Pete Lawson.

Like I said, I went to community college, but then focused on becoming a police officer. My weight was an immediate issue to be dealt with and as an adult I dealt with it. Pizza, along with soda were cut out of my diet again and again. Exercise filled me out in better ways for physical inspection and while I've had some slips of indulgence over the years, fat I am not.

Pizza is my kryptonite. I have stayed away from it as best I can. I have not had any in at least a year. Any time I fell off of my diet in the past year it was some other sinful treat, though I will state for the record that pizza bagels or microwave pizza pocket sandwiches don't count as pizza to me when I say that I've stayed away from pizza.

At police academy I discovered that the other candidates were normal folks just like myself, chasing employment opportunity and for some "a calling." There was not a Pete Lawson in my class and the fastest runner doesn't come to mind, though it wasn't me. I posted satisfactory report cards, but I graduated knowing that I had more to offer, being graded has never been a strength of mine.

Law enforcement as a career had always interested me as a child, perhaps the steady stream of action movies I spent time with cultivated that interest. It also seemed like the type of job that would help me grow, help me strengthen myself within structure to battle life in general along with my weight fluctuation issues. Also, I won't lie, I have heard the saying that "women love a guy in uniform," and quite frankly I hoped I might strike an action figure pose and become a fantasy made real for some woman as lonely as I was.

Eventually I landed a job with the Columbia city police department. Columbia is a much bigger city than the town I grew up in, but it's not really all that far down the road. You might say that I didn't run very far. However, that's the truth for the majority of the small town kids. Pete Lawson though, he seemed long gone and on to better things. He didn't show up at the ten year class reunion and no one knew where he was.

Lindsey Perry was at the reunion and I heard her say she married some doctor and that they split their time between two homes, one in Florida, and one somewhere else that I didn't hear. She never spoke to me.

Joey Wall, my best friend all through school, showed up late to the reunion. We caught up a bit. We talked about all the music we used to listen to, all the video games we played, and all the pot we used to smoke. We marveled at how funny it was that we were both such potheads, yet I became a police officer and he became the foreman at the Frazzon plant. Frazzon is a factory where they manufacture parts for industrial refrigeration units.

It dawned on me that night how structured I had indeed made my life, which was the total opposite of the adventure I thought life would actually be. My job provides me excitement, absolutely. I get satisfaction on a job well done, on a community served, but where was that Tag King of the playground? I no longer knew how to duck, jive, zig, or zag, it was a straight forward run even when there were hurdles to jump. A lot of things dawn on a person when they are put into a room with the past and some spiked punch.

Comradery is one thing that I knew had been missing in my life. Heck, I had not been aware that Joey still lived in the region. However, it seemed that he recalled the music, games, and drugs more than who I was. Married and with two kids, he didn't swap phone numbers with me before leaving the reunion. I mean, I left knowing where he worked but that would be weird if I called his work to ask him out for a meal.

My days have been counted by my work schedule more than not. I don't socialize well. On my days off I like to watch movies. I go to the theater alone and experience the emotions of those larger than life people on the big screen. Comic books never appealed to me as a child, but comic book movies sure are a nice bang for the buck.

Many superhero stories are about coming into one's powers, accepting responsibility, and then forging a commitment to the art of selfless dedication. Superheroes falter in their journey when it comes to knowing right from wrong, when it comes to dedication, and while I may not have their special powers, I think I have been no less heroic when it comes to being "dedicated."

I can appreciate myself a little more after watching an adrenaline rush of a movie. However, sometimes I can walk out completely in the blue and feeling underappreciated. Happy or sad, that fleeting burst of energy after walking out of a movie is what I'd call my second drug of choice. My first drug, of course, being the thrill that comes with the pursuit of criminals while wearing a lawman's badge. Those moments are few and far between the paperwork, but I get to have a gun.

Eating junk food is not my drug of choice, I can quit anytime I want, I have proven that. At the theater I do not have popcorn and a soda, I have bottled water and a hot dog. One hot dog as a meal is not going to bloat me back up to blimp size.

The people I work with call me an asshole behind my back and to my face, no repercussions. Bullies did not bother me all that much growing up and it's a shame that as an adult I am surrounded by them. There's a lesson in there somewhere. Don't let the bullies get you down as a kid because you'll have to face them all of your life, get used to it.

Complaints get filed against me at work, both from within the department and from the public I work to protect. Occasionally I get a talking to about being more personable, but my hard work is appreciated on some level. Too many people dislike me and I have too much value to ever get promoted, which is a shame and something to be proud of.

I've been put in charge of the evidence room, inventory tracking, and light janitorial duties. It's not like the department is trying to put me "out of the way," because dealing with the evidence gets my fingers brushing over most cases. It's really just the position I am in due to some blow back over that dog I shot during a traffic stop. Chihuahuas are just as vicious as any breed if you give them the chance.

Policy is policy for a reason and when it comes to protecting and serving I go by the book and won't apologize for that. It's not a popularity contest. It's not up to me to explore the gray areas of philosophy. The law is the law and if a person doesn't like that then they can try to change the law. My focus is on enforcing the law; it is hard work without superpowers, selfless dedication. The thanks I get is knowing that I followed the dotted I's and crossed T's as man dictated the law to be in pursuit of order.

Or so that's how I WAS approaching my job.

I am not married. I am not a father. I don't really want to talk about that intimate stuff. Basically, I have gotten us to the point in this story of where I was at in life, more or less, on the day that Pete Lawson died.

Friday the thirteenth means nothing to me. I am not superstitious. It is a day like any other day and no matter what happened, it didn't happen due to the numerical designation of the day aligned with the given name of the day of the week. If anything, for most folks, the positive aspects of Friday should overpower any negatives formed by unlucky thirteen. It is the last day of the common work week, a day when you have something to look forward to— the weekend, being off of work, etc. It's rare to have something solid to look forward to in life.

On a Friday the thirteenth I awoke and went into my normal routine. I am not a fan of breakfast; I take a pill and some coffee. The pill is for my acid reflux. The pill stops my stomach from producing too much acid, prevents the overabundance of acid from regurgitating up my throat to eat through my esophagus. The doctors say it is a condition that can be brought on by genetics and stress. Doctors sure are paid a lot to make educated guesses.

I popped my pill. And then I stuck the barrel of my .40 caliber Glock 22 into my mouth to wash it down with a bullet. I did not consciously choose to stick my gun in my mouth. Suicide had not crossed my mind when I got out of bed; there was not premeditation of self-execution. Surprised, but not shocked, I lingered in a moment of stasis, thoughtless, yet somehow aware that some part of me was contemplating whether or not to pull the trigger.

I did not pull the trigger. Instead, I slid the gun out of my mouth and holstered it to my side. Then off to work I went. Or, so I thought.

As I drove I got lost in a middle school memory that was less event and motion and more emotion and a snapshot. A photograph exists of a young me sitting right next to my crush Lindsey Perry in the bleacher seats of the school gymnasium. I can see this picture in my mind, though I cannot recall the exact motions gone through by me as a person during that night. I can, however, feel the excitement, the nervousness, and the embarrassment that was destroying me inside.

There I sat, right next to the girl of my dreams, hoping that in some way our destinies might suddenly intertwine into inseparable threads of existence. Well, obviously little me wasn't thinking that exact thought, I'm interpreting it for him, little me just felt awash with too many feelings at once.

Lindsey and I sat waiting our turn with the rest of the class to take the stage for a school musical performance. I never sang at those events, merely moved my lips to appear like I was singing; skipping the events altogether was not permitted. There I am captured in the photograph, looking toward my mother who snapped the shot. And there is Lindsey, looking at something that is just short of being the angle needed to be looking at me.

As much as I wanted to be acknowledged by her, I may well have imploded if such had occurred in my state of dress. I wore black sweat pants, a yellow and black striped sweater, and a fuzzy yellow beanie on my head featuring black pipe cleaner antennae on top. I was a bumblebee with zero confidence. There were probably wings, I'd have to double check the photo—it's stored in a box of albums somewhere.

Lindsey wore black tights, a dark shirt, and the pink petals surrounding her neck made her a flower. Boys were bees and girls were flowers. It is me in that picture next to her and Pete Lawson is nowhere to be seen. One could imagine that I was her bee and she was my flower. It is a painful fiction really, a picture, a memory worth a thousand wishes unfulfilled. My flower sang near me, but never spoke to me.

As I drove, I longed for a time machine. Go back to being that child and buzz something sweet into her ear! Or at the very least, sting her, damn it! Die knowing what it was like to be inside of her, knowing that she felt you! Bzz bzz bzz. Your past self never hears you though.

Instead of heading to the station and reporting for duty I drove around town aimlessly, time of no meaning until it was too late to be on time. As I realized where I was, where my mind had been, I also realized that from the start of my morning routine up until that point I had not been in control of myself at all. What would I do next? Or, not do next? It was scary. Right at that moment I could have had the breakdown I should have had after putting my gun in my mouth.

And then a call came out over the radio. A man had committed suicide at the mall. That is how much time I had wasted drifting, long enough that the main shopping mall had been opened for business and someone had offed themselves in front of shoppers. My mind made up my mind for me when the call came over the radio. I went to the mall.

When I arrived on the scene no one stopped me from crossing the yellow tape to get a closer view of the gore. A fellow officer even filled me in on the quick progress the detectives had made on the case.

A man had managed to climb up on to the roof of the mall. He then threw himself through a skylight and plummeted to his demise in the food court. It was not just any man; it was Pete Lawson.

The detectives found Pete's ID tucked into a suicide note left behind with his clothing on the roof. Yep, his clothing. Pete took his final swan dive in the nude. "Naked came I out of my mother's womb, and naked shall I return thither," Job 1:21.

His suicide note read: "Goodbye. Good luck."

As of this writing the motivation for suicide and the life lived by Pete Lawson as an adult are still shrouded in mystery. The context with which to interpret the words of his note are as open as the theories on why he chose to end his life to begin with. I am not kept in the loop on the investigation nor am I doing work toward filling in any of the details myself. I've never mentioned to anyone that I actually went to school with the deceased.

When I found out that the dead man was Pete Lawson, not revealing my knowledge of Pete's glory in youth was not deceit on my part, I merely shrunk inside myself, stunned by the end of his story. If a person like Pete, given everything easy as you please on a platter, could be driven to suicide, what truly were any of the rest of us holding on to?

The glass from the skylight sliced and diced Pete into a mangled hunk of rare steak. The impact of the fall broke him apart. Much of Pete splattered, yet near a table struck by Pete, I discovered that his brain lie on the floor as complete and perfect as a movie prop brain might appear. There was some blood and slime, sure, but nothing icky enough to bring nausea with my intrigue.

The top of his head must have popped off and the brain popped out. It lay partially on the floor and partially on a slice of pizza that had been knocked off of the table. The paper plate that once held the pizza lay nearby advertising the food court pizza joint of its origin.

Someone had been about to dine at the table when they decided to walk away to get a fork. They had thus avoided injury once Pete came crashing down; however, their pizza was now a part of a crime scene. It is perhaps some sort of miracle that no one other than Pete was seriously injured in the suicide. His inconsiderate act had given some people minor cuts from sprinkles of glass, but nothing hospital worthy.

The oversized slice of pizza touched by Pete Lawson's brain is a brand that has been around the mall ever since I was a kid. In my late teens, empowered with my license and access to my step-father's truck, I'd sometimes make the drive to Columbia seeking movies and the sense of energy only alive in more populated areas. Dining on pizza at the mall was a common activity for me. It was never the best quality pizza, but the location made for some quality people watching.

There I was all grown up and working in the city and there Pete was all cut up and dead in the city. My brain in my head, his at my feet, brought together by what? Twist of fate? Grand design? Cheap pizza?

A paramedic walked by me and I stopped him, tried to break through the turmoil in my head by speaking to him. I pointed at Pete Lawson's perfect brain.

"Look at this brain. Should we put it on ice in a cooler or something?"

The paramedic went from smirk to scowl before giving me his reply.

"Yeah, go ahead. I'm sure someone's waiting for it. If you get it there quick enough maybe they'll let you perform the transplant."

He shook his head and walked away having "heard it all," I am sure, the condescending cunt. Maybe my question was stupid, slowly vomited out past my lips by a rattled psyche. However, why was he still on scene? It's not like a paramedic was going to be bringing Pete Lawson back from the dead. What a self-important jerk he was, there to hand out some band aids, yet thinking himself the pinnacle of emergency services knowledge and wit. He could have used a brain transplant and I would have said as much if I had thought of it in the moment.

Something was meant to be done. Something had to be done. I stood at a crossroads.

There was still activity around the crime scene, people chatting, probing, but no one seemed to be as transfixed by the brain as was I. No one seemed to be paying attention to my presence, no eyes were on me. I almost reached down to grab the brain with my bare hands in order to whisk it away for further study. However, as a police officer I knew that a missing brain might become an issue at a later date in the investigation. The stress of trying to return the brain or explain my role in its disappearance should someone happen to recall my standing near it was not something I was prepared to take on.

I reached down and pulled the slice of pizza out from under the brain. The pizza was too stiff to fold and fit into my pocket without an awkward moment in which I could draw attention to myself, therefore, I casually held the slice and walked away from the food court. The pizza take out was a success.

The slice of pizza rode in the passenger seat of the car all the way back to my apartment. Then I took it inside with the utmost care not to disturb the toppings and I placed it on a kitchen counter.

The pizza had been ordered as pepperoni, but the meat was not in the exact style of my preference. The pepperoni lay thin and flat indicating, along with the hue of the crust, that perhaps the product's time in the oven had been too short. The cheese and tomato sauce were also both spread thin. Some of the sauce may have been blood. Also, there was a smear of some snotty substance across the pizza surface and a small chunk of what looked like discolored egg. The gray egg matter being a crumb of brain meat of course.

I don't know how long I stared at that pizza. Time was lost for sure. The day had been so abnormal that if I were put under hypnosis it would not surprise me if I told a tale of alien abduction in those missing moments in my kitchen. More than likely, however, my brain merely shut down all processes and a hypnotist would be related one boring story about standing in a kitchen staring at pizza. Maybe my brain rebooted to try and establish a link to the slice of pizza, a type of psychic wi-fi to find any remaining signals coming from Pete's minuscule piece of brain.

When I broke out of my trance I went to my computer to do some brain research. I learned that the brain is seventy-three percent water and at two percent dehydration a person can experience degraded cognitive skills as well as depleted memory and attention span. The brain is the fattiest organ in the body and holds twenty-five percent of the human body's cholesterol. A brain generates about twelve to twenty-five watts of electricity. The average brain is thought to have at least 50,000 thoughts a day. Stress and depression can cause brain shrinkage. The brain can focus on only one thing at a time, meaning there is no such thing as multitasking, merely going back and forth quickly, which can harm short term memory and attention span functions. There is no such thing as a left brain or right brain personality. Studies show that an extrovert's brain has a larger dopamine reward system and an introvert has more gray matter. Human brain tissue is squishy. The brain floats in cerebrospinal fluid. Brain cells will cannibalize themselves to stave off starvation.

We are born with our brains, but we can expand them and shape them, train their computing abilities or perverse their functionality. The human brain seems to be the master of our existence, our world engine. A hub where understanding and confusion fold over one another, science and spirituality. Where is one to focus inside of themselves to find answers? I considered that maybe I did not have enough spirituality in my life. However, I did not think of that in terms of religion, rather, connection to myself, others, the world, and the grand scheme of having emotional value and permanent gratification.

My research pivoted into the act of cannibalism. Specifically, I sought out studies on the potential integration of another individual's powers should you eat them. Mostly I found stories of famine and taboo, while the special powers angle got worked up mostly in fiction, nothing much new aside from what I had already seen in movies. Logically speaking, however, when we eat food it converts into energy, therefore, if we are indeed beings of energy, to consume another being seems to imply the gaining of some power. Then again, food converts into poop also.

At one point I found myself delving into serial killer biographies. My ability to suppress emotion may in turn suppress my acting out in an outrageous manner such as how infamous killer Jeffrey Dahmer did. He ate portions of his murder victims so that they would never leave him. My gun had gone into my own mouth, but perhaps in the logic of Dahmer, my gun would better serve me by being pointed outward. Tears came to my eyes as I realized the desperate loneliness that afflicted Jeffrey Dahmer was all too familiar to me.

Dahmer also experimented with trying to turn a person into a zombie by drilling a hole in their head and then pouring some acid inside. He wanted to gain complete control of the person. It is there that I disconnected and dried my eyes. I don't want to enslave the world. I just want it to be perfect and for me to participate in that. However, that is not to say there is no value in taking what you want. If you don't take it, you may never have it. You may find out that when you take what you want, that something always wanted you to have it.

B-movie zombies are not merely monsters, they are reflections on ourselves. Most would agree that at times they feel enslaved or dominated by forces outside their control, stuck in a loop. Zombies want to eat brains and maybe that is a commentary on our seeking of enlightenment.

Inside of me I know that I can be as fast, smart, and as likeable as Pete Lawson if I work at it. Oh, but wouldn't it be nice to have some of his magical privilege?

I returned to the kitchen and stood at the side of the counter to gaze at the slice of pizza once again. For a moment I decided that I would eat the pizza. Then I would set out to find Lindsey Perry, whatever home she may be at, and lose my virginity to her once and for all. Pete Lawson is dead, I won. Around and around it goes, ego, identity, fantasy, reality, wants, needs, ah, ah, ah!

"Goodbye. Good luck." Did Pete win the race? Did he know something that the rest of us do not and slip off to a wonderful afterlife? I wouldn't follow Pete Lawson off a cliff. As much envy as I have harbored for his gifts and status, it's not like I've ever set out to literally be him. I've never said I wanted to be him. Switch places with him? Sure, but as me still. Me is all I know. Maybe a better me.

Even if Pete meant for his last words to read as sarcasm, I choose to believe his wishes were genuine. We need to work hard, but we need all the luck we can get too, because the world is going to try and eat us all, Pete Lawson included. It's all a balancing act and you don't want to let yourself tilt too far to one side or the other, and what side is what is anyone's guess at any given time because the Earth is spinning.

I did not succumb to my moment of weak, demented fantasy. I don't want to talk about the intimate stuff, but even on my worst days I have hopes just the same as I have erections. We are all capable of perseverance in the face of adversity coming and going.

I did what most any of you would do. I called into work to apologize and let them know I was running late, but that I would be in. Then I picked off the bite of Pete Lawson's brain, popped it into my mouth, and swallowed it before tossing the slice of pizza into the trash.

Cover photo by Denise Terriah

Check out her book *As It Ends*

How would you survive the collapse of society? All Tara really wants is for her life to return to normal. She's unemployed, impoverished and newly married to a man who isn't what he'd seemed. When their power is turned off and her husband brings home an injured young woman it will test the limits of Tara's patience and their dwindling resources. But as Tara's life is coming apart the society that they live in collapses around them. The devastating loss of everything she holds dear forces Tara to pick up the pieces in a world unlike anything she's ever known. With no running water, grocery stores, hospitals, or electricity and the appearance of a killer who leaves behind a series of grisly murders, Tara will need all her wits and skills just to survive.

Available everywhere books are sold